FRANCES T. BOURNE
JACARANDA PUBLIC LIBRARY
4143 WOODMERE PARK BLVD.
VENICE, FLORIDA 34293

THE HOTEL DICK

THE HOTEL DICK

AXEL BRAND

FIVE STAR
A part of Gale, Cengage Learning

GALE
CENGAGE Learning™

Detroit • New York • San Francisco • New Haven, Conn • Waterville, Maine • London

3 1969 01771 7280

Copyright © 2008 by Axel Brand.
Five Star Publishing, a part of Gale, Cengage Learning.

ALL RIGHTS RESERVED
This novel is a work of fiction. Names, characters, places and incidents are either the product of the author's imagination, or, if real, used fictitiously.

No part of this work covered by the copyright herein may be reproduced, transmitted, stored, or used in any form or by any means graphic, electronic, or mechanical, including but not limited to photocopying, recording, scanning, digitizing, taping, Web distribution, information networks, or information storage and retrieval systems, except as permitted under Section 107 or 108 of the 1976 United States Copyright Act, without the prior written permission of the publisher.

The publisher bears no responsibility for the quality of information provided through author or third-party Web sites and does not have any control over, nor assume any responsibility for, information contained in these sites. Providing these sites should not be construed as an endorsement or approval by the publisher of these organizations or of the positions they may take on various issues.

Set in 11 pt. Plantin.
Printed on permanent paper.

LIBRARY OF CONGRESS CATALOGING-IN-PUBLICATION DATA

Brand, Axel.
    The hotel dick / Axel Brand. — 1st ed.
        p. cm.
    ISBN-13: 978-1-59414-676-3 (hardcover : alk. paper)
    ISBN-10: 1-59414-676-4 (hardcover : alk. paper)
    1. Police—Wisconsin—Milwaukee—Fiction. 2. Lookalikes—Crimes against—Fiction. 3. Nineteen-forties—Fiction. 4. Milwaukee (Wis.)—Fiction. I. Title.
PS3573.H4345H68 2008
813'.54—dc22   2008019783

First Edition. First Printing: September 2008.
Published in 2008 in conjunction with Tekno Books and Ed Gorman.

Printed in the United States of America
1 2 3 4 5 6 7 12 11 10 09 08

THE HOTEL DICK

CHAPTER ONE

Joe Sonntag knew the victim this time. He never liked the man and wasn't surprised that someone put a bullet through his mouth and another through his heart. There would be maybe two hundred suspects.

J. Adam Bark lay on the barbershop floor, a white barber's apron covering his face and most of his body. Gorilla was taking photos with his Speed Graphic and spraying used flashbulbs all over the black and white tiled floor. The ambulance guys were not allowed in, and they stared through the plate glass windows from the hotel corridor. The reporters from the *Milwaukee Journal* and the *Sentinel* were gawking there too. They'd get their story when Sonntag was good and ready.

Bark's legs projected from the barbershop apron, the pants pinstriped black broadcloth, pressed so sharp they could cut cold butter. The newly shined black wingtip oxfords hadn't a scuff on them. That was Bark for you. But now his white shirt was all mussed up, and so was his graying hair, and there weren't many teeth left in the ruin of his mouth.

The Lakeshore Towers was a flossy hotel, and this was a flossy barbershop, and J. Adam Bark was a flossy hotel dick. He had his own suite around the back, one story down from the lobby. That was his home. He liked it there. The hotel was his parlor.

Whoever shot Bark knew the man's ritual. The house dick arose late and retired late. There was no one to nab in the mornings anyway, except an occasional towel thief. Promptly at ten

7

each morning, J. Adam Bark entered the barbershop for his morning shave, after which he repaired to the coffee shop for his ritual eggs benedict and orange juice and java, and then toured the lobby, and finally retreated to his small office with the unmarked door. It wasn't until evening that Bark's job got interesting.

Lieutenant Sonntag had been there many times. He constantly had business with Bark. The amount of crime in the Lakeshore Towers was astonishing. That was what troubled Sonntag.

He thought to get Bark's wallet out of his pants before it disappeared. He tugged the sheet aside, found the pocket, unbuttoned the flap, and withdrew the wallet. Like everything else belonging to Bark, it showed no signs of use. Not even the soles of Bark's oxfords showed signs of use. Two singles and a fiver. Maybe not strange if you lived in a hotel and didn't need cash. He pulled Bark's social security card out. The man didn't have a driver's license.

"Jesus," he said.

"Yeah, it's bad," said Corporal Feeney.

"No, that's his name. The J in his name. Jesus Adam Bark."

"Yeah? He's been J. Adam long as I've known him."

"I think his parents wanted to cover all the bases."

Sonntag dropped the wallet and its contents into his evidence bag.

"J. A. B. Jab. That's what he did. A name is destiny," Feeney said. "Call a man Hubert and he's a sissy."

"Yeah, Feeney, call a man Jesus and he's a house dick."

The corporal looked a little miffed. "It fits," he said. "A Jesus would make a good house dick."

There was blue everywhere, too many cops, some of them wrecking the evidence. Sonntag was waiting for the medics to slap a few plasters on the barber, Damon Barbara.

At a few minutes after ten that Tuesday morning, someone had barged into the barbershop off the main lobby of the Lakeshore Towers and pumped two shots into the house dick while Bark lay back in the chrome-plated and leather barber chair with a hot towel over his face. Two shots, both fatal, both messy. Blood and brain had splattered over the chrome-plated chair and the neighbor chairs. The bullet had fragmented when it hit the chair, spraying lead all over, including several pieces into Barbara. Fragments had broken the mirror behind the chair, the one the barbers used to show off their work, wheeling the customer around to admire himself. Other fragments had wiped out a bottle of witch hazel and spilled talcum powder.

Barbara was the only witness.

"You can talk to him," the med said.

"You sure he doesn't need a ride?"

"We offered him a ride, x-rays, whatever. Some lead caught his forearm. Simple laceration. No lead in the wound. We patched it. He's okay, and itching to spill whatever he knows."

Sonntag nodded.

The barber was sitting in the third chair looking heroic. There was blood on him, blood and gray stuff. A thin guy, wiry sort of, with receding black hair pomaded down.

"I'm glad you're okay," Sonntag said.

"You ain't the only one."

"What happened? Just start at the beginning."

"Mr. Bark, he came in as usual, you can set your clock by it, and I did the usual, pumped the chair so he was sort of lying down, soaked his beard, plenty of hot water, lathered up, stropped my razor, and set to work. He didn't say nothing. Hardly ever does. I scraped off his beard, always taking care special, because he hates a nick. But this was a regular morning, no one else in my shop, and I finish up and wipe his face and then leave the hot towel over him for a minute, he likes it, and then bam!"

"Bam?"

"Yeah, bam. This guy, Spencer Tracy, barges in, pulls out an automatic, army forty-five I think, and bam, bam, that's the ball game. He's gone before I know what's happening. Loud, bam, bam, loud, and my ears are ringing and something stings my arm."

"Spencer Tracy?"

"Yeah, himself. Spencer Tracy comes wheeling in, gray fedora, Eisenhower jacket, bam, bam, bam."

"Spencer Tracy did it?"

"No one else."

"What does Spencer Tracy look like?"

"Jesus, everyone knows what he looks like. Big nose, big jaw that juts out like that."

"You're telling me that the actor, Spencer Tracy, killed Bark?"

Barbara shrugged. "I saw what I saw."

"How'd you know it was a military automatic pistol?"

"I wasn't in the 82nd Airborne for nothing."

"How close was Spencer Tracy?"

"Close! Six feet maybe. Them automatics, they ain't known for putting a bullet where you want it."

"You ever fired one?"

"We carried them, army airborne."

"Show me how close. Bark's lying back in the chair. Show me how it went."

Barbara leaped up, eager as a pup, headed for the door where cops blocked a milling crowd in the hall outside. Barbara paused there, then piled in, lifted his arm, and yes, about six feet from the chair, lowered the arm.

"Bam, bam," he said, wheeled away, and plunged toward the hall.

"Spencer Tracy," Sonntag said. "You sure?"

"Listen, man, I've seen him twenty times. He even stayed here once. They told me he checked in and we slid out to get a look. He was giving a valise to a bellboy."

"The assailant didn't wear a mask?"

"Hell no."

"Barehanded? Did he wear gloves?"

"White gloves, skinny gloves. Kid gloves, I'd say."

Sonntag noted it. The assailant had been around, it seemed. The automatic was probably lying in the bottom of the Milwaukee River, but gloves were harder to get rid of.

"You done? You gonna let me clean up around here? How's anyone gonna sit in a dead man's chair for a cut and a shave? No one will sit there now."

Something stirred in Sonntag's memory. Yeah, that was it. Spencer Tracy and Pat O'Brien were Milwaukee's gift to Hollywood. Two cut-ups at Marquette Academy. The actor knew Milwaukee, all right.

"Was there anyone else? Someone hanging around the hall, did you see?"

"Nope."

Sonntag sighed. "You remember when Tracy checked in here?"

"Nah, two, three years ago. Right after the war."

"Was he on a tour? Publicity?"

Barbara shrugged.

Sonntag pulled a pad and made a note to himself. He would look at the hotel records and a lot more. He didn't like this case. He didn't like Bark, he didn't like the fancy Lakeshore Hotel, he didn't like chasing down an actor.

"Do me a favor, Barbara. Don't say a thing to the press about Tracy, okay? Not a word."

He looked disappointed. Sonntag knew he was ready to spill what he saw into headlines.

"Yeah, for a little while anyway."

"Until I tell you."

"It's a free country," Barbara said.

"I have to check things out. We're going to get some photos of Tracy, and some others like him, and then we'll see how you do."

"I can pick Tracy out of any lineup," Barbara said.

"Okay, good. My guys'll drive you over to the station and show you some photos soon as we get this together."

"I'm ready. I'll finger him, all right."

"Maybe you will," Sonntag said, but he sensed that Barbara wouldn't.

Sonntag corralled Sergeant Vince Packard. It was time to set things in motion. "Go report to Captain Ackerman," he said. "Take Barbara with you. And Vince, tell them to get some mug shots ready. Anyone looks like Spencer Tracy. And tell them to wire the Los Angeles PD. We need to know where Spencer Tracy was all this week. Ask them to call MGM. I want a fast answer."

Packard nodded. A request like that had to go through top-dog channels, captain to captain. "I'll take Barbara."

"Yeah, and keep him away from the press. This Tracy thing, not a word."

"If I can."

"You will."

Packard grinned.

The big blue uniforms hustled the barber out, past the jostling reporters, and away. They shot a few questions at the barber, but Packard bulled his way out to his cruiser, parked in front of the hotel.

"Are you done, sir? This is disturbing our guests," said a gaunt gray gent.

"You the manager?"

"Yes. Please put this in order, just as fast as you can."

"You employed Mr. Bark?"

The man nodded. "Casper Reinhold; I run it here."

"I'll talk to you in a bit. We'll give the press their story. There's some things I want from you: keys to Bark's office, key to his suite. And your absolute promise to touch nothing, disturb nothing. I'm posting a man here."

"I'd just as soon there was no police presence here, sir. It really disturbs—"

"There will be cops here for a day or two. We'll stay out of sight as much as we can." There was something in this that bothered Sonntag. "Say, Mr. Reinhold, did you know Bark?"

"Of course."

"Like him?"

"He was very good at it, his work, you know, lieutenant."

Sonntag smiled. That was answer enough. "I'll be talking to you later."

"Whatever you say. But please, please, take that body away."

Sonntag thought that Reinhold wasn't grieving for J. Adam Bark.

CHAPTER TWO

Matt Dugan of the *Journal* would ask the best questions. He always did. The cops were his beat and he'd been around Milwaukee's streets for twenty years or so. And unlike the rest, he knew Bark.

"Lieutenant, have you any suspects?" Dugan asked.

"Not a one."

"Before the day's over you'll have a couple hundred."

Sonntag nodded. Reporters never knew how to deal with a nod. He would say as little as he could, for now. The brass didn't like detectives in the field giving interviews, but this time it couldn't be helped. Pantella was on vacation, and Saltz was in court testifying.

"Did Bark have enemies?" Dugan asked. "Like hotel guests?"

"It would seem that way, Matt."

"I mean, like guests that got their name in the papers?"

"You mean for court appearances? We're looking into it."

"Like people Bark yanked out of bed?"

This was getting into turf Sonntag didn't want to make public. Not yet, anyway.

"We have yet to establish a motive, Matt."

"Like people who forgot to bring their marriage license?"

"We're looking at all possibilities."

"Like famous people getting caught in bed?"

"Hotel dicks try to keep things up and up, Matt."

"How many? Two hundred, three hundred?"

"How many what?"

"How many guests did Bark catch, doing stuff?"

"We'll cover all the bases, Matt. We've hardly started."

"Fifty a year? Hundred?"

"Court records are public information."

"I thought maybe you'd put it right on the line, lieutenant."

Sonntag stared. He had an unrelenting stare that he found handy sometimes, like just then.

"You think this was a crime of revenge?" asked Peterson, the lightweight at the Hearst *Sentinel*.

"I repeat. We've barely started. We'll keep you posted. For now, all we can say is that hotel security officer J. Adam Bark was slain in the Lakeshore Hotel's barbershop a few minutes after ten, by a single assailant who escaped. He was shot twice, died immediately. The barber, Damon Barbara, was slightly injured and released. We will pursue every lead, and welcome tips. That's it, gents. We have work to do here."

"Hey, lieutenant. How many suspects did you say?"

Sonntag shook his head. They looked angry and combative. This was big stuff, and at least Dugan knew it. The rest probably sensed it, but didn't know the half of what Dugan knew. Sonntag wondered how the *Journal* would play it. Second section front page, he guessed. The Hearst paper would make it front page news with war type for a headline, and steal Dugan's story.

"All right. Camera guys can go in there. Take your pictures and don't touch anything. That's it."

Three rummies shoved in, all armed with the press cameras the size of an accordion, and pretty soon the flashbulbs were sizzling.

"Hey, you mind if we pull the sheet off?"

"Get out," Sonntag snapped.

They stared a moment, and retreated. Sonntag had a way of

laying down the law. He figured it was because he had raised boys.

The blue shirts hustled the press out of the barbershop.

"All right," he said. The sergeant would take over. Load the body, off to the morgue, seal the barbershop, drive their cruisers back to the station. Sonntag watched them, making sure no one screwed up, making sure no one flipped the sheet from Bark, no flashbulbs went off, no fresh plates were shoved into the Graflex cameras. They had their story. The *Journal* would run it that afternoon.

Sonntag watched them pull out. He turned off the lights in the barbershop. The windowless place slipped into twilight, lit only from the hotel corridor. He shut the door and put a police seal on it, a gummed notice not to tamper.

The hotel seemed almost normal. But there were solemn people in the lobby. He ignored them and headed for Bark's little office off the back of the registration area. He was hot suddenly, and ditched his trench coat. It was an odd death. No one wept. No one grieved. No family materialized. No hotel staff sat there, holding each other, wiping away tears. Jesus Adam Bark was a loner. Maybe a man without a family. It occurred to Sonntag that in all the years he had known Bark, and it was just about forever, Bark had never mentioned a family. No wife, no parents, no children. In fact, Sonntag didn't even know where the hell Bark was from.

Sonntag slid the big key into the heavy lock and pushed Bark's office door open, warily, ready for anything. The office was lit. Bark's Philco radio was playing, as usual. Bark loved and hated that radio. He loved band music, Tommy Dorsey, Benny Goodman, Harry James, Les Brown and his band of renown. Doris Day, Helen Forrest, Dick Haymes, Don Cornell, you name it. Sonntag heard the familiar voice of Rob Thomas, WTMJ's disk jockey. Thomas always played "The Sunny Side of the Street" as his theme. Sonntag liked that. It lifted his spirits, and most of the time his spirits needed a lift.

Bark kept that radio going night and day. They wouldn't let him play it loud. It might disturb the serene silence of the lobby, might scandalize guests. So Bark played it in his cubicle, and low, but anyone who had ever visited Bark there always got the best that the Hit Parade could offer.

On the shelf next to the radio was Bark's supply of spare tubes. He always kept a few on hand, especially a little devil half the size of the other tubes that kept burning out. When you had a burned out tube, you had to take it or other suspects to the hardware and have the clerks run them through the tube tester, and then replace the bad tube. For a price, always for a price. But Bark hated the delay, the silence, the hissing of the malevolent wounded radio.

"It's always that little stinker, the U5K72, with five prongs. They last about a week if I'm lucky. I go through more of those stinkers than all the other tubes put together," he had explained. It got so he simply kept spares on hand, lest he miss the latest Frank Sinatra warble or a Claude Thornhill arrangement.

But the Philco hummed away in its wooden cabinet. Glenn Miller's "Sunrise Serenade" now, which suited Sonntag just fine. He closed the door, just as Bark always did when they talked. If the music reached the irate ears of management, the music would cease.

The office was immaculate. Sonntag had never met anyone as immaculate as J. Adam Bark. There were wire baskets containing newspaper clippings. Mimeographed hotel directives had been pinned to a cork board on the door. Several days of Milwaukee's two papers were neatly stacked, awaiting Bark's scissors. There was a stack of recent movie magazines. Along one wall was a bank of four-drawer black file cabinets. On Bark's desk, where there should have been a photo of a wife or a child or two, was a studio publicity photo of Ava Gardner. It was signed, too. "To Adam, lots of luck, Ava."

Sonntag smiled. Ava knew her man. Sonntag doubted that Bark ever got lucky. Or wanted to.

The clippings heaped in one wire basket were entirely from the local society pages. Sonntag picked up a few. Debutante party for Miss Cecilia Gant, and in attendance were Janice Hopkins, Marsha Teague, Gail Hofsteadter, and so on. Sonntag knew most of the family names. Milwaukee was a big, muscular industrial town. These were the prim daughters of its captains of industry. Daughters and sons. Each name in the story carefully red-lined by Bark. Sonntag lifted a Dorothy Parnell column from the Hearst paper. Dorothy Parnell was its society editor. "Mesdames Perkins and Fellowes held a tea at the Women's Club of Wisconsin in honor of Miss Jane Fellowes, upon the announcement of her engagement." Bark had underlined every proper name, twenty-three names. Wives of lawyers and dentists, insurance executives, leather and tanning people, heavy equipment builders, hospital administrators. These were the ones who lived up in Whitefish Bay or Shorewood or Fox Point, along the lakefront. Their homes did not lack for space or comfort or view. Here was word that Peter and Maria Baskerville had returned from Palm Beach after checking on their property following a hurricane. The Baskerville names had been red-lined.

Not a day's paper escaped Bark's busy scissors.

The next wire basket had stories of a different sort, local and sometimes national business news. Corporate announcements. The new secretary-treasurer of the Wilmot Leather Company had been announced. Fortney Tire and Rubber. Spearhead Fertilizer and Phosphorus, on and on. Red-lined names. J. Adam Bark must have known the name of every prominent citizen of Milwaukee County, and their offspring as well. The other wire basket had stuff about celebrities, movie people.

The stuff in the baskets depressed Sonntag. What a shit Bark was. There were maybe fifty people waiting in line to kill him.

Robb Thomas was playing a new one, that woman Rosemary Clooney singing, and Sonntag wasn't so sure about her. He thought he'd better check in, so he lifted the earpiece off the upright phone and waited for the operator. "Broadway 5-7777," he said. He heard a click and the ring. Agnes, the chief's secretary answered.

"It's me. Tell him I'm in Bark's office. Anyone want me?"

"You got any leads?" she asked. "He wants something to give the radio people, five o'clock news."

"I have leads," he said. "About two hundred, but I'm closing in. I'll finger the killer at four-fifty."

"Big deal," she said. "He'll love that. Say, while you're on the line. We need next of kin. We need to notify someone. Could you—"

"Personnel file. I'll get back to you," he said.

He replaced the receiver on its hook and headed for the manager's suite.

His path into Casper Reinhold's sanctum sanctorum was blocked by a formidable woman with football player's shoulders and pince-nez parked on a pulpy nose.

"I'm Lieutenant Sonntag, homicide," he said.

She eyed him warily and nodded.

"I'd like Mr. Bark's personnel file."

"That's confidential, sir."

"Is Mr. Reinhold available?"

"He's busy just now."

"This is a homicide. I'd like the file. Show me where it is and I'll get it."

Her glacial obstructiveness slowly melted, but she wasn't going to fetch the file without a tussle. Slowly she rose, towering two or three inches above Sonntag, and set sail. Sonntag followed her into a side room, where she punched the light button. She slid open a cabinet and withdrew a manila folder, but she didn't hand it to him.

"You'll have to sign for it. We make everyone sign for it."

"I'll look at it right here," he said.

She reluctantly handed it to him.

Bark's file was thin. There were annual performance evaluations. Some salary calculations. His hotel suite was part of his compensation. Everything else was missing. His employment application, name, address, next of kin, background, war record if any. There was something else missing. Complaints. Had no guest of the Lakeshore Towers ever complained about the man in the eleven years he had worked there?

"I'll have to borrow this," Sonntag said. "Tell me something: did Mr. Bark ever talk about his family, his history?"

"I refused to talk to Mr. Bark, detective."

Her glare put a stop to that line of thought. "They want next of kin. Can you help me?"

"I think Mr. Bark's parents were anteaters, sir."

"Did he leave any baby anteaters behind? Did he have any brother or sister anteaters?"

A faint smile built on the woman's face. "Return the files when you're done, Mr. Sonntag."

The lieutenant carted the file back to Bark's office and worked through the scanty material. The file had been purged.

He called Agnes. "There's nothing in Bark's files. Tell them to try the army. Tell them that his parents were anteaters. That comes straight from the executive suite."

He waited for a response but Agnes didn't bite.

"No ID. I'll tell them," she said. "If you find out anything, call me."

"I have a hunch I won't," he said. The man he thought had been J. Adam Bark was no such person. Was nobody at all.

CHAPTER THREE

Joe Sonntag pulled Bark's incident logs off the shelf. They were kept in gray ledger books, and filed by years. Eleven in all. Sonntag had seen some of these in the past when Bark had answered police questions or responded to investigations.

The hotel detective had a variety of duties. He investigated the hotel's own staff, looking into theft from guests or from the hotel. Bark had caught an assortment of chambermaids, bellboys, bartenders, maintenance men, and kitchen staff over those years. He looked into security complaints from guests. Intruders in their rooms. He nailed guests walking out with towels. Ashtrays were okay; the hotel regarded them as advertising, just the way the Stork Club in New York liked to see its distinctive ashtrays disappear from the premises.

Sonntag had once watched Bark stop a salesman who was checking out with a satchel full of monogrammed hotel bath towels. He'd been cued by the desk clerk, who had been clued by the chambermaid.

"Mind stepping in here, sir?" Bark had asked.

The salesman had followed Bark, simply because Bark had the presence to command it.

"I know you meant to pay for those towels in your bag; we enjoy having our hotel monogram in people's homes. But I guess you forgot."

"Yeah, uh, I guess so. I didn't mean to."

The salesman looked abashed. It cost him twenty-seven dollars. The hotel always made a tidy profit. Twenty-seven was cheap compared to a petty theft complaint in municipal court.

Theft, a domestic shouting match that had to be quieted down, an occasional nut, an arsonist, pickpockets, a few con men in the bar fleecing patrons, a chambermaid who claimed she'd been ravished, vandalism, a barkeep who was cleaning out the till. Bark dealt with that sort of stuff.

But the hotel dick had other agendas, and as Sonntag pulled the gray ledgers off the shelf, a wave of melancholia gusted through him. It always did. Every meeting he ever had with the house dick resulted in the same gust of pain. Bark was a stalker.

Sonntag knew what he would find in those ledgers. There would be a complete description of each incident, time, date, nature of offense, action taken, and charges pressed in municipal court. These were written in Bark's spiky hand, blue ink, amazingly disciplined penmanship with not a blot or crossed-out word, and only one to a page. He had a Parker fountain pen, made over in Janesville, and two bottles of Parker blue ink.

Bark wore no badge. He was not a sworn peace officer. The great hotel, in its rectitude, was ever vigilant to prevent offenses against public morals in its rooms: adultery, fornication, rape, and prostitution. It had the law on its side, and used it.

Sonntag knew the drill. Older man, young babe check in. Clerk tells Bark. The hotel dick stalks them through cocktails and dinner. Watches them enter elevator, elevator stops at eleventh floor. Bark calls cops, a pair of patrolmen stop in, Bark and cops raid the room. Bust right in, catch older man and younger woman compromised. Maybe take photos. No marriage license, eh? Let's see, this time it's adultery for you and fornication for her, old man, municipal court, nine tomorrow morning. Sonntag had seen it. Seen photos. Seen testimony. Seen names and charges show up in the papers.

Sonntag didn't buy it. He didn't like the law, he didn't like

hotel dicks in general, and Bark in particular. He opened a
ledger at random:

May 27, 1947. Guest registered at 9:02 P.M., single.
Grover Milledge. 57 West Denver Ave., Kenosha, Wisconsin. Rm 907. Milledge, age 52, had no luggage; I was
alerted by desk. 9:30 P.M. Mary Beth Kean, 23, observed
in lobby, wearing dime store glass ring, took elevator to
ninth floor, entered room 907. 9:45 officers summoned,
Patrolmen McClary and Collier responded. 10:15, forcibly
entered 907, witnessed Milledge flip away from Kean. Both
naked. After questioning, charges preferred. Defrauding
innkeeper (two persons at single rate), adultery for
Milledge, fornication for Kean. Pair allowed to dress and
taken to station for booking. May 28: Action: guilty on all
counts, fined $87 Milledge $26 Kean. LT billed Milledge
$17 for double occupancy.

Eleven annual ledgers full of stuff like that. Sonntag set them
aside. He needed air. The majestic lobby caught the westering
sun, which gilded its green marble columns, brightened the pot-
ted palms, and made the waxed green and gold tiles of the floor
glisten. The hotel was built to last forever. The first two stories
were quarried gray stone, loosely dressed; the rest, Milwaukee's
own cream-colored brick, twelve stories except for the penthouse
towers north and south. From all the east-side rooms, one could
see far out upon Lake Michigan, watch boat traffic. The west-
side rooms offered a view of downtown Milwaukee and a sea of
green trees that hid the residential districts. This was the premier
hotel in Wisconsin, solid, muscular, a fitting place for the city's
moneyed guests.

Joe Sonntag patrolled the lobby, studying the clothing
boutiques, the florist, the magazine stand, the shoe-shine stand,
the bell captain's desk, the two brass-bound elevators operated

by wiry elevator men. He drifted toward an empty elevator. The elevator monkey stood just inside, his green pillbox hat matching his green uniform, five feet, wizened, maybe half Filipino.

"Floor, sir?"

"You see Spencer Tracy here today?"

"Your people already asked me that."

"He around before? Ever been in here?"

The elevator man beckoned. Sonntag stepped in. The elevator man swung the mesh doors shut, pushed the brass rotor handle forward, and Sonntag felt the cage rise upward. Then the elevator man stopped the machine. The needle pointed between three and four.

"Everybody says Spencer Tracy shot the house dick," the elevator guy said.

"We're looking into it. You ever see him in this hotel? Ever?"

"Never. But I seen Frank Sinatra once. I took him to the north penthouse. Private entrance. Last stop, goes right into the penthouse."

"I don't think Sinatra did it, right? You see anyone today who even looked a little like Tracy?"

"Mister, I see ten guys an hour look like Tracy."

A bell clanged. The elevator man rotated the brass handle forward, and the elevator climbed to the seventh floor. He swung the mesh gates open. A nervous woman in a wool suit eyed them, and reluctantly entered.

"I'm half afraid to go to the lobby," she said.

"It's safe," the operator said. He pulled the brass handle toward him. The elevator plummeted and then bounced slightly. He opened the gate, found he was two inches low, and nudged the cage upward until its floor was flush with the lobby floor. The woman left.

"That it?" the man asked.

"If you think of anything, get ahold of me. I'll be spending time in Bark's office."

"You ever been in his suite?"

"Not yet."

"No one has. Maybe some cleaning ladies."

Sonntag made a note of it.

He spent the rest of the afternoon culling the suspects in the three most recent ledgers. Every single person in the ledgers was a suspect, but he would focus only on the ones who were caught in bed, the ones whose lives and reputations were likely demolished both by their own conduct and by getting caught by the hotel dick. The ones who ended up in municipal court. There were, all told, two hundred and twenty-seven over all those years.

Sonntag would confiscate the ledgers for the time being, but meanwhile he compiled a list on a legal pad.

The phone rang. It was his captain, Ackerman, homicide and vice.

"You going home?"

"No, why?"

"It's ten. You're going home. You can get the last streetcar still."

That amazed Sonntag. Ten. Dark out. "I didn't know."

"What have you got?"

"Two hundred twenty-seven prime suspects, maybe another hundred towel thieves and cheats."

"We got some poor ballistics from the rear of one slug, the one in his chest."

"Dredge the river, then."

Ackerman laughed. "Go home. You're off."

Sonntag closed the ledger he was studying, put the ledgers back on their shelf, collected his trench coat and fedora, and slid out of Bark's office. He tucked the list of suspects into his breast pocket. The darkness amazed him. The lush lobby, glow-ing in lamplight, was silent.

He stepped out the double doors into a cool eve. A row of checkered taxis waited there. He was tempted to go back to the station to collect his black lunch bucket, but decided not to. He was only a block from the east terminal of the Wells streetcar line. And he had just time enough for the last car if he hurried.

It was there, a pool of bright light. He entered, showed his two-dollar monthly pass, punched for October 1948.

"Evening, lieutenant."

The motorman knew him. Sonntag had caught this last car many times. He was middling everything: middling height and weight and tincture. Middling lantern-jaw ugly. He wore his wavy brown hair longer than the rules allowed, but no one docked him for it. People took him for a cop, and he didn't know why. Like the motorman calling him lieutenant. Maybe it was the stare. Lizbeth said he had a disconcerting stare.

Another man boarded, dripped a dime into the glass collection box where it rested on a trapdoor. The motorman eyed the dime long enough to make sure it wasn't a slug, flipped a lever, and the dime vanished into the steel money box below. The man headed for the rear, passing rows of lacquered yellow wicker seats.

A moment later the car ground west, its familiar ozone smell wafting through it. Streetcars always smelled like burned-out electric motors. The overhead trolley snapped and crackled as it conveyed juice to the motors.

Lieutenant Sonntag thought he would study the list of suspects as he rode, but then he didn't want to. Somehow it was painful. But that was his job: exchanging pain with other people. Names, names, some of them familiar names, were on that list. Names of mortified, guilty people with plenty to hide were there. Names of Milwaukee industrialists, names of debutantes, names of lowlifes, names of a couple of politicians, names of celebrities, each of them diligently stalked, stalked, stalked. Bark had been a stalker. And the bigger the catch, the happier he was.

The Wells streetcar ground west, past downtown buildings, past mixed old neighborhoods. The other passenger got off at 27th Street.

"Guess you're looking for the killer," the motorman said.

Sonntag grunted. He didn't really want to talk about it.

But now the car was coming to the viaduct. This was the bad part. He resisted pulling the cord, getting off, walking three miles home. Instead he gripped the seat in front of him, hung on hard. All he could see from the windows was streetlights at the intersections, night lights in shops.

The viaduct was a long trestle that spanned the Menominee River valley. Down below eighty feet or so, heavy industry sprawled along the riverbanks, punctuated by warehouses, a brewery, equipment lots. A half a mile of terror.

He felt his pulse leap and hung on tight. By day it wasn't so bad. He could see the valley floor. But now it was bad. The motorman slowed to ten miles an hour and then suddenly there were no lights, just darkness, the Wells car floating slowly through air, rocking sickeningly with every minor gust of air, crawling forward with that odd streetcar whine, and then at last the earth rushed up, and there were lights beside him, and he was on land again. His hands were sweaty.

He and Lizbeth lived in a bungalow on 57th Street. His older son, Junior, had been drafted. His younger boy, Will . . . polio, 1947, on the football team, gone.

He pulled the cord before the next stop, 56th Street. The Wells cars stopped on even-numbered streets. The motorman didn't stop there, though. He stopped the car at 57th and let Sonntag off. The motorman always did that when no one else was aboard.

Lizbeth wouldn't be up. Sonntag would fill the stoker with coal and go to bed.

CHAPTER FOUR

It was still dark when Sonntag walked into the Kilbourn Street station. He had scraped out of bed an hour early and fixed his own lunch. Lizbeth had barely stirred.

"You got a big push again," she said, half groggy.

"I'll get home tonight. We can see a movie."

She opened her eyes, smiled at him, and flipped to her side, lost in sleep before he even finished dressing.

He stood twenty minutes in the mean cold before the orange streetcar squealed to a halt. By the time the car reached the viaduct a hint of light grayed the world, but the light didn't help much. He white-knuckled across the Menominee Valley, never looking down. Sonntag couldn't fly, either. Once he was assigned to a law enforcement conference in Denver, but he declined: he couldn't put a foot into a DC-4. He couldn't even walk through an airport without busting into a sweat.

He reached the downtown station at six-thirty.

"Go home and go back to bed, Sonntag," Lammers, the night dispatcher, told him.

Sonntag ignored him, studied the messages and reports on the spindle, found nothing, and headed out the door.

"Say, Sonntag. There was something. In the captain's in-basket. A telex from Los Angeles."

"Mind if I look?"

"You didn't hear it from me."

Sonntag punched the light switch in the dark office. The yel-

29

low sheet lay coiled in the wire basket. Sonntag plucked it up. The Los Angeles cops didn't know of Tracy's whereabouts. MGM didn't know. Tracy wasn't scheduled for a film until November. They thought he was out of town. Should they take further action?

He dropped the curling sheet back in the basket. Spencer Tracy, fugitive killer, blasts a hotel dick and runs for cover. They would track him down. A life sentence for an actor would entertain the world. Tracy would walk into Waupun prison jut-jawed and handsome.

"Thanks," he said to the dispatcher. "I'm at the Lakeshore."

"You gotta report here at seven-thirty."

"Tell them."

This was a ritual. They didn't like for him to start ahead of shift. It upset their orderly universe. Cops report on time. They stand at attention for roll call. They get looked over, receive instructions, take assignments. No overtime. No bending rules. No exceptions. Obey. Do your job the way you've been taught. They had threatened to fire him for coming to work early, but he paid no heed. It was in his personnel file: disobeys instruction to appear promptly at the beginning of the shift.

He hiked to the Lakeshore Towers, a dozen blocks, with a lake wind probing through his trench coat. The great hotel was silhouetted by the blue first-light sliding across Lake Michigan. Now, before full day, all but two or three lights were dimmed. He plodded through the shadowed lobby, his footsteps echoing hollowly on the tiles, descended a tile-lined stairwell that took him into the executive office area, headed along a corridor until he reached a row of ground-level suites with windows opening on the lake. The southernmost one of these was Bark's home, if that was the word for it. He let himself in with the master key, and punched the light switch.

Bark's lair was immaculate. Except for one thing, it looked

like a showcase apartment; a furnished suite devoid of idiosyncrasy, colors and styles muted to offend no one. But the exception was striking. Every wall was crammed with studio portraits of Hollywood actors and actresses. These were the glossies sent out by the hundreds of thousands to fans who clamored for them. Bark had filled the living and dining area, kitchen, bath, hallway, and single bedroom with them.

Sonntag opened the anonymous tan drapes, revealing a gray lake and the yellow coaches of a Chicago and Northwestern passenger train in the station. He examined the rooms for disorder, but there was none. There was not a dirty dish in the kitchen. Not a wrinkle in the carefully made bed. Not even underwear in the wicker hamper. A cigar smell permeated the rooms, but not a butt burdened an ashtray.

There was nothing of J. Adam Bark here, nothing that stamped the man, nothing that gave Sonntag an insight into the house dick—except those photos. Lucille Ball, Van Johnson, James Stewart, Gary Cooper, Jean Peters, Katharine Hepburn, William Holden, Rita Hayworth, Betty Grable, Errol Flynn, Lana Turner, Deborah Kerr, Douglas Fairbanks, Mary Pickford, all on one wall.

Loraine Day, Red Skelton, Elizabeth Taylor, Brian Donlevy, Nelson Eddy, Charley Chaplin, Montgomery Clift, Greta Garbo, Henry Fonda, Jane Wyman, Frank Sinatra, Keenan Wynn, Robert Young, Stuart Whitman, Ward Bond, James Cagney, Harry Carey Jr., Joan Blondell, Mary Astor, Wallace Beery, Humphrey Bogart, Ethel Merman, Lionel Barrymore, Ethel Barrymore, John Barrymore, all in a row.

Franchot Tone, Preston Sturges, Ronald Coleman, Bette Davis, Delores Del Rio, Gary Cooper, Rosalind Russell, George Raft, Tyrone Power, Donna Reed, Ronald Reagan, Jane Russell, Carole Lombard, Laurence Olivier, David Niven, Ida Lupino, Jeanette MacDonald, Adolph Menjou, Jennifer Jones, Danny

Kaye, Arthur Kennedy, Burt Lancaster, Myrna Loy, Greer Garson, Robert Taylor, Angela Lansbury, June Allyson, Clark Gable, Gene Kelly, Robert Mitchum, and yes, Spencer Tracy over there above the sofa.

Sonntag paused, studying the studio portrait of Tracy. Lanky, male, a great crop of sandy hair barely disciplined, clean jaw, long nose, a certain tough look. There on the wall, no special place, surrounded by stars and stars.

Sonntag made a hasty survey. No picture was missing. No empty slot on the wall. He studied the photos closely as the light quickened over the lake. No real signatures; just the printed variety. Ask for a star photo; get one from the studio in the mail. How many? Two hundred? Not enough wall for so many. Maybe a hundred and fifty. Anything else? Yes, no female stars in the bathroom. John Wayne, George Sanders, Ricardo Montalban, Paul Henreid, Richard Widmark, Wallace Beery, James Cagney in there.

Strange. Sonntag thought women ought to be just the thing for a man like Bark. But there were no female smiles when Bark took a leak. Lizbeth had done their bathroom in antiseptic white without a hint of decor. White tiles, white enamel walls. White towels. Sonntag liked that. Body functions required white.

He glanced at his Bulova. Seven twenty-nine. They'd all be standing in lines now, and would snap to attention when Day Captain Ackerman barreled in.

The Chicago and Northwestern engine, a Pacific four-six-two, humped smoke, and the yellow snake rolled out of the station. The lake was glistening in morning sun.

Sonntag turned to the small polished desk with an unabused green blotter on it and pulled the drawers. Payroll receipts, rubber band around them. A hundred ten a week. Not bad. The hotel put him up, changed his sheets, did his personal laundry, ironed his shirts. No rent, no utilities, and food on the house.

Not even a bar bill. Manila payroll envelopes, pure cash. No bank account that Sonntag could find. The hotel was Bark's banker, too. All a man had to buy was a Palm Beach suit now and then, and some wingtip Florsheims.

The black cradle phone rang. Sonntag eyed it, knowing it hadn't been dusted for prints. He lifted it.

"Did you dust it first?" Ackerman asked.

Ackerman always read his mind.

"No."

"Next time you miss roll call, I'm busting you."

"Yes, sir."

"What did the telex in my basket say?"

"Should I know?"

"Are you a detective or not?"

"Track him down. I want to know where he was."

"I already told the LAPD to keep looking. We'll get a handle on Tracy. Think he did it?"

"I'm not ruling out anything."

"He's a lapsed Catholic."

"What's that supposed to mean?"

"He had reason to shoot the hotel dick." Ackerman laughed and hung up.

There was more to look at. In an end table drawer were some *Photoplay* magazines. Every issue, in perfect order. Bark not only had acquired signed photos of half of Hollywood, but kept up with all the glitter, the alleged romances, the occasional scandals. Beside the magazines were manila envelopes, each with a year written on it. Inside of these were clippings: Louella Parsons, Hedda Hopper, Sheila Graham. The man stored every scrap of gossip the mavens collected, each column neatly clipped and dated. And Walter Winchell, too, clipped from the *Sentinel*, machine-gun journalism, the bullets linked by a series of periods, gossip, celebrities. Who hadn't heard Winchell's radio gossip, that always began, "Good evening, Mr. and Mrs. North America and all the ships at sea. Let's go to press." Who didn't know that Winchell held court at table 50 of the Cub Room at Sherman Billingsley's Stork Club in New York.

And here were Winchell's ra-ta-tat-tat clippings: divorces, marriages, arrests, breakups, flings, drunks, parties, movies. Why? What had J. Adam Bark seen in all that?

Sonntag punched the light switches and let himself out. An elderly chambermaid was vacuuming the gloomy corridor. She barely noticed him. He pulled a pad of gummed stickers from his suit coat, licked one, and pasted it to the door. "Do not enter," it said. "Sealed by order of Milwaukee Police Department. Violators will be prosecuted."

The lobby had come to life now. Guests were checking out, waiting for taxis, collecting in the dining room for breakfasts served on white linen–clad tables.

He clattered across the shining tile floors at the registration area, headed for Bark's office, and let himself in once again, intuitively studying the room to see whether anything had been altered. It was just as he had left it. It was odd, maybe the result of years at his trade, that he always had in his mind an imprint of any room he was leaving, and how he called it to mind when he reentered that room.

Ackerman would be wanting suspects. And right now. And Joe Sonntag knew where to find them. He settled in Bark's swivel chair and opened the incident ledger for this year. In it was recorded in minute detail, the sort of detail that made lawyers happy, exactly what had transpired.

9/17/48 Alban Conover checked out 7:48 A.M., one-night single. CM notified desk two bath towels missing. I waylaid Conover as he was leaving, pulled him into office, suggested that he had forgotten to pay for the souvenirs.

What souvenirs, he said, following the usual script. Would he care to open his valise? He wouldn't. The price would be seven each. He protested; I urged him to pay or face consequences. Restocking charge. He paid, check #478, $14.00, which I sent to accounting. I gave him receipt #1690 for same.

Seven clams for a dollar towel. Sonntag thought it was a racket.

Alban Conover, Green Bay, Wisconsin, suspect. Not a very likely one, Sonntag thought as he wrote the name on a legal pad.

There were hundreds more to examine. Indeed, this was 1948 Incident 101. There were scores of suspects from this year alone, but only a few really good ones.

He would call Ackerman and tell him to send help. Ten detectives wouldn't be enough.

CHAPTER FIVE

Most of the stuff in Bark's ledgers was routine. He nabbed some kitchen help stealing flatware. He collared a chambermaid who was lifting cash from guests. He stopped a brawl in the restaurant. He threw a confidence man named Alonzo Podesta Salazar from Buenos Aires out of the bar. He nailed people skipping out. He caught hookers up from Chicago. He found a lost purse. He caught a pimply boy hiding in a stall in the women's room. But the leitmotif threading through Bark's incident reports was something else entirely: he regularly caught people in bed and hauled them to municipal court on fornication charges, or worse, adultery charges, and usually these involved defrauding an innkeeper. Case after case: "Observed so and so checking in, single room. Later, so and so was discovered climbing stairs instead of using elevator." Bark would fetch a cop or two for the bust, and they took photos and preferred charges. The victims ended up paying $25 to $80 plus costs, and got their names in the papers.

That was obviously Bark's game. The man boasted of it; he told cops that he knew every hump in the hotel. Sonntag sighed. There were laws he hated even if they upheld public decorum.

Bark had his ways, all right.

Sonntag ignored most of those. He was looking for the unusual, the odd. That's how he was. Whenever he hit upon something that awakened his curiosity, that's when he took a closer look. He knew he wasn't at all like the other cops, not even like the other detectives. He couldn't explain it; he was alert for things that weren't routine. He thought maybe it was because he was dumber than the other investigators.

Like the Stebbins incident, 12 March. Marcia Stebbins, twenty-one, hauled before the magistrate for soliciting for immoral purposes. Complaint from Bark.

That one bothered Sonntag. The Stebbins Motor Company, down in the Menominee River valley, was a big, sprawling tan-brick plant, ancient buildings but modern interiors. Biggest manufacturer of diesel engines in the world.

Marcia Stebbins, from Whitefish Bay, fancy executive outpost north of Milwaukee, on the lake, society suburb. Whitefish Bay people got written up by Dorothy Parnell at the *Sentinel* a lot. Why the hell was that girl soliciting? Her daddy could buy and sell the Rockefellers. He could also hire a hit man for a few nickels.

Sonntag reached for Bark's phone, found the name in the directory, and called: Lake 5-3256.

A woman answered.

"Marcia Stebbins, please."

"May I ask who is calling?"

"Joseph Sonntag, Milwaukee police."

There was a lengthy pause. "Miss Stebbins no longer is here."

"How can I get ahold of her?"

"I'm not permitted to say, sir."

"And you are?"

"I'm in domestic service to the family, sir."

"And your name?"

It came in a rush. "Miss Stebbins has an apartment on Lake Shore Drive. She's attending the Layton School of Art . . . I'm Agnes Kowalski."

"I'll need a phone number and address, and then I'll let you go, Mrs. Kowalski."

Sonntag got what he needed and called the apartment. No answer. Layton, maybe. He'd leg it. Only three or four blocks.

The stately old gallery and museum had been a fixture of Milwaukee's cultural life for years. Sonntag had scarcely been in it; he preferred to read a good mystery, sort of a busman's holiday, he figured.

He tracked her to a fashion design class, and picked her out of the students without having ever seen her. What other art student would be wearing a tweedy suit, leather pumps, nylons with seams that ran like arrows up her calves, and a pearl necklace? He whiled away the last five minutes of the class hour absorbing his lifetime quota of oil paintings.

"Miss Stebbins?" he asked as the class fell away.

She turned, suddenly, a hard scrutiny in her brown eyes.

"Joe Sonntag. I'm with the police. Have a minute?"

"I don't . . . look, I have to go."

"You could help me. I'd like to ask you a few things about that hotel detective."

"Him? You think I . . . look, I've got to go."

Sonntag pulled his fedora off his head and smiled. "I think maybe you had some bad luck last March. Maybe we could help each other."

"Do I have to?"

"Why don't you sit down with me for five minutes and see?"

She paused on the edge, and then tumbled. "Okay."

"Where?" he asked.

"It's not true, it's not true! The whole thing was . . . like, a lie."

He steered her into a silent gallery, toward a bench. Gray light flooded through a skylight. A room full of fat Flemish art. Milwaukee went for fat.

"I think it was probably a lie, too," he said.

"How do I know who you are?"

He pulled his badge, flipped open the black leather folder.

"Mr. Sonntag, you've come to haul me away," she said.

He smiled. "Not like that. March twelfth. Start at the beginning."

She didn't. She sat mutely, staring at him, the recollections flooding through her.

"That's my birthday," she said. "I turned twenty-one that day. Finishing up at Madison. A BA in design. Home for Easter break. Twenty-one! I could order a drink. My parents were in Palm Beach. That's where they go, you know. Daddy said here's a hundred, have a party, have fun, sorry we can't be there. So I thought and thought, and what I thought was, I would like to go to a big hotel and have a drink and dinner all by myself. So I did. I checked in."

"A single, right?"

"Of course! There was this man reading a paper in the lobby. I didn't pay him any heed. But I guess he was keeping tabs on me. The bellboy took me to my room, I tipped him, he gave me the key and smiled and said if I wanted anything, anything at all, just let him know. He winked. I thought that was pretty bold. But single women in hotels are fair game. I laughed. He wouldn't have said that around my parents."

"Did you mind?"

"Mind? On my first fling? A night on the town. Twenty-one and legal at last!"

"You had a good time."

"I started to. I got myself all dolled up, put on the Carmen Miranda lipstick, and then headed down to the bar. Maybe I'd drink too much. Maybe I wanted to. Maybe I'd meet a guy. Maybe I'd just sit there and watch the boats go by. That's a nice view, you know."

"Six o'clock, seven?"

"I don't know. I was going to have some fun. So I rang the

elevator and the little guy took me down to the lobby, and I drew a few looks. I was ready for a whistle or two. That would have been a nice birthday present."

"You're a very handsome woman."

"Yeah, too handsome, it seems." Her humor vanished into an odd bleakness.

"Were you looking for a date?"

"I was looking for a few birthday presents. A guy, well, if he was just the right type."

Sonntag hesitated, then plunged. "And do what?"

She stared hotly. "Maybe dance the night away. Maybe just to meet someone interesting. You ever had a birthday? Or a dream? You want any more? I'm tired of this. The hotel man's dead. Go pick on someone else."

A bunch of Cub Scouts piled into the gallery and spread out like Mrs. Stewart's Liquid Bluing in the wash water. One kid was making grunting noises, but a toothy mama was shushing him.

Marcia sprang up. "I gotta go."

Sonntag smiled. "I'm hooked. You can't leave me dangling. Finish the story?"

"I don't know why," she said.

"For my next birthday."

She smiled suddenly. He liked her smiles, which came like a string of sun dogs across the sky.

"So I ordered a Manhattan in the bar. The bartender, he looked, the gears rotating in his head, and then nodded. He didn't ask. That was my first Manhattan, my dad's favorite. I was just sitting there at a little table, having a birthday, when that man . . . that man . . ."

"Mr. Bark."

"He wandered by, a drink in his hand, and says something like, 'Hey, buy me a drink?' "

"I just shook my head. He was three times my age."

"Then he sat down, uninvited, and I froze up. 'Whatcha doing, honey?' he said, and I knew I was going to have a problem with a masher. You don't know what it's like, mashers. They just come on, and think they're God's gift to women. But he scared me a little. He looked like he could order a girl around, even if I was absolutely legal and just having a night out."

"He didn't leave."

"No, he was pretty funny, a little bold, sort of, you know, risque, and I just sipped. He stuck like glue and I was thinking maybe I'd go to my room, just to get rid of him but he was halfway entertaining and I didn't know what to do."

Sonntag knew. What interested him most was how Bark operated.

"I'm so dumb," she said. "I think I'm the dumbest woman on earth. Two drinks later, when I was looped, I finally got free of him, told him I had to find a restroom, and went to my room. I was going to freshen up and maybe have a late dinner."

She looked about ready to stop, but then she continued.

"He came to the door. I was in the bathroom and he knocked and knocked until I opened. He thrust a twenty in my hand and said the evening was on him. I just sort of took it. Next I knew, a cop took a picture, and they put handcuffs on me and said I was soliciting for immoral purposes. I guess you know the rest."

Sonntag felt the old pain, the pain when being a cop is no joy. "Thank you. One more question, Miss Stebbins. How did your parents react?"

"They . . . never knew. They were in Palm Beach. But everyone else knew. There was my name in the *Journal*. For that! For that! I didn't get invited any more. I lost . . ."

"A night in the tank, twenty-five and costs, a magistrate who was amused and told you to plead guilty to save yourself some grief, yes?"

She blinked, fought off the tears, stood abruptly, and bolted from the gallery.

Not a happy lady, Sonntag thought. He had a lot of questions still. He really wanted to know more about how Bark had trapped her. And why. What did Bark say? Was he gloating? Who was the cop with him? A young lady from a prominent Milwaukee family, nailed for hooking? What happened after? What was she learning here? She'd had a college education in Madison. Did she have a beau?

He watched Marcia Stebbins sail past Cub Scouts and vanish through the double doors. Jesus Adam Bark, you sonofabitch.

CHAPTER SIX

Sonntag called Ackerman from the hotel.

"What have you got?" the day captain asked.

"I've got too many leads. What I need is three or four men."

"Can't do it. I've got a Schlitz truck hijacking, a baseball bat murder of a paraplegic, a Railway Express robbery at the Milwaukee Road station, an unidentified female body at the Milorganite fertilizer plant, and eleven burglaries, four on Vliet Street."

"I still need three men."

"What am I going to tell the press?"

"We'll have our man tomorrow. We're narrowing down two-hundred twenty-three leads."

Ackerman paused. Then, "Sonntag, just keep at it a couple of days. Okay? No one's hollering. It can wait. The papers are calling it the Close Shave Killing. Maybe you can get something more from that hair cutter, Barbara."

"I'll try. That reminds me, what about Spencer Tracy?"

"Oh, yeah, I forgot. Movie star Spencer Tracy was in Chicago four days ago; came to town on the Super Chief out of LA. Left from Union Station for New York last night on the Twentieth Century Limited. He's going to England."

The phone crackled. "How do you know?" Sonntag asked.

"MGM, they keep a leash on all their pets."

"The timing fits," Sonntag said.

"Fat chance." Click.

Ackerman hung up. He always did that. Talk, click, dead line. Sometimes Sonntag had to call back to finish up what he was saying.

So Tracy was ninety miles south in the Windy City the morning Bark ate two bullets. Or was he? What an odd case. Spencer Tracy, maybe the biggest star in Hollywood, biggest at MGM anyway, known for his tough-guy roles. People flocked to any Tracy film, especially when it had Katharine Hepburn in it. The two made magic. But wasn't Tracy supposed to be a serious boozer, in fact a drunk? Unreliable? Unstable?

Sonntag peered around Bark's orderly office. Too orderly. The man was obsessive about it. Sonntag punched the radio. It squawked to life. Frank Sinatra singing "All or Nothing at All." Then "Tangerine" with Dick Haymes and Helen O'Connell. Then the DJ, Rob Thomas, pitching run-stop nylons. You get a run first thirty days after buying them, ladies, give 'em back and get free replacements.

Marcia Stebbins, prominent family in Milwaukee. Bark knew that; cared enough about it to frame her. Did he keep score? The bigger they are, the harder they fall? Get a rich girl like that for soliciting. That was a big score for Bark.

Sonntag felt the beginnings of an ulcer churn his gut. Cop work: get pain, give pain, roll in pain, watch the whole world's pain. He wished he had an Alka-Seltzer.

He emptied the wire basket of local clippings and worked through them. Almost all of them society news. Parties at Brown Deer Country Club. Teas at the Woman's Club of Wisconsin. Bridge parties, canasta parties, pinochle parties, dances. Lots of names. Sonntag swiftly spotted scores of leading families. Pinchot, Marley, Hoffmann, Dresden, Selligman, Borg, Olson, Grundy, on and on. Bark had cut them each day, blotted them up, memorized those names. There was another wire basket of business clippings, another of politicians and civic leaders. Why?

To catch them fornicating in the Lakeshore Hotel? "Business-man's wife caught with lover." Or, "Prominent surgeon fined for soliciting girls." Or drunk in the hotel? "Son of industrialist arrested for drunk and disorderly." Or cheating it? Or stealing an ashtray? Jesus Adam Bark scores again.

Sonntag heaped the clippings back into their baskets. He needed more time with Bark's incident ledgers, and maybe look at city court convictions. Did Bark go after prominent people and not even bother with small-fry?

"June 14, 1948. Marcel Wolle, Anita Bergstrom. Wolle rented a double, nine P.M. Bergstrom with him. Nine-fifty, J.A.B, with Officers McClary and Meyers, entered Room 472, a corner suite, unannounced, found Wolle and Bergstrom naked on bed. Photos taken by Meyers. McClary told them both to dress, cuffed them and took them to station for booking. Bergstrom on fornication, Wolle for adultery. Out on bail, both pleaded guilty in municipal court."

Marcel Wolle ran a tannery, family business for three genera-tions, down in the river valley. Another prominent man. Berg-strom? Sonntag didn't have any idea. Wolle was married then. Not now. It was in the *Sentinel.* His wife had headed for a Nevada dude ranch and gotten a six-week quickie in Reno.

Sonntag decided to talk to the man. He hiked down to St. Paul Avenue, caught the rapid transit, flashed his badge—cops on duty got a ride for free—and was soon gliding west, past Marquette University and up the river valley, under the 27th Street bridge, and past the tannery. The first stop was a half mile west. He'd hike. It was a fine fall day. Football and gold-colored leaves were in the air.

The tannery, in an old building of Cream City brick, exuded odors and tradition. Cowhide had been tanned here forever, and by god nothing would ever change. Prime Wolle leather was snapped up by half the shoemakers in the country. Bark was probably walking on Wolle leather the day he was shot. Sonntag found the offices under a weathered sign, entered, found a receptionist, said "Lieutenant Sonntag, police," and that he wished to talk to Marcel Wolle, please. He remembered to remove his gray Dobbs fedora. Half the time he forgot.

He was admitted at once, not the slightest delay.

Wolle was built like a barrel, bald, bushy-browed, and a lot of black chest hair boiled up around his collar.

"I knew you'd show up, Sonntag. I'm a suspect. I hated that sonofabitch, and I don't mind saying it. And I don't mind saying by god he got what was coming."

Sonntag smiled. He already liked Wolle. "Tell me," he said.

Wolle wheeled around his ancient desk—this office was strictly utilitarian, not a dollop of ego in it—and shut the door tight.

"Everyone around here has funnels for ears," he said. "All right. I had a little thing going with the lady. I like women. She's not married. I was. Not that it was much of a marriage. We went to the Lakeshore. It's water-cooled, you know, they pump lake water right through the radiators on hot days, and that made it the place. Anita, she'd gotten herself a Woolworth ring, you know, glass that looks like a ten-carat rock, that was to make it look okay, and I had my marriage license too. Agnes and Marcel, that's what it said."

Sonntag nodded. What was it about Wolle?

"I suppose you disapprove, and I don't give a damn. I like women and follow my pecker wherever it takes me. Anita was a hell of a good time."

"You sure you want to tell me all this, Mr. Wolle?"

"You're damn right I do. We live in a cuckoo world. It's none of the public's business how I live my private life."

"Then?"

"We get to our room and bam!"

"Bam?"

"Bam, bam! Twice in twenty minutes! I'm not so old, not yet."

Wolle looked mighty proud of himself. He looked like a thirty-year-old barrel, not a fifty-year-old one.

"Then we're just lazing there on the bed, getting up steam, and bam!"

"Bam?"

"Bam! The door swings open, there's the hotel dick and the cops, and one cop, he's got one of those big Graflex Speed Graphic cameras, and poof! He pops a flashbulb, and poof! He's got another shot. Anita, she howls, heads into the bathroom. Me, I smile. 'Take another shot, boys,' I said, and by god the cop did.

"They tell us to dress. There's that hotel dick, little pointy mustache, dark suit, shiny shoes, knife edges in his pants, looking smug at us, like nothing gets past him. Then you know what he says? 'That ring. That dime-store ring. It's all I need to know. You could afford to give the lady a sapphire.'"

That sounded like J. Adam Bark, all right.

"The rest, you want the rest? I'll tell you even if you don't. You know what? We get paraded through the lobby in cuffs, like felons, and hauled in a cruiser to the jailhouse, booked in. They ask about our marriage, and warn us not to lie. Fornication for her, adultery for me. That's the law. So I holler for a bail man, and he springs us, and next day in municipal court, before that oily-haired judge, we plead guilty, and get our names in the papers, so Agnes can head for Reno and clean three hundred grand out of my pockets. So, you bet, I'm no friend of the house dick."

"Where were you that morning?"

"Right by god here in this office where you and me are standing." He pointed at the door. "Ask her."

"Do you know anyone looks like Spencer Tracy?"

"I'm glad I don't. You know my secret? Women like uglies like me. Okay, so arrest me."

"You did it?"

"I sure as hell admired it."

Sonntag laughed. He wasn't supposed to. Ackerman warned all his detectives to be professional. Be stern. Keep 'em nervous. Never say anything. But Sonntag was never able to keep his trap shut and had given up trying.

"So who do you know looks like Spencer Tracy?"

"One person for sure. Yep, he looks just like Spencer . . . couldn't be anyone else. That's himself. Him and me, we were in the same class at Marquette Academy."

"He been around here?"

"Not since he got famous and started chasing skirts. Like Katharine Hepburn. *State of the Union.* The title made me laugh."

"Okay, I've gotta talk to Anita Bergstrom. You point the way."

"She . . . I've got a hide like a rhino. She doesn't."

"I have to talk with her, better sooner than later."

"Okay, here." He rounded the desk, wrote an address, and handed the slip to Sonntag. "Treat her nice, all right?"

Sonntag nodded.

"Am I a suspect?"

"I've got two hundred suspects."

"Two hundred? Some hotel!"

That's what Sonntag was thinking.

The secretary, a veritable dowager with pince-nez, sat just outside Wolle's door.

"Say, you mind if I phone my office?"

"We provide a phone for salesmen over there," she said.

"He keep you busy, does he?"

"No, sir, I'm mostly a gatekeeper. When he closes the door,

he wants privacy. He's in there all day, before I arrive and after I leave. He's a glutton for work."

"Doesn't he ever take an hour off?"

"He sets an example, sir."

"Do you know anyone who looks like Spencer Tracy?"

"I don't associate with actors, I'm afraid."

"Bad stuff, actors."

"I think very highly of Mary Martin."

Sonntag smiled, clamped his fedora over gray-shot hair, and drifted out. He'd call Ackerman later. Anita Bergstrom lived on North Prospect.

CHAPTER SEVEN

Anita lived in a small second-floor walk-up on the East Side.

"I'm Lieutenant Sonntag—"

"I know. He called. Come on in."

Anita Bergstrom was a Viking, taller than Sonntag, worried blue eyes, bright blond hair off her shoulders. She led him into the small living-dining room of a one-bedroom apartment, with a view west. She didn't radiate anything feral, and Sonntag wondered why he thought she would. In fact, she gave the odd sensation of being smaller than her lush body.

"Coffee or something?"

"No, just a visit for a few minutes."

"We're on your list."

"There's a lot of people on my list."

"Victims of a bunch of laws I never heard of."

"What do you do, Miss Bergstrom?"

"I don't do anything. I was a receptionist at St. Luke's hospital until I got my name in the paper, and then they fired me. I've done bookkeeping too, so I tried lots of places. They all say no, we can't hire anyone like you, not with your name in the paper. So now, well, Marcel gives me a little. For the time being. I don't know how long that's going to last. He uses up a woman every six months. I've got no illusions. But I'm glad for the help. I guess I'm a kept woman. Is that illegal too?"

Sonntag chose not to answer. It could be, under Milwaukee and state statutes. "You want to tell me what happened at the hotel that night in June?"

"No, I don't, but I guess I have to. You know something? Once you get put in the spotlight, it never stops. Now I've got a record. Now it's like being in the crosshairs. You won't be the last. There'll be police coming up those stairs the rest of my life. You know what I can't do now? I can't marry. I can't work."

"Things get better. By helping me you can make them better."

"You want the story. Well, okay, you've got it."

The funny thing, that husky quality in her voice was stirring him. She was going to talk about sex. Joe Sonntag was all ears.

"I got a shiny dime-store ring, lot of good that did. When they see the local address and the cheapo ring, that's all they need. We checked in, double, Mr. and Mrs. Wolle. We get up to our room, hardly put the bag down, and away we go. Is he something. You don't want the details."

"No."

"You know something? It takes a little prepping not to have a baby, and there wasn't time."

This time she grinned. "I don't know about women like me," she said.

"Just lucky, I guess," he said, and wished he'd kept his mouth shut.

That surprised her. Her mouth slid toward humor until she straightened out and flew right.

"Okay, I don't care what the world says. And Marcel . . . woowee!"

Sonntag wasn't sure he wanted the discussion to head where it was heading. "Ah, so the hotel dick busts in."

"Yeah, him in his black suit and little Adolphe Menjou mustache, and big cops, one with a big camera, one of those press cameras with a big flashbulb thing on it, and pop! Pop! They shoot me naked, and the cop yanks another plate, and

51

pop again when I head for the bathroom, but I have a nice butt and I don't care. Your whole Milwaukee PD has admired my butt by now. I hope my mother never figures it out. She lives in Beloit."

"You were angry?"

"Oh, mostly afraid. Why do they have laws like that? No one cares! Why should the hotel care?"

"I ask myself the same question."

That stopped her cold. "You do? You really do?"

Sonntag knew he was blabbing too much. "What did Marcel say?"

"Oh, him. He glared at the house dick. 'Big fish, eh?' he says. And the house dick, he just nods and smiles."

"Big fish?"

"You know. Marcel's a big executive."

"Why would he say that?"

"Would that house dick have bothered if it was just Rudy the Welder?"

"A good question."

"They let us dress, handcuffed us, paraded us through the lobby right in front of people, put us in a cop car, and off to the State Street station. They booked us, municipal code this and that, it's illegal to pee in Milwaukee, and Marcel, he had no cash so he hollered for a bail bondsman and about midnight we were sprung, and had to appear the next morning. I guess you know the rest."

"I guess I do. Now, Miss Bergstrom, did Marcel make any threats? Remember, you're talking to an officer."

She visibly cooled. "I thought I was talking to a friendly guy. Dumb of me."

"There was a murder."

The light went out of her eyes. "Yes, he did. He said he'd like to grab that hotel dick by the shirt and punch him in the nose."

Sonntag liked that. A punch in the nose was about right.

"Anything else you want to tell me? That would help me?"

"I'd just incriminate myself," she said, and laughed suddenly. He waited. She would spill it.

"I told Marcel I'd like to turn the hotel dick into a soprano." He permitted himself a smile.

"Did Mr. Wolle say anything later? Anything at all?"

"Yeah. He said if you have the right address, Fox Point, Whitefish Bay, Shorewood, you were fair game. I asked him where he heard that, and he said he didn't; he just figured it out."

"He said that? Actually, the house dick moved in on anyone. I've been going through his reports. There's salesmen from Racine, and doctors from Chicago, and a professor from Madison. A few ladies who made the mistake of registering without a husband, looking for a temporary."

"Well I think those didn't interest him. He loved to nail celebrities."

"That reminds me. You know anyone that looks like Spencer Tracy?"

"That sure changed the subject, didn't it. No, but I wish I did. A Clark Gable in my closet wouldn't be bad, either."

On that note Sonntag retreated. He found a pay phone in a Rexall on Farwell, and called Ackerman.

"Anything for me?"

"Yeah, Chicago can't nail down Tracy. He was there, they know that much, but he didn't appear anywhere. He didn't register at some hotel. Maybe he booked himself to here."

"Fat chance."

"I sort of hope it's Tracy. That'd be a feather in our cap, pinching a movie star for murder. Milwaukee boy makes good. Where are you?"

"East Side. Questioning some leads. Two hundred left."

"Anything hot?"

"Yeah, an inspiration. Repeal the vice laws."

"What are you, some Communist? I want the killer booked by next Wednesday. The reporters are asking why nothing's been done."

"Captain, tell them the department wants to ditch all laws about fornication, sodomy, adultery, and soliciting. We've got more important stuff to do. Tell 'em that."

Ackerman grunted like a hog. "Go home. Lizbeth needs you." He hung up.

"I've got ten minutes more on my shift," Sonntag said into the dead mouthpiece.

He hiked down to Wells Street and caught the streetcar, and sat behind some bobbysoxers who were making oinking noises. This car clanked. It had a wheel out of round or something. When the car reached the viaduct, Sonntag gripped the seatback and hung on as the car rolled into space and the valley floor fell away. Then out of the slits of his eyes he saw the thing he dreaded most, an eastbound car coming toward him. It rattled by, inches away, with a great thump of air rocking his own car, so his heart leapt and he knew that the papers would say that a PD officer had plunged to his doom.

But then it was okay. The car rolled onto solid land, a quiet neighborhood where the bobbysoxers got off and began goosing each other as they hiked home.

He got off at 56th and hiked to 57th. It was still daylight.

"How come?" Lizbeth asked, after planting one of her wry kisses on his five o'clock shadow.

He shrugged. "I guess we can go to a movie."

"You got fired or something?"

"What's playing?"

"Take me out to dinner, Joe. I gotta get used to you all over."

He pitched his old rain-softened fedora onto a hat rack. It

was a skill he'd acquired. The tan trench coat was looking a little worn, but raising two boys had consumed all he could earn and then some. He loosened his tie, the one with Evinrude outboards on it, but didn't whip it off. He'd tighten it up for dinner.

She appeared with two drinks in hand. She loved a rye Manhattan on the rocks; he always settled for a bourbon and water. This used to be a ritual until recently, when he was always too busy.

It tasted just fine. She was smiling. It was like it had been years ago. Often she had fed the boys in the kitchen and shooed them upstairs to do their homework, and then poured drinks when he got home. She and Joe liked a cocktail together. That's when they reconnected; when they resolved her problems and solved all his cases before *Fibber McGee and Molly* started.

She sipped. "So, who shot Bark? Or is this one of those don't-talk-to-wives deals?"

He was reluctant. He could talk about murder, about torture, about doping, about heists, about crooks in white collars, but he couldn't talk to her about vice.

"Pretty rough, babe."

"You want to hear my theory?" She didn't wait. "This house dick. He had something personal going in the hotel. You check in, he looks you over without you even knowing it. He's really good at spotting people who don't have marriage licenses. He's got a regular system. The clerks tip him, the elevator man tips him, the shoeshine boy tips him, the bell captain tips him, even the maids."

"That wasn't in the *Sentinel.*"

"No, but everyone knows about the Lakeshore Towers. Very, very respectable. So there's a long list of people who got their names in the papers. I always feel sorry for them. Elizabeth Jones, charged with, you know what. So who're you going after?"

"Prominent ones. Lots of names everyone in town knows. Businessmen."

"That's it! You see?"

Lizbeth sometimes puzzled him with her Eurekas.

"It's not businessmen," she said. "They don't have much to lose. They shrug it off. It's got to be someone who had so much to lose he shot the house dick. Not some salesman. Not an actress. Not some football player. Not some socialist. They haven't got reputations. Skip all them."

The Jim Beam was just fine. "Such as?"

"People who got really, really ruined. Who had reputations that got blasted. People whose lives got wrecked by this guy. Like a minister or a bishop. Haul a bishop before municipal court on charges, you know, and he'd likely go off like an atom bomb."

"Bishops don't shoot people."

"But there's a lot like that. Governors, congressmen. A governor's wife. A nun. The chancellor of a university. A judge. Especially a judge. Judges have to be above it all. Judges have to be perfect. Start with judges."

"I'll hunt down judges."

"And police chiefs. Don't forget police chiefs."

He downed his bourbon. "Chop suey or Greek?"

She arched a brow. "Greek," she said.

That suited him just fine. It was an ancient signal. Go to the chop suey joint on North Ave, and she'd wear a white flannel nightgown to bed. Go to the Greek restaurant on Lisbon Avenue and she'd wear a little black transparent nothing.

CHAPTER EIGHT

Sonntag was a half hour late for work.

"What happened?" asked Captain Ackerman.

"The streetcar ran into an American Flyer coaster wagon. The kid ran. By the time the motorman got it straightened out, there were three more cars backed up."

"Well don't do it again. I won't give you a demerit if you put in an extra hour tonight. Now. Where are you with the barbershop butcher?"

"I could use two more men; give each a list for questioning."

"Can't do it, Sonntag. The mayor's got a stalker. We think it's an SAR."

"What's that?"

"Sons of the American Revolution."

"I don't get it."

"The mayor's a pinko, Sonntag."

"I guess that explains it," Sonntag said. He always pretended he knew something about politics. "I'll be at the hotel."

Ackerman nodded. "Catch him. I'm getting heat. Why do you think it's one of the guests? It could be anybody. It could be Bark's auntie."

"Like who?"

"Spencer Tracy. Like, well hell, it's your baby. Premeditated murder."

Sonntag hiked through a mean chill to the hotel and headed for Bark's apartment. There were things he should have done but didn't. The damned movie star pictures had deflected him. He let himself in with the hotel key. The suite was quiet and shadowy, drapes drawn. He eyed the place, wondering if anyone had tampered. No one had.

Then he saw Loretta Young. She was right there on the wall, staring at him, proper and virginal in a blouse up to her throat, pearl necklace, boxy suit, a fake smile, her face soaked in Pond's. He hated Loretta Young. "You should elope with Peter Lorre," he said to her. "Then you'd be halfway a woman."

The movie stars on the walls were a distraction. He headed for Bark's prim white bedroom and rolled the closet door open. It was just a closet, and these were just clothes, except . . . Jesus Adam Bark had his ways. Each ironed dress shirt hung exactly two inches from its neighbors. Each pair of suit pants hung exactly three inches from the suit coat. On the floor were three pairs of shoes: two black wingtips and one round-toed pair with thick soles, for bad weather. Each pair pointed straight out, each shoe two inches from its mate, the row of shoes precisely six inches back from the sliding door. Bark's stodgy ties hung from a rack, a tie occupying every other prong.

Sonntag pulled a dresser drawer open. There were Bark's white boxer shorts, in a neat pile, each separated by a layer of tissue paper. Every black sock had been rolled into a ball with its mate.

What was all that supposed to mean?

Sonntag tried the suit coat pockets. Empty, empty, empty, and then a slip of pasteboard. He pulled it out. A torn ticket stub, purple, half the word missing, the remaining letters ". . . press" plus a number.

Sonntag smiled. J. Adam Bark had a little secret of his own. The stub was a ticket to the Empress, the burlesque theater on Third Street. It sort of humanized the man. And it was worth looking into. Churchy Milwaukee was the end of the line for burlesque queens; the young and pretty girls played Minsky's in Chicago. The old ones with varicose veins and sagging buttocks played the Empress, where truant sixteen-year-olds could puzzle how the gals made the tassels on their pasties whirl in opposite directions.

Sonntag pocketed the stub. The number might tell when Bark was there. It was worth a few questions.

That was the only thing he found. He started to leave, but Loretta Young bugged him. He pulled her off the wall and laid her face-down on the kitchen counter. Smile at the counter, babe. So much for the Virgin Queen. She sure would never occupy wall space in the Sonntag residence.

He locked behind him, feeling good, and headed for Bark's office.

Lizbeth's idea was a good one. He punched the light switch, hit the Philco, and got WTMJ again. They were doing a sports roundup, and next would be some organ-music soap operas, bible stories, and ads for Fels-Naptha. He opened the ledger, planning to look only for those whose life was ruined. Bark's spidery hand was as regular as his closet; there was not a crossed-out word, not a blot. Each incident was reported in flowing sentences, each sentence perfectly wrought. It was unreal. Sonntag's own file reports, hastily typed on the station's Woodstocks, were loaded with deletes and typos and misspellings. Bark had an odd gift.

Who were these people caught in bed with someone that made it illegal? Fallowes, a Studebaker dealer. What about him? Bramble, a Singer salesman. Margot Messenheimer, a saleswoman at the perfume counter of Gimbels. Laura Dilworth, a florist. Gerta Heine, a Wisconsin Synod Lutheran Church secretary. That one was interesting. He pulled a phone book from Bark's drawer and looked her up. The number was Bluemound 8-1122. He dialed; an operator intervened. "That number is out of service, sir."

"Got a new one for her?"

"No, sir. You could try Information."

Information didn't have one either. Gerta Heine probably had skipped town after being fined for fornication in municipal court. That would wreck a church secretary's life, all right. She probably had moved to San Diego or some other obscure place. He wrote her name on a list of possibles.

Rasher Kinnets, associate professor of biology, University of Wisconsin. Tried a little biology at the Lakeshore with one of his graduate students, a Miss Abby Wool, during a freshwater marine biology conference at Marquette. No, make that Mrs. She was hitched. The old story: he rented a single, she rented a single on the next floor up. He visited her room and didn't notice the bellboy carrying room-service dinner to someone. Didn't know that the bellboy, Willie Kaspar, was listening at the door. There it all was, in Bark's regular and spidery hand. Every incident had a story. Kinnets was fined $25 and costs for fornication; she was fined $80 and costs for adultery.

Sonntag pondered that. Why was adultery worth $80 to the City of Milwaukee, while fornication was much less? Why eighty? Why not seventy-five? Was fornication about two-thirds less serious?

He dialed information.

"Number for Rasher Kinnets, K-I-N-N-E-T-S, Madison, please."

"That name is not listed, sir."

"Was it disconnected recently?"

"I can't answer that."

"It's Lieutenant Sonntag, Milwaukee police department."

Silence. Then, "This is the supervisor. Mr. Kinnets discontinued Wisconsin Bell phone service last July, sir."

"Did he supply a forwarding address for his final bill?"

"I believe he paid it here, sir."

Another wrecked life. Maybe two. He put Kinnets and Wool on his short list.

Wool's Madison number rang but no one answered. Just as Sonntag hung up, he thought he heard an answer. He tried again. A man responded at once.

"Is Abby Wool there?"

"No, she no longer lives here."

"Where can I find her?"

"Who's calling, may I ask?"

"Lieutenant Sonntag, Milwaukee police department."

"You going to charge her with something else?"

"Who am I talking to, sir?"

"Tom Wool."

"You her husband?"

"Was. Until she ran off."

"I'm sorry about that. It must have been tough for you."

"Lieutenant, I can't even begin to tell you."

"She got a divorce?"

"A Nevada quickie. I got the papers. They said I'm divorced. I don't know where she got the money. I don't even know if Wisconsin recognizes them. So I'm in some kind of limbo."

"I'd like to talk with her, if that is possible. Can you put me in touch?"

"No, I don't know where, and I don't care where she is."

"That bad, eh?"

"Listen, have you ever had your life blown apart? She took a course from that bastard and he—in a hotel room. They got caught. I'll never be the same. Say, why do you want to talk with her?"

"An investigation. We're looking into things at that hotel."

"Oh, the hotel dick that got shot. He did me a favor. I trusted her. I'd never have known if he hadn't busted in on them. It would have been a big secret, right under my nose."

Wool didn't sound like he meant it.

"Say, Mr. Wool, you mind sending me a photo of her? Maybe both of you?"

"Yes, I'd mind. But I guess I will. You got an address?"

"Sure. I'd like a nice photo of her and you too."

"She's a suspect. That's the funniest thing I've heard in weeks."

Maybe he would look like Spencer Tracy.

Sonntag called the university in Madison, got hold of the personnel office, and asked about Kinnets.

"Lieutenant, Professor Kinnets left us the end of June, after the semester," the lady said.

"Discharged?"

A small hesitation. "For cause, lieutenant. He wasn't tenured, you know."

"A relationship with a student of his?"

"I . . . am afraid that's correct."

"And where did he go?"

"We have no idea. But most academic disciplines have directories. Try the American Biology Association. Here, I can get you the address. Hang on."

Two minutes later Sonntag knew how to reach a professional society Kinnets might belong to.

"One last question, ma'am. What does he look like?"

"This is a big university, sir. I hardly know."

"Have you a file photo?"

"I have his personnel folder. Just a moment. Yes, there's a photo here. What a handsome man."

"Does he resemble anyone?"

"That's a funny question. No. He's good looking, at least I think he is. Nice face, clean jaw, long nose, horn-rimmed glasses."

"Could I borrow that photo?"

"I could have a copy made. But I can't release the file materials."

"You don't suppose he looks like, oh, Spencer Tracy, do you?"

"He could. I don't quite see it. But I don't go to films very much. Professor Kinnets is more Tyrone Power."

"Bill us for the photo," Sonntag said.

He put Kinnets, Abby Wool, and Tom Wool on his short list.

He owed the Lakeshore for some long distance. There were proper procedures for this and he had violated them.

He headed for the front desk. They knew him by now. "I've made some long distance calls to Madison. Let me know the toll."

He would pay them himself. Ackerman would rebuff him if he tried to run the bill through the department. Follow the rules or take a hit.

He itched to bust out of the hotel. A bright afternoon beckoned. He'd eat at the station from his lunch box and try something new.

Chapter Nine

It was tuna salad day. Lizbeth followed a ritual: Mondays, egg salad sandwich. Tuesdays, ham and cheese. Wednesdays, tuna salad. Thursdays, bologna sandwich with mayo. Fridays, Swiss cheese, mustard, and lettuce. Cookies and fruit. Birthdays, chocolate hearts wrapped in red foil and a Kleenex with her lipstick kiss imprinted on it, a lunch box billet-doux.

Sonntag munched at the station house, ignoring the world, at least until Ackerman interrupted his lunch.

"We still don't know about Bark. No relatives. No history. Nothing in the hotel files. The original application's missing; the one that lists previous jobs and references. Social security says his first job was in Akron, undertaker's assistant. We checked Akron. No Barks. At least none ever heard of him. We're looking for other Barks. You got a clue?"

Sonntag masticated the last bit of tuna salad and shook his head. "His suite, like nothing's there. No person, no history. No prescriptions, no letters, no bills, no personal photos, no bank account—he was paid cash in manila envelopes, the hotel supplied all services. Nothing in his pockets except a stub to the Empress."

"Empress?"

"It's on my list."

"The hotel's anti-vice man. That's something. Let me know."

"I think he had a past. Try the FBI."

"Yeah, well the morgue's done with him. Coroner's done.

They want to bury him. We called the hotel. They'll spring for a funeral. We're going to announce it, papers, radio. Friday at one. You attend and see who shows. That's the old game, you know."

Sonntag nodded and chomped on the sandwich.

"And keep on digging. Maybe, we get a history for J. Adam Bark, we get the killer too."

"Could be," Sonntag said. "I'm going to need a cruiser this afternoon. Amanda Gruen, Fox Point."

"Gruen? Yeah, Gruen. That's a good idea. Take four-oh-six. It might even get you there."

The detectives got condemned patrol cars for their use, some of them repainted, the PD decals removed. But it didn't fool anyone.

Ackerman was gone before Sonntag could take another bite. That was Ackerman for you. He said what he wanted to say and beat you out of a reply.

Stanley Gruen was on Bark's incident list. So was Amanda. Who could forget it? Gruen was the top dog at Milwaukee Fire and Casualty Insurance Company. Was, past tense. He committed suicide.

Gruen's company threw a big Christmas party at the Lakeshore Towers in 1946. Those were tough times, price controls, shortages, quagmire. A peacetime economy was slow in coming. So Gruen thought to boost his company morale with a dandy party. He got one of Tommy Dorsey's road bands, ordered a ton of champagne, and rented the ballroom. It was a hoity-toity affair, all right, the biggest thing in Milwaukee for years.

Amanda got looped, decided to stay over at the hotel, took a room, and had a visitor, the corporate counsel, Archer Hoffmann. As usual, J. Adam Bark got wind of it, busted in, caught them en flagrante, and that one made all the papers for days, but carefully buried in the classified section. A dozen reporters hied themselves to municipal court to watch Amanda Gruen and Archer Hoffmann get theirs. A week later Stanley Gruen shot himself with a Luger, a war prize he had been given. And the whole business was rehashed again. But there was more. In the space of a few months, Amanda Gruen became a new person, abrupt, radicalized, brimming with opinions that no paper dared to print, and often funny. The whole town had traded Amanda stories ever since.

She was entirely capable of blasting J. Adam Bark out of his worldly life.

Sonntag was all too familiar with car 406. He pulled the choke rod, cranked it over, pushed the choke back into the dash, and cranked again. The engine caught, sputtered, and came to ragged life. He let it warm, punched the clutch, shifted to low, and eased out of the bullpen, onto State Street. The worn-out transmission whined cheerfully. This was a good afternoon, just right for a drive up Lake Shore Drive, with glimpses of the bright blue lake to entertain him.

If she was in, he was going to have a good time. A half hour with Amanda would give him twenty stories to tell over lunch and a dozen more he would clean up slightly and tell Lizbeth.

Fox Point was the northernmost of the flossy suburbs. The Gruens had a ten-acre piece of lakefront, their house high on a bluff over the lapping waters. The house, a radical Frank Lloyd Wright structure, sat low on the ground, but with a burst of glass to the east, making it seem like the bridge of a lake steamer.

He parked in the circle drive, the brakes squealing, and he pulled the parking brake up. A seductive sloe-eyed maid of about twenty opened even before he rang.

"Mrs. Gruen is expecting you," the maid said.

"How . . ."

"No one but police drive cars with bad brakes. The screech awoke Alfie. That's her Jack Russell terrier."

The maid led him through an entry, a low foyer, a dining room, into a spectacular lake-view parlor, the acres of window glass divided by a fieldstone fireplace.

Mrs. Gruen was dressed in a purple caftan and wore furry pink slippers.

"You've come to arrest me," she said, offering a soft hand.

"I'm Lieutenant Sonntag, Milwaukee police," he began.

"I'm sure you are. Have a seat. Do you like tea? Or something more cheerful?"

"Ah, we'll just visit a little, if I may."

He settled into an awning-striped Louis XV chair, parked his fedora on his knee, and admired the lake view.

"Of course you may. Amanda likes to blab. I will stop at nothing. I'll start by saying that J. Adam Bark deserved to be shot, and I envy the shooter. Lucky dog. He was simply first in line, that's all."

"Who else is in line?"

"I'll get to that. First you're going to hear my story, straight from the mare's mouth. I think I like you, but we'll see."

"This is a Frank Lloyd Wright house, isn't it?"

"Frank Lloyd Wrong. The roof leaks, the plumbing quits, and the lakeside windows crack. Why are you diverting me from my purpose, which is to talk your ear off?"

"I wouldn't mind living here," Sonntag said.

"It all starts with Stanley. He was a dear old bore. But he had a problem. Why am I telling you this? Because I feel like it, and any man with a fedora is worth knowing. Stanley always wore Homburgs and they made him look too bankerish. Anyway, dear, Stanley had his little problem, and what's a girl to do? I'm a good girl at heart, a patient girl, and I was patient year in and year out. But I kept my eye on, you know, Hoffman at the company, and I always thought that if I decided not to be a good girl, I might just seduce him. Well anyway, that's another story. Stanley Gruen would come home, listen to H. V. Kaltenborn, down his Ovaltine, and vanish into his suite. Now what kind of life is that?

"So when Christmas rolled around, and it was party time, I was ready. I had been a good girl long enough. No more H. V. Kaltenborn. No more Ovaltine. I got looped on all that champagne, and that's when I propositioned poor old Archer. The Dorsey band was swinging that night, oh my, did we dance, and I told the poor goose that the evening was young and would get better and better, especially if he would get himself a room. He could be my Santa Claus."

She smiled, enjoying the memory. She was one hell of a woman.

"I got a room too, you know. I told Stanley I planned to dance the night away and would take a room. So I did. Fourth floor, lake view. Charged it to the company. He was grateful, and climbed into the Packard for home. So this was my Christmas present to myself. At last, at last. Are you sure you wouldn't like something cheerful?"

"I'm on duty, ma'am."

"You sound like Stanley. I pitied Stanley. For years, he would try once in a while to please a lady, namely me, but the poor old dear had no iron in his spine or anywhere else. Then he would look at me like a tired beagle, apologies tumbling from his lips, and I responded very cruelly, with a yawn. That's me. It's right on my sleeve, daddy-o."

This was all new to Sonntag, and best of all, he didn't even have to ask questions.

"Well, luck of the draw. There we were, creeping down hotel corridors, intent on original sin, and eventually he wound up in my little boudoir. Poor dumb girl that I am, I had no idea that Archer had the same problem, at least that night. The booze did it, he was looped, or maybe he was scared, poor thing, but all I could think of was that I had run out of luck. So I rolled him onto his back and did him a few favors, and then he got into the swing of it, and I thought finally, after years of H. V. Kaltenborn, old Amanda's going to go over the top."

She eyed Sonntag levelly. "Only it never happened."

"Bark?"

"The entire Milwaukee gestapo. Flashbulbs. Blue coats. And that swine leading the parade. I started yelling. 'Who are you, Heinrich Himmler?' but that hardly slowed him down. Instead of scurrying under sheets, I yanked mine away. Let 'em stare, baby. Poor Archer, he clasped his big gentle hands over his parts, and quaked. So I not only didn't get laid, I got arrested for adultery. Oh, was that a corker!"

"And the reporters had a tough time writing the story."

"Poor dears. How do you write that up for a family newspaper in Catholic Milwaukee? Well, they hustled us down to the lobby, which emptied the ballroom. The cops and me were a better show than Tommy Dorsey's second-string band. There we were, waiting for the paddy wagon. I told Bark he was a fascist, and he smiled. I told him that was a phony name, Bark, Bark, Bark, like a dog. No one gets to be called J. Adam Bark, so who was he? Barker, he said. He'd started life as Barker, but that reminded him of a watch dog."

"Barker? He said that was his name?"

"So what's the big deal? We all invent ourselves. I'm not the woman I was before that Christmas party. You know what I am? A flaming, evil-tongued liberal. I'll vote for Henry Wallace. Harry Truman's a tough little bastard, but I want a Progressive. Henry Wallace wouldn't arrest me for getting laid. I'm just sick of a gestapo world. The whole city's full of brownshirts. Especially the cops."

Involuntarily, Sonntag checked his clothing. White shirt, baggy blue suit.

She saw it and licked her chops. Another canary swallowed.

She turned somber. "A week later Stanley shot himself. I felt so bad, like it was my fault. That started it all over again, this time the papers got a little more bold. You know how they are. They never say rape, they say an illegal act. They never say I was getting laid, they say I was engaged in illicit congress. Oh, I got to laughing. You know how the rich are, dear. Like me. I'm going to do what I want, when I want."

"Why did Bark tell you he was originally Barker?"

"Because I was laughing at him. He wasn't used to that. Laughing. Usually they're in tears, got caught with their pants down, please don't tell anyone, have mercy, hush this up. But I was laughing, and he turned red. Why? Is he related to Ma Barker or someone?"

"Not that we know. We've been trying to give him a funeral and no one claims him and he left no records. Do you know anyone?"

"That would be like claiming Josef Goebbels, sweetheart. Would you like me to come to the funeral and do the eulogy? When is it? Where is it? I'm serious."

"Ah, no thanks."

"Coward. As long as I didn't get to shoot him, I thought I could shoot his reputation."

"Don't leave town, okay?"

"Why not? Am I a suspect?"

"I don't know, but you improve Milwaukee and I'd hate to see you leave."

"You're the first cop I ever liked, Sonntag. Bring your wife for a visit. Or don't. Your choice."

"Maybe we'll invite you out for chop suey, Mrs. Gruen," he replied.

CHAPTER TEN

More people showed up at the Carnahan Funeral Home than Sonntag expected. He thought only a few hotel people would come.

Even Captain Ackerman made an appearance, resplendent in his dress blues, his alert gaze assessing degrees of criminality in the throng. He settled beside Sonntag in the back row, making it obvious who Sonntag was.

"Nothing on Barker yet," Ackerman whispered.

"Maybe it won't pan out," Sonntag replied. "Maybe Spencer Tracy will show up."

There were no Spencer Tracys among the people settling into their chairs in the chapel. Sonntag couldn't finger any of them except hotel people, but intended to find out who they were afterward. This was the hotel's show. Even the barber, Damon Barbara, was there, three rows forward.

"Who are these people?" Ackerman asked.

"Beats me. We'll find out."

"You should know."

A minister materialized from a curtained door. A Reverend Harsch. Sonntag thought he was as close to being a Spencer Tracy as anyone in the place. Light from a mean-cold November day streamed through the small windows, glared off the coffin, and made the place too bright.

Harsch pulled out a fat pocket watch, saw that the time was ripe, and proceeded to the pulpit.

"We have come to say farewell to Jesus Adam Bark," he began. "Most clergymen have been called now and then to bury someone we have never met. That usually gives us the opportunity to talk about the voyage of the soul to its eternal reward, because so little is known about the departed. Mr. Bark is a stranger to me. But I have indeed, thanks to the hotel's staff, hastily gleaned a few facts about this man who now commands our respectful attention. So I shall share with you what little I do know of him.

"Even his age is uncertain because the employment records have been lost. But this man faithfully, for many years, guarded the Lakeshore Towers against all sorts of tribulations; against theft, against predators preying on its guests; against violence and disorder. Because of his watchful guardianship, the hotel was and is a safe place. Because of his zealous enforcement of good order, the hotel's reputation is flawless, and the place of his employment glistens brightly among the world's great hostelries. He watched over the hotel he called his home. The laws he so zealously enforced are intended to protect women, and his innate chivalry toward the gentle sex was present in all he did. Because of his vigilance, women were and are safe in the Lakeshore Towers. Woe to any society that does not protect its women!

"I am told by the hotel's managers that at times he put himself in harm's way to protect guests, to help them to safety at a time when electrical power failed, to find medical help for those in need. He was a hero.

"About his personal life we know so very little. He has no known family, though somewhere in this world are those who knew him and loved him, perhaps parents, perhaps brothers or sisters. Possibly even children. I am told he had a great love of movies, and enjoyed collecting the photos of actors and actresses. He loved the music of the popular bands, and listened to it in his hotel office, and had a special fondness for Tommy Dorsey and Glenn Miller and Les Brown. He apparently served in the army in the first world war. But he kept to himself, and when I chatted a little with his colleagues from the hotel, I learned how little they really knew of Mr. Bark.

"So let us celebrate a life well lived . . ."

Sonntag thought it was a gracious eulogy, built upon the thin realities of the man no one knew. The minister finished with a prayer, and then the service was over.

There would be tea and pastries in the adjacent parlor.

And a guest book.

"You won't get anywhere with me hanging around," Ackerman said. "Let me know if you've caught the white whale."

The captain collected his hat and coat and vanished through the doors into the glaring light.

Casper Reinhold, the hotel's general manager, assailed him at once. "Say, lieutenant, when will we have our square footage back? I wish to retain a new security man, and have no place for him until you're finished."

"I'll clean out Bark's office, sir. Some things will temporarily go to our evidence room. I'll give you an itemized list. The apartment, I need a day or two."

"We'd like to put his possessions in storage."

"I'll finish there as fast as I can."

In truth, he was done with the place—except for one of those intuitions detectives get. He wanted to go over Bark's living quarters one more time, and couldn't say why.

"We would appreciate it. Are you any closer to solving this case?"

"I'm making progress."

The standard answer.

The manager abandoned him. The hotel was the host, the neighbor, the family of Jesus Adam Bark, or Barker, more or less, and the manager wished to greet the guests.

Sonntag wanted to talk to Damon Barbara, who was scooping up pastries.

"Mr. Barbara, how are things? Back to normal?"

"Oh, it's you, lieutenant. No, it'll never be normal. People come in there, they want to sit in that chair. I finally says, no one sits in that chair. That chair is off limits. You want a haircut, you got it; you want to sit in the dead man's chair, you're out of my shop."

"Lot of 'em?"

"No, but it's steady. They want to see the place."

"I don't suppose Spencer Tracy's been in."

"If he was I'd be on the phone to you in two seconds."

"Did the killer really look like Tracy? Maybe someone else?"

"It happened fast, you know. Bam, bam."

"Let's pick a few movie stars. Did the killer look like, say, Tyrone Power?"

"Nah. It was Tracy."

"What does Tracy look like?"

"You know, long nose, well built, shock of light-colored hair, good sharp jaw."

"He was wearing . . ."

"Eisenhower jacket, gray hat."

"Tie?"

"You know, I don't remember. What you look at, see, is that big piece of black metal in his hand, nothing like ties. I saw that gun, did I ever see that gun."

"You really saw the gun more than Tracy?"

"Well, it came to me the guy's Tracy. Bam, bam!"

"Could he look like Howard Keel?"

"Him?"

"Yeah, the singer. He's a possible. We think maybe Bogart. The hit man looked like Humphrey Bogart."

"Yeah, could of."

"More like Bogart than Tracy?"

"Hey, I saw Spencer Tracy, bam, bam!" Barbara's teeth clamped on a croissant.

There was no changing Barbara's mind. Sonntag eyed the mélange and discovered a couple of people he knew after all; he would get to them after he had talked to a few strangers.

One couple intrigued him, if only because they were wearing outmoded and dark clothing, and were squinting uneasily at the rest of the crowd.

"You came to say goodbye?" Sonntag asked.

"Why, yes, we think highly of the late departed," the gent said. "We gave him one of our public service awards, you know."

"Oh? Tell me about it."

"The Wisconsin Watch and Ward Society. Mr. Bark, he did so much to keep Milwaukee wholesome, you know. No man ever fought harder against looseness."

"Ah, yes, I've heard of you. I'm Joe Sonntag."

"Why this is Olive Percy, and I'm Wayne Percy. This city's in such dire straits. It's the Great Lakes Naval Base you know. Wherever there are sailors, there's ruin. But there was Mr. Bark, a warrior in the front lines. So we came to honor him."

"Pity how he died," Sonntag said. "Who would do it?"

"Well, we thought the police would solve it by now. Maybe someone's buying them off. I wouldn't put it past them."

"We think a sailor did it," Olive said.

"Or maybe an actor?"

"Oh, they're quite capable," Wayne said. "They sell their souls, you know. But no, this was the work of a navy man, maybe a chief petty officer. That would be the sort to walk into the Lakeshore Towers. Not some enlisted seaman."

"Enjoy the croissants, Mr. and Mrs. Percy," Sonntag said.

"Oh, we're not married. We're brother and sister," Wayne said.

"Yes, well, I'm glad to meet you."

"You're not a navy man, are you?"

Sonntag shook his head. The crowd was already thinning. He beelined toward the two gents whom he knew, if only slightly, both of them hotel dicks. Peter Mapp, for the Pfister Hotel, and George Dolfuss, for the Schroeder. Both of them urbane, middle-aged, overweight, and boozy.

"Imagine finding you here," Sonntag said.

"Just lucky, aren't you?" Mapp retorted.

"Whodunit?"

"We wish we knew. This time, it was Bark. Next . . ." Dolfuss shrugged.

"I hadn't thought of that," Sonntag said. "If someone has it in for hotel dicks, you won't want to get a haircut or a shave."

"Who do we look for? I want some advance warning," Mapp said.

"We have only one eyewitness, and that's the barber, Damon Barbara. And he stuck to one description—Spencer Tracy. The guy looked like Tracy. And don't spread that. We're keeping that under wraps. I'm telling you so you can keep your eye peeled."

Mapp looked friendly, for a change. "Yeah, that's a real favor, Sonntag."

"If anyone looks like Tracy, he wanders through the Pfister, you call us, okay?"

"Tracy, the actor Tracy, or some other?"

"We're checking. The actor Tracy was in Chicago, and his time's not accounted for. But he's off to London."

"We get Tracy types in the Pfister all the time."

"Never saw one in the Schroeder," Dolfuss said.

"I've pushed the barber on this, and it's Tracy. He did say he was too busy watching the gun to get more than a glimpse."

"If I see a genuine Tracy, by god, you'll hear from me in ten seconds," Dolfuss said.

"You friends of Bark?"

"Oh, we used to exchange stuff. Deadbeats, crooked maids, silverware thieves, towel snatchers, whores, you name it. That's how we knew Bark."

"Were you guys close to Bark? We're still trying to ID him. Was his real name Barker?"

"He was in the navy once, he told me," Mapp said.

"Did he ever talk about his life? What about his movie photos?"

"He was going to be an actor once."

"He said that?"

"Yeah, he talked about it once."

"He liked actors? Actresses?"

"Well, that's the thing. I don't think he liked them; I think he was obsessed with them."

"Like they were scores, people he might bust if they came to the Lakeshore?"

"Got me, Sonntag, I just don't know."

"Think about it. You've known Bark for years. Some time, in all those coffees, all those bar rail talks, he probably told you things that could help me now."

"He never told anyone much of anything about himself, Sonntag," Mapp said.

CHAPTER ELEVEN

The funeral had yielded nothing. Sonntag hiked through a mean-cold day to the hotel, collected the incident ledgers and the three fat file folders he intended to look over when he could. One was stuffed with clippings about prominent Milwaukee people; another, entirely movie people; and the third, fat with clippings about people of consequence nationwide.

He hand-wrote a receipt listing the evidence he was confiscating, dropped it at the hotel's business office, told the lady it was okay for the hotel to reclaim Bark's office, and then toted his pile of evidence to the front doors, where a red-nosed hotel lackey swept a door open for him.

"Need a cab," Sonntag said.

A shrill whistle brought a Checker cab, and Sonntag piled his stuff and himself inside. The cab had a heap of legroom and smelled of wet wool.

"Cop station, Kilbourn door," he said.

The cabby eyed him in the mirror. "You catch that barber shop shooter yet?"

"Not yet. You have a fare that looked like Spencer Tracy recently?"

"They all think they look like Spencer Tracy."

"I'm serious. Anyone looking like him hire this rig?"

"Naw, the ones I get look like Bess Truman."

At the station, Sonntag paid the cabby, tipped two bits, got an expense receipt, and hauled his stuff to the evidence room, where it was recorded and shelved.

He found a message spiked on his desk. Package awaiting him at the Badger Bus depot.

That was fast, he thought. Badger Bus ran a shuttle between Milwaukee and Madison, heavily patronized by students. He settled his fedora. It felt tight. He needed a haircut. If it got any longer, he'd be docked for violating the dress code. He headed into the bone-chilling day.

The package, a manila envelope actually, was awaiting him at the baggage window in the odorous terminal. He slit it open and found what he had hoped: a black and white photo, with "Rasher Kinnets" blue-inked on the back and a note from the personnel lady. "Lieutenant Sonntag—Please return. This is the file original. I thought you might want it fast so I bused it. Sincerely, Laura Sinclair O'Byrne."

Good for her. He eyed the photo in the light of those flickering fluorescents and was intrigued. Pull those horn-rimmed spectacles off of Kinnets and you might have a Spencer Tracy. Except that Kinnets had wavy dark hair, maybe even curly. Still . . . jawline, nose, forehead, all matched up. Sort of.

Maybe a break at that. He hiked back in numbing wind, cursing the cruel day, and gratefully plunged into the heat of the station house. He climbed two flights to the photo files, and got hold of Harry Bailess.

"Listen, Harry, I want you to do a mug display for me. This guy here is a suspect in the Bark case. Kinnets is his name. Put a bunch of good-looking guys around him, but not all looking like Spencer Tracy. Fast?"

"Two hours if you're lucky. Not Tracy? That barber fingered Tracy in about two seconds, last time we brought him in."

"No, not Tracy. I'll bring the guy over in a while. I want to see if he fingers Kinnets."

"The barber Barbara," Harry said. "I'll get it together."

Sonntag plowed down the marbleized stairs to his grimy carrel in the bullpen, yanked the receiver off his black phone, dialed the AT&T long-distance operator, and gave her the Baltimore number of the American Biology Association. While he waited, he made a long-distance log entry. If you don't keep the log, you pay the LD. Lots of rules. He heard the clicking of connections down the line, and at last, through static, he heard a voice. "Johns Hopkins Department of Biology."

"I'd like to find the address and phone of a member of the ABA," Sonntag said.

"Who's calling?"

"Lieutenant Sonntag, Milwaukee police department."

"Professor Watkins is lecturing, sir."

"I just need the address of a member, Professor Rasher Kinnets."

"Well, I'm not supposed to do that."

"You're a sweetheart for sticking to the rules. But maybe you can do me a favor."

She turned into an icicle. "I will give your request to Doctor Watkins, sir. He will decide."

The wires were freezing up.

He'd try later. Maybe after he got Barbara in to look at those mug shots.

He leaned back in his swivel chair, thinking maybe he had a break. But it didn't make a whole lot of sense. Why would Professor Kinnets plug the house dick? What good would it do?

Maybe Tom Wool was the one. But what good did it do him to plug the house dick? Still, this little triangle had some potential.

It didn't make sense, but murder didn't make sense either. He'd learned that a few times over. Murder made sense to someone's feelings, but no sense at all when you tried to rationalize it. Maybe a bullet into J. Adam Bark made Kinnets feel good.

Sonntag was snatching at straws and he knew it.

Then, surprisingly, the phone rattled. He pulled the earpiece off.

"Long distance for Lieutenant Sonntag."

"Speaking."

"Go ahead, sir."

"Hello? Hello? Mr. Sonntag? You called? Watkins here."

A bit of luck after all. "Professor, I'm looking for a way to reach Dr. Kinnets, Rasher Kinnets. He's a member of your society, I believe."

"Oh, Rasher, yes, I know him. Fine fellow. Why do you ask?"

"A routine investigation. We'd like to talk to him. He's left Madison and we can't trace him."

"Well, that's fine, let me see here. I should have it in my Rolodex. Yes, here. But it's Madison. Last address is Madison, Wisconsin."

"We believe he left Madison last July, Dr. Watkins."

"Well, he didn't let us know."

"Do you send out mailings? Have his come back?"

"Well, the secretaries handle that. I could ask."

"Where might Mr. Kinnets go, if he were to seek another position?"

"Biology department somewhere. Or zoology. He's well qualified."

"Where would he go if he had been fired? Is that the word? By the University of Wisconsin."

"Kinnets was fired?"

"That's what we understand."

"That's biology, for you," Watkins said. "He probably taught evolution."

"You must know something I don't know."

"I don't know anything, sir, and Doctor Kinnets is a promising talent in our field."

"What's he done?"

"Well, for one thing, an exhaustive survey of ungulate breeding habits, broken down by climate. He probably knows more about deer demographics than any other living person. He once did a paper on bachelor deer."

"If he rejoins, or surfaces, would you let me know at once?"

Watkins agreed to it.

Sonntag clamped the earpiece on its hook. Kinnets had vanished, and maybe with Abby Wool. He'd put the FBI onto it. He slumped into his chair. He'd been on this case for days, and still hadn't anything worth pursuing. But that's how it went.

He lifted the phone and called.

Damon Barbara grumbled about the lost time. "I got three people waiting, and you want me to close up and come over there," he said.

"I'll pick you up in an hour. It won't take long."

An hour later Barbara was waiting. He had clipped his customers, locked up, and was perched in the lobby. Sonntag drove him over to the station and led him up the marbleized stairs to Harry's bailiwick, where the display, mug photos stuffed into a glassine wrap, were waiting on a battered table.

Barbara didn't bother to pull off his war-surplus naval pea jacket. "If he's here, I'll finger him. I know what I saw, lieutenant."

Actually, the barber was obviously enjoying it. He knew how important this was.

Harry had done a good job. Kinnets was in the number-five slot, surrounded by some clean-jawed types.

"All right, you look them over carefully, take your time. If anyone looks like the killer, give me the number," Harry said. Sonntag stood aside, watching carefully.

"None of these. That one there looks sort of like Spencer Tracy, but that's not him." He pointed at number two. "Tracy doesn't quite look like that. I've seen him in twenty films."

"You want to look a while more?"

"Yeah, I'll look." He examined the mugs again. "That's him, right there," Barbara said.

"Which?"

"Right there."

The finger was on Kinnets.

"How do you know that?"

"I just do."

"Was the killer wearing horn-rims like that?"

"No, he wasn't wearing glasses."

"Try to imagine this man here without the glasses."

"It's him. What's his name?"

Harry smiled. "Good question."

"You're positive this man's it? This man shot Bark?" Sonntag asked. "Now's the time to change your mind."

He saw a flash of something, hesitation, then resolution. "I think that's the man," Barbara said with dignity.

"Thank you, Mr. Barbara. We'll take you back to the Lake-shore."

"I'm done for the day. I got to catch a Cudahy car. Glad to help."

Barbara trotted out.

"Looks like we have another suspect," Sonntag said to Harry.

"That's the way it is. I don't see much resemblance between the Kinnets and Tracy, but people see what they see," Harry said. "Are you satisfied?"

"No. Can you try a few things? Blank out the horn-rims on Kinnets? Put some horn-rims on Tracy? I'm not happy with this, but it's all we got."

"I'll do it, Joe, and I'll see what other Spencer Tracy photos I can find."

Sonntag reported to Captain Ackerman. "We've a suspect, but not much of one. Barbara fingered him, sort of. You could call it a lead if you want. He's vanished, and we'd better put some resources on it. Family, friends, his girlfriend's family, friends, the whole nine yards."

"I'll do it."

"I don't see a motive. That's what bugs me," Sonntag said.

"You know something, Sonntag? Most killers don't need a motive. They just need to be mad."

"Mad enough to plan it perfectly," Sonntag said. "Choose the right moment, figure it all out, get to know Bark's rituals, plan an escape, do it in broad daylight but not get caught. That's some kind of mad."

CHAPTER TWELVE

Frank Silva would do. Captain Ackerman let Sonntag borrow him for a morning. Silva was the youngest investigator on the force, and how he got to be a detective, jumped over about thirty guys more senior and qualified, was a mystery in itself. Sonntag had opposed him. Over my dead body, he had announced. But Silva got the slot.

But that was only half the story. Young Silva had, in two years, proven to be the best man in the investigation unit as far as Sonntag could see. It might have been his old man's office—he was an alderman—or his old man's socialist connections that got him an investigator's badge, but it was talent that got him plenty of respect from Ackerman and the chief. Now Sonntag wanted him.

He unlocked the door to Bark's suite, which was silent and airless in the November dawn's light reflecting off the lake.

"This is Bark's residence. Hotel wanted a dick around full-time. Look around and tell me what you think. Nothing's been disturbed except for that photo on the counter."

"What's that?"

"It's Loretta Young, face down where she belongs."

Silva, almost bald at twenty-nine, studied Sonntag from under bushy brows, and smiled slightly.

Sonntag watched the young detective meander through the place, blotting up Bark's life and habits, saying nothing. Except for Kinnets, there were no leads. And now Sonntag was falling back on his intuition, thinking he needed to know more about Bark, but unable to say why. That was the reason for Silva. Sonntag hated to admit it, but the case was wide open.

Silva was absorbing Bark. Silva had an instinct that bordered on the spooky. Absorbing the clothes hung in rigid perfection. The shoes lined up like racehorses at the starting gate. The rooms entirely devoid of anything personal. Rooms without souvenirs, without mementos, without a heap of various magazines, without photos of loved ones. A medicine closet without medicines, save for a bottle of Bayer. The minimal shaving gear; a straightedge, crockery mug, brush, and soap. One toothbrush. One tube of wintergreen-flavored Pepsodent, its base carefully rolled upward with use. This man never shaved himself except on Sundays, when the barbershop was closed. The hotel towels, hotel soap, hotel sheets and blankets and pillows.

Then Silva studied the vast gallery of movie stars, the photos cramming every wall, row on row, from waist height to ceiling. Sonntag had found no order in them, except that the bathroom photos were only male. Here, in the living area, the photos hung without rhyme or reason, men and women, young and old, not by studio, not by fame or prominence. Silva studied them, one by one, until he got to Spencer Tracy. He pulled that off the wall and examined the back. The Hollywood studio photos had all been stuffed into black dime-store frames. He freed the cardboard backing and pulled out the photo of Tracy. There was nothing. No notations, no codes or numbers. For comparison, Silva pulled apart the Loretta Young display. Nothing there, either. Just studio photos, hung randomly on walls, perhaps in the order in which Bark had gotten them. What did it mean? Silva just shook his head.

"This guy either was hiding something in his past or he just didn't have any interests," Silva said. "Except for the movie stars. He's got the hots for actors. There's nothing here. I don't get a sense of a real live person. Now why's that? If someone's got a past, he's real careful. There's not a clue around here who he is, where he's from, what class of people, what his education is. No family, no friends. Now, if the personnel records are missing, that probably means he pilfered them. So he probably does have a past. But I don't get that from this place, either. What I get is someone who's so dead inside he's living his life through the movie stars. They're more real to him than he is to himself. The stars have lives; he doesn't. If he had a past, he would be creating a different one here. Camouflage. But I don't get that, either. This is the place of a man who's living life vicariously."

Sonntag wasn't so sure. "He was obsessed with the rich, the prominent, the famous. And not just movie people. I've got his clipping files in the evidence room. Why was he clipping articles and photos of everyone in this town? Maybe he's a stalker."

"Money, maybe. There's no money in here," Silva said. "How much was he carrying when he was shot?"

"Seven and change. I've covered that. He kept cash in the hotel safe; had his own lock box and free access to it. There were two hundred seventy in bills. All the rest was hotel book-keeping. No checking account. No bank savings. Most services paid by the hotel, including meals. A bar bill, mostly. I couldn't find anything amiss. Odd, though. No savings account. No stash."

"Did he pay Barbara cash for his morning shave and hair-cuts?"

"No, that went through the hotel. A tip was added monthly, too."

"You think Barbara shot him?"

Sonntag felt a jolt run through him. It was something he hadn't considered, and should have.

Silva pursued it. "Barbara's the sole witness, gotta good story, Spencer Tracy shoots Bark and runs out. There's Bark, hot towel over his face, lying back in the chair. Barbara pulls a rod, takes his time, bam! Then when cops arrive, he has a story."

"Well, but a running man was seen in the lobby after the shots."

Silva smiled. "Maybe. Let's suppose Barbara shot him. Why?"

"Beats me," Sonntag said.

"Here's Barbara the witness, saying someone like Tracy shot Bark. Here's Bark, with a suite full of movie publicity photos. Why didn't Barbara simply say Bark was shot by a lean, red-haired guy with a clean jaw and wide shoulders and a long nose? Why Tracy?"

"It's shorthand, Frank. Witnesses are always saying, the thief looked like Bogart, or the hit-and-run driver looked like George Raft. Just shorthand. It beats a long description, and anyone picks up on it. I've had that happen. The pickpocket looked like Marlene Dietrich."

"So everyone's looking for Spencer Tracy. Nice."

"Maybe this is just a dead end," Sonntag said. "I keep think-ing that someone shot Bark because of something Bark did or threatened to do."

Silva was running his finger along the frames, looking for dust. He eyed his forefinger now and then. He found some. "You take a guy like Bark, who's got no self. What does he do. He dresses up. Man, he gets into those knife-edged pants. His shoes, you can see your own face reflected in them. What else does he do? He wanders around looking for celebrities. They have lives. He doesn't. He needs them. He needs to know who they are, what they've done. But let me tell you, life can't be lived vicariously, see? The celebrities, they're living their own lives, not Bark's life. So he needs them and he hates them, got it?"

Silva studied his finger, where a gray smudge of dust had grown like a cancer. "You see? He didn't take these down. There's nothing secret about them. If he took 'em down, did some mumbo jumbo, he'd clean them because he has to; he has to line up his shoes in the closet, and he'd have to clean these frames. But he doesn't, see? These have been on the walls for years, I imagine."

Sonntag gaped. This was the first time in his life that someone had deduced some evidence from a little dust. Silva was like that, putting things together. Boy genius.

"So here's Bark. Got no life. Obsessed with other lives. Cuts out articles about sorority parties, debutante balls, travel plans, life in Palm Beach. Now there's two ways we can go with this. Maybe he collects stuff so he can pounce; he sees a name in a hotel register, and he's prowling. He's got the most complete set of names of big-timers in Milwaukee, maybe better than the papers. So maybe he clips this stuff so he is omniscient, see? Some local person checks in, and there's Bark, knows the whole story. Maybe.

"But maybe that's not it. Maybe he collects names of prominent people because he needs to live like them, some vicarious thing in him, okay? But it's futile. He can't find a life crawling into someone else, see? So he needs the rich and famous and prominent, and hates 'em, and busts 'em, and has the meanest way to do it; catch 'em in bed, wreck their lives. They're ruining their own marriages, and wrecking their own lives, but there's Bark, helping them right along and feeling pretty cheery about it. He scores!"

Silva banged his dusty fingers on the kitchen counter. Then he pulled inside of himself again. He would do that, hunt around within him, like pulling a pail of water up from a deep well, and then he would reconnect with the world.

Sonntag prompted him. "Lizbeth says, look for the ones who

really got hurt. Not some traveling salesman, but maybe some minister nailed by Bark. Maybe some politician whose career was ruined. Not some floozy who doesn't care."

Then Silva began to inflate. Sonntag had seen it before. His face brightened, an idea bloomed in his brain. "It's the photos!"

Suddenly Sonntag knew where this was heading and dreaded it.

"Tell me how it was done. The busts," Silva said.

"I think I got this right. Bark would spot a likely, as he called 'em. See what they were up to, maybe dinner, all that. It wasn't hard. Then he would call the station, get some cops in."

"Who?"

"The camera man, Meyers. Duty men, often McClary and Bernoulli. That's been their evening beat for a couple of years. I don't remember, before that."

"You're going to have to talk with them, Sonntag."

"I'm afraid so."

"Tell me what you know."

"Bark would ring in some cops and make sure Meyers was on hand, with his big Graflex. He was a genius at organizing these things. He had to pick the moment, you know."

"No, I don't know. There's half a dozen statutes."

"It depended on what they found. In the act or not. Fully dressed but occupying a room. Or defrauding an innkeeper, two people in a single. There's laws for every occasion. You could always get them for something."

"Yeah, and then what?"

"Bark listened first. They collected in the hall. He had a handy-dandy listener, a Dixie cup. Just lay that cup to the door and stick your ear to it and listen. If it was talk, he waited. He wanted silence or other noises. You get the idea."

"Then what?"

"He's got a passkey. In they go, Meyers first with the camera.

He usually got a shot before anyone knew what was happening. Then the patrol cops, but Bark, he often didn't even go in, just hovered around the hall."

"A cop deal! The couple hardly knows the hotel's involved."

"Not at first. They figure it out. I was talking with a gal yesterday who had it all figured out. She wanted to turn Bark into a soprano."

"It's the pictures. What happens to them?"

"They're rarely admitted as evidence. People plead guilty. So they get locked up. Theoretically, no one can have a peek without written permission from the chief and good cause."

"Do you believe it?"

Sonntag was feeling more and more uncomfortable. He just smiled weakly.

"You don't want to give me an opinion," Silva said. "So I'll give you one. I believe some of those shots get floated around. I think some of those shots have been seen by Bark, maybe pedaled by Bark, maybe used for blackmail. Maybe not just Bark. Maybe someone on the force. Maybe someone dirtying the badge. Photos like that, they're worth something, right?"

Sonntag didn't want to hear it. Hated it. Hated what was coming. Hated what he had to do. Hated interviewing the cops involved with the busts. Hated looking at the photos. Hated even asking for a look. Hated pointing the finger at any man in the department.

Silva was grinning.

CHAPTER THIRTEEN

Captain Ackerman's glare was known to wilt collars. Now the man glared at Sonntag, his brows knitted into formidable ridges and canyons, the heat so intense it threatened to melt the Brylcreem out of his straight jet hair.

"You want to interview cops? Why?"

"To find out exactly how Bark's busts worked."

The captain's unwavering gaze pinioned Sonntag. "Why?"

"Because they angered someone enough to kill Bark."

"You mean the cops angered someone enough."

Sonntag stood rigid.

"Tell me the exact damned truth, Sonntag. Are you investigating my cops? Are you going to point any fingers?"

"It's possible."

"Possible! Possible!"

"I need to talk to Gorilla Meyers. And two beat cops, McClary and Bernoulli. Maybe others if I have to go back further. I want to know how Bark operated. I want the whole deal, step by step."

"The photos. You want to see the dirty pictures."

"I don't want to see any pictures if I can help it. I do want to talk to Meyers and find out how he got his evidence. And who got mad. Mad enough to threaten the hotel. Threaten Bark. We thought the photos might be the key."

"We! You mean Silva did. Someday that little weasel will go too far. So you're going to look at pictures. I need to get the chief's okay for that. What'll I tell him, eh? You tell me."

"Getting pinched is one thing. Getting photographed is another. It could lead us to the killer."

"This is your deal? You're going to start investigating the department?"

Sonntag suddenly just shut up. No matter what he said, it would be turned into a probe of some cops.

Ackerman suddenly grinned. "I'll buy it. Go talk to the beat cops and Meyers. Tell 'em I said so. I'll talk to the chief about the dirty pictures."

"The evidence."

Ackerman laughed nastily. Not one jet hair, combed straight back and oiled down, had come loose.

The beat cops wouldn't come on shift until four, but Gorilla Meyers might be around. Technician Corporal Meyers was one of the busiest men in the place. If he wasn't photographing a crime scene or doing a suspect's mug shot, he was probably in the darkroom running off copies of wanted men or running some evidence photos for the district attorney.

He was in his darkroom, an odorous place in the basement.

Through the closed door: "Meyers, this is Sonntag. Can you talk a minute?"

The door opened. A light was on. "I was just going to load some film. Come in."

Sonntag stepped in. On the table was a big enlarger and developing trays. Paper was stuffed into black Kodak light-proof envelopes. Bottles of hypo and fixer lined the shelves. The overhead light clicked off, and suddenly Meyers was a disembodied voice. Sonntag heard clicks.

"I made sure this was okay with Ackerman. I'm working on the Bark case, and thought you could help."

Sonntag waited for signs of hostility, and heard none. He knew from the sound that Meyers was winding exposed roll film onto a reel.

"I never liked that job," Meyers said.

"We're out of leads, mostly, and looking to find out who was angriest. Someone got awfully mad at Bark."

"I'd say so, lieutenant." The response out of the blackness was cool, distant.

"You sure could help, corporal. I guess I just want to know what happened on these deals. What was Bark's MO? How did these busts work?"

"I don't know how he lined up who he was after. I never paid attention. But he sure had the goods on most of 'em. My job, the instant that door swung open, was to point my lens at the bed and shoot, don't wait. So I did. There were usually three of us. A beat cop, me, and Bark. Sometimes two beat cops. He slid his house key into the slot, swung the door hard, I pushed in, shot, flipped out the bulb, stuffed in another, and put in a plate and tried again. That's all the time I had. After that the woman would be in the bathroom."

"That's what I figured. You usually got what you were looking for?"

"No, if you mean caught in the act, not often. Not even Bark could figure that out."

"What did you get?"

"People, hell lieutenant, how do I talk about this? I always ended up staring at my shoes. I didn't even want to look at those people."

"I need to know how it worked. We're looking at all the ways people could get mad at Bark. Mad enough to kill. You sure could help me."

"Yeah, they'd get mad at him, And me. Mostly they were afraid of me. I had the camera and I'd just used it and they knew what was on film. You know what? I didn't even need film in there. One time I had a jammed shutter, but the flashbulb went off, and they thought I got the picture and pleaded guilty, even though there wasn't any picture."

"Anyone threaten you?"

"Not at first. Everything happens too fast. Mad and naked don't mix. Naked they're like sheep. Once they got their underwear on, they get mad. Some of them real mad."

"Threats?"

"A few, yeah."

"Those would be valuable to me if you can remember names."

"I don't remember names. These photos, they get identified by the beat cop if I don't remember, and usually they just go into the sealed files. They hardly get used. It's enough so that the subjects, they plead guilty and get out of court just as fast as they can. Who wants photos like that floating around a court?"

"But some did threaten. You remember any?"

Meyers's hands clicked something to something in the utter dark, and suddenly the light went on. Sonntag blinked. Meyers was the color of salmon. A pink gorilla. On the counter was a fat black canister with some film being developed inside it. Meyers rinsed his hands in the sink, his back to Sonntag, and Sonntag knew that Meyers was wrestling with this.

"Not a happy way to make a living, I guess," Sonntag said.

It was the right thing to say, for a change. Meyers smiled. "Most of it I like. I like doing crime scenes, mug shots. I get them into sharp focus, and that helps. My photos have solved crimes, put crooks into the pen. Those things make me feel like I'm doing something good. But busting in on people when they . . . Well, I hear jokes all the time. 'You lucky dog, you get to see all that stuff,' and dammit, I don't like to see that stuff, it's not what you think, it's pathetic, and I don't like to go home after seeing that stuff."

"Me, I wish there were some laws that got scrubbed from the books," Sonntag said, and wished he hadn't. Let a cop complain about a law, and the chief heard of it ten minutes later.

"It's no one's business," Meyers said. "There's no good reason. It's between husbands and wives. It's between lovers. It's their problem, not ours. It doesn't belong to the public."

"Lot of people think there are good reasons."

"Yeah, I'm afraid so. But who am I? Pictures are my trade."

Meyers checked his watch, clicked off the light, night returned, and Sonntag heard gurgling as the photo man poured off the developer and poured in fixer. Sonntag didn't ask questions. He just stood patiently. Then the light clicked on.

"I don't remember names," Meyers said. "But there was plenty of yelling sometimes. I heard a threat or two. You know what I heard most? A lot of weeping."

"Well, tell me the drill. The beat cop would tell them to get dressed, and the women would hide in the bathroom. Did they lock the door?"

"Often. Bark could flip a bathroom door open. Then they'd be charged. Under arrest for this or that, it's illegal. If there was any likelihood the gent would run, the beat cop would put cuffs on him. But there wasn't. I mean, a time like that. They'd get paraded through the lobby, past grinning guests, and taken to the station in a cruiser, and booked."

"Meyers, do you remember a real bad one?"

"Ah, yeah, there was one a year or so ago. I wished I wasn't around there."

Meyers opened the canister and pulled out the spooled negatives, all thirty-five millimeter. He rinsed them and stuffed them into a dryer of some sort. The hum of a blower filled the cubicle.

Sonntag kept quiet. The man was having trouble enough talking about this.

"You got to understand, Sonntag, that ones caught in the act, they don't get mad. It was the others, people dressed, people not touching each other, those are the ones that were bad."

"A year ago?"

"Yeah, we busted into a room, and there's this couple, they're dressed. Nicely dressed. Some money in those outfits. She's got a hat on the dresser. This room has twin beds; he's on one, she's on the other, six or eight feet apart. She had kicked off her pumps. He had his suit coat off, tie loosened, shoes off. Wingtip oxfords. So there they were, talking, and that's the picture I got. He got angry. He stood there lecturing us. This was his former wife. They were thinking of getting back together. They were going to talk it over. She had a room down the hall. They both were in bad marriages. They just wanted a private place. See how it was, sort of experimental."

"So what happened?"

"Booked for adultery. Partly dressed, shoes off, and that was all it took. This poor dodo couldn't believe it. I couldn't believe it. But this time Bark was reciting law at them, chapter and verse. It turned out he was some sort of big shot, this guy, rich and all that. Bark knew the name. I don't know what happened after that."

"Could you get me that photo? The two of them lying in twin beds, dressed except for their shoes?"

"No, Sonntag. Those photos and the negatives are all under lock and key. Not even I can get into that file."

"But there's a picture, maybe a year old, of this couple on their twin beds?"

"Far as I know."

"What did the man say?"

"The tone was icy, I remember that. That gent was going to sue and wouldn't quit, and Bark had better watch out."

"This was in 1947?"

"I think so. Last year."

"Has a name come to you?"

"No, I'm bad at names. It was fall, maybe October."

"October? That helps. They were charged with adultery?"

"I don't know what happens after I'm done with a case."

Sonntag knew he was on to something. It would be in Bark's incident ledger. "Any others?"

"I'll think of a few. Mind if I get to some printing now?"

"Meyers, thanks. This helped." Sonntag edged out of the darkroom.

"Those are crappy laws," Meyers said, and shut the door.

CHAPTER FOURTEEN

Sonntag caught Billy McClary ten minutes before the shift roll call, while the beat cop was waxing his shoes against the predicted rain. McClary was big and pink, like so many Milwaukee cops. Sonntag couldn't explain it. Maybe it was socialism.

"Need to talk."

Billy peered upward from the gray enameled bench in the locker room, wary.

"It's nothing, just help me a moment. We're mostly out of luck in the Bark case, and I want to find out if you remember any really angry people in those hotel busts. People mad enough to pull a trigger."

Billy's little blue pig-eyes focused on a steam pipe. "Those were fun. We really nailed those humpers. Man, you should have heard the yelping." He grinned. "Pinch a babe with her skirts off, that's what makes life worth living."

"Yeah, well, Billy. What was the deal?"

"Oh, Bark had it all figured. He always knew. If he wasn't sure, he'd listen at the door with his Dixie cup, his ear right on it, you know? Man, you can hear anything with a snooper-duper Dixie cup. Then he'd give the signal, and he'd unlock. Meyers would go in first, flash, click. Then I'd follow, usually see a female butt vanish. And there would be the hairy gent, yanking a sheet over his hot dog."

"And you pinched them, right?"

"It never failed. There was always something."

"You remember the time last fall when you busted into a room with twin beds, and the man and woman were dressed, one on each bed?"

McClary chuckled, the scene playing on the screen of his memory. "Oh, that was a corker, all right."

"That was Grayson Bartholomew, right? And Andrea Story, right?"

"Who knows? I'd have to look it up. A rich bastard. Bark told me he was an investment banker out of New York."

"What happened?"

"Oh, he gave me a song and a dance, but meanwhile I looked in her purse, and there it was, a diaphragm, know what I mean? That was all I needed, that and the two of them in a single, defrauding an innkeeper. So off they went, and was he ever pissed. I thought maybe I'd get him for resisting when I cuffed him, but he started to behave so I let him cool."

"You booked them?"

"Yeah. That's the story."

"I've looked at Bark's incident book and court records. They got bail, appeared the next morning, had to wait to noon, pleaded nolo, and got fined."

"I never knew. Me, I prefer to catch 'em at it, you know?"

"I'm sure you do. Bark was with you, right?"

"Yeah, this was a big one for him. He was grinning. He was going to nail a big-timer, and told us to get it right. This guy, he's pouring moolah into Europe, helping it rebuild. He's connected, you know? Talks to presidents and kings, and maybe he's the biggest big shot to check into the hotel in months."

"And Bartholomew tried to explain that this was his former wife?"

"Oh, yeah, they all say that. All that stuff, and how she's got her own room, and all they were doing was talking, and there's

Bark, hovering around, slowly shaking his head. I pinch 'em, tell them we have photos, and that's that, and off we go."

"Did Bartholomew threaten Bark?"

"Oh, yeah, he'd sue Bark; he'd sue the hotel. He'd sue me. He called it a racket. A shakedown."

"Definite threats? Violence? Did he say he'd break Bark's kneecaps or something like that?"

"Nah. But he was pissed, all right. Me, words just bounce off."

"Is that the maddest anyone's been? Have any other people threatened Bark? You could really help me here."

A bell clanged.

"Roll call, Sonntag, gotta go."

Sonntag watched the big pink cop lumber off. Well, it had been interesting.

Maybe they were headed for bed. Maybe she was ready for whatever might happen. Maybe Bark broke in an hour too soon. She wouldn't have brought that stuff otherwise. She was thirty-seven, from Minneapolis. He was forty-five, from New York. They had both landed at Billy Mitchell, but separately, and caught cabs to the Lakeshore. They had obviously wanted to be in a city where no one knew them. Maybe to talk, maybe not. Bartholomew was a suspect, all right.

Sonntag phoned Rudy Espana at the *Journal*.

"Rudy, Joe Sonntag here. You free to talk a little?"

"Sure, Joe."

"What do you know about a financier named Grayson Bartholomew. Background stuff, what he does."

If anyone knew anything, Espana would. He ran the business pages.

"Oh, him. He was in the State Department, one of the architects of the Marshall Plan, putting Europe on its feet, and then he took a top slot at Chase, I think it was. The Rockefeller bank. He's doing loans. European businesses need cash, bad, and he's the man with the checkbook. You could call Chase, I suppose. Is he coming here or something? I'll interview him."

"No, not that I know of."

"Before the war he was banking here. First Milwaukee Savings."

"Has he been back?"

Sonntag started to lie and then caught himself. "If he has, I guess you'd be the first to know about it."

"Guess I would. If there's a story brewing, I'd like a tip. That guy makes headlines."

"You got it, Rudy. Say, do you have a file photo of the man?"

"Let me look."

Espana was back in five. "No we don't. You could call AP."

"What does he look like?"

"Bartholomew? Oh, like a banker. Clean square face, graying at the temples."

"Like a movie star?"

"That would be stretching it. But handsome, I suppose. Sandy hair. I don't remember."

"Thanks Rudy."

Sonntag hung up. That explained the nolo. They wouldn't plead guilty, and they wouldn't plead innocent and call attention to themselves. They would plead whatever way they could escape unobserved. No contest, fined eighty apiece and left town.

The other beat cop, Bernoulli, wasn't on duty. Ackerman had left. The day shift had died. It had been a long day and it wasn't over.

Sonntag spooled a form into his ancient Woodstock and typed with his index fingers. It was a request to the chief. He wanted a photo, dated 17 October 1947, of Grayson Bartholomew, of New York, and Andrea Story, Minneapolis. Reason: suspects in

Bark murder. Photo in restricted files.

He carried the sheet to the chief's office, presently dark and unoccupied and redolent of witch hazel, and dropped it into the wire in-basket. It should have been endorsed by Ackerman and any other rung on the ladder, but Sonntag was never one to follow protocol.

He felt lousy. This wasn't good guys against bad guys. This was weak people and rotten laws and people looking for a few scraps of happiness, and twisted things, and making cases out of birth control stuff, and peepers on the force. Maybe he should ask Ackerman to switch him to something else before he got ulcers. And he wasn't getting anywhere anyway. It took Silva to see through to something. Lieutenant Sonntag, twenty-odd years Silva's senior, was just muddling along and the kid saw the opening. Maybe Joseph Sonntag ought to retire before his brains quit entirely, but he couldn't. Not yet.

He collected his black lunch bucket, drained the cold coffee from the thermos, crawled into his trench coat, and headed into a hard cold twilight. He'd be late again, and Lizbeth would keep food warm again. Probably meat loaf. She made good meat loaf, with beef and pork in it.

He boarded the Wells Street car as it started to drizzle. The acrid interior comforted him. He settled into a hard wicker seat and watched raindrops trace across the windows. It wasn't snow; not yet.

Then suddenly he knew. Knew! Get off the car. There were iron bolts in the viaduct that had worked loose. This time the trestle would cave in and dump the car over the side, and the orange streetcar would plummet through the roof of a Miller Brewery warehouse, and shatter in a sea of glass and foam. He sprang up, pulled the cord, but it was too late. The car was creeping out on the viaduct, edging along, its wipers washing away rain so the motorman could see. Sonntag reeled back into his seat and waited for death. But death passed him by. The car squealed to a halt at the first stop west of the valley, and the motorman cranked the door open.

"Sorry," Sonntag yelled. The seven other passengers ignored him.

The car groaned on. Sonntag cursed himself. He got off on 56th Street and walked home through a cold drizzle that collected on his hat brim and unloaded ice water on his collar.

He must have seemed beat, because Lizbeth looked at him sharply after his perfunctory kiss. He hardly noticed when she busied herself to serve their dinner. Before he was halfway through the comics and the Green Sheet, she summoned him.

It was tasty. She made good meat loaf.

"This is good," he said.

"What was it?" she asked.

"Meat loaf."

"No, stroganoff."

"I thought it was meat loaf."

She carted the empties into the kitchen and he heard the clatter of dishes and the rush of tap water.

Then she appeared in the parlor. "They'll keep," she said. She always said that when she let the dishes soak.

This time she sat on the arm of his chair.

"You won't contaminate me," she said.

He stared.

"Whenever you're wallowing around in stuff that you think women shouldn't know about, you wear it. I absorb it. You're wearing it, buster."

"It's the Bark case."

"Of course it is. He made a career of busting in on people when they were doing what comes naturally. And someone shot him."

"That sums it up."

"Yes, but you're so far down inside of yourself I wish you'd surface. I'm pretty lonely around here. My guy's being the strong and silent type." She paused. "My boy's gone, my husband's gone too. I get to read *Reader's Digest* and wash the dishes."

"I'm sorry."

She stared at him. "Gin rummy?"

"Sure," he said.

She got a deck and dealt ten each. She melded first and won.

"Whenever it's about sex, you don't want to tell me anything. I love being protected," she said, dealing another. "Bark caught someone cheating, and got killed."

"Bark may have caught people who weren't cheating, and got killed for it."

She stopped dealing. "Really?"

"People who were thinking of putting an earlier marriage back together."

She sorted her hand and pushed cards around. "You live in the middle of torment. I'd be blue, too," she added.

It was mostly pain, he thought.

CHAPTER FIFTEEN

Sonntag met Peter Mapp in the lobby of the Pfister, and followed the security man to his warren in the rear of the ornate hotel. Mapp's crammed lair could barely hold two people, and Sonntag settled into an old wooden office chair.

As always, Sonntag surveyed the man's habitat, looking for insights. He found plenty; shelf after shelf of books, some leather-bound, some in bright modern jackets.

"Making progress?" the hotel man asked.

"A little. I'm not happy with it. Blind alleys. I'm looking more and more at Bark himself; it seems to be leading me somewhere. We've gone through a lot of names, mostly people Bark nailed in the Lakeshore." He shrugged. "So . . . you knew him as well as anyone."

Mapp smiled briefly. "In one way, I did. Bark talked about his little triumphs. In other ways, I didn't. He just didn't talk much about himself. He's a blank slate. Always deflecting the conversation away from himself. I'm not going to be very helpful."

"You already are. What don't you know about him?"

"Now that's a good cop question. Let's see, I don't know where he's from. Who his parents were or what they did. Brothers or sisters. Family stuff. Hometown. What he did when he was a kid. What interested him back then. Whether he was a good student. Whether he played football. Whether he had a girlfriend. Whether he ever was married or even engaged.

Sonntag, there's a hell of a lot I don't know about Bark."

"Yeah, it's what he doesn't talk about that interests me. He came over here a lot?"

"All the time. It's just a few blocks. I'm the closest thing he had to a friend. When he got tired of the Lakeshore, he'd show up around here. We always talked shop."

"Shop?"

"Yeah, hotel security. We didn't see eye to eye, and frankly, I wasn't too happy to have him around, but he was happy to have someone to talk to. You know something, Sonntag, house dicking is a lousy job. I got the job during the war, after I took a load of shrapnel. This arm's no good any more. You know what I do? I try to keep the place honest. You get to deal with petty thieves mostly, stealing kitchenware, food, towels, linens. Drunks who puke on the dining room linen, people who get sick as hell and need an ambulance. But mostly you deal with boredom. That's why I have these," he said, waving a hand toward shelves of books.

"Is that the way Bark saw it?"

"Bark." Mapp laughed. "Bark loved his job. He always had a yarn for me. This person did this, that person did that. Some cabbie swore at him, so he had the cabbie fired. Some maid tried to seduce him when he caught her digging in customers' purses. Stuff like that. Stories, Sonntag. My God, the man had fifty stories."

"But you didn't see eye to eye? About what?"

"Oh, Sonntag, can't you guess? If I did what Bark did, nailing all those guests, this hotel would fire me in two seconds."

"The hotel doesn't care how its rooms are used?"

"Of course they care. This isn't a dive. We chase floozies out of the bar now and then. But we don't try to drive trade away. You know why I'm here? Paid for this? It's to protect women. These morality laws are hard on rogues. I'm here to make sure that any woman in this hotel is treated with respect. That's what I do. I believe in it."

"What do you do differently from Bark?"

Mapp stared at the books a moment. "Okay. Suppose a pretty young woman checks in. She's got no luggage. She's local, local address. Nothing for the bellboy to carry. He escorts her to her room and gives her the key, and she tips him two bits. That would set off Bark like a five-alarm fire, and that woman would be in trouble one way or another at the Lakeshore. But me, if I really think she's there to meet a lover, or stuff like that, I'll just go knock on her door. Low key. She's smiling. Expecting someone when she opens the door. The smile vanishes when she sees me. I tell her I'm the hotel security, and I noticed she was alone, and I'd say if she needs anything, call on me. I'm here to keep her safe. The Pfister is a safe place for unescorted women. And I'll be available to make sure she's fine." Mapp smiled. "So, you see, we're doing her a service, watching over a single lady, keeping wolves away. So she understands she's watched, and conducts herself accordingly. Better, isn't it? She's not going to be angry at the hotel, not even if I've thwarted her intent to try a little hanky-panky. Now Bark, he'd get cops and bust her."

That interested Sonntag. "Why did the Lakeshore Towers let Bark rampage the way he did? He must have hurt their business."

Mapp smiled. "He didn't. He wasn't good at the job. He couldn't read people. He was too busy checking to see whether his Florsheims were polished. Here's the scoop, lieutenant. Their operations man, Greaves, had marketed the hotel as a party place. A celebrity place. That's the hotel's deal, you see? If Bark had seriously dampened that, they would have booted him out. But they never had to. Just to pull a number out of the blue, he probably caught one couple in a hundred doing some hanky-panky. All he nailed was the obvious ones. That's a party hotel, lieutenant."

"A party hotel? Hard to believe, Mr. Mapp."

"Weddings, fiftieth anniversaries, retirements, balls, celebrities, big bands, opera stars, string quartets, you name it. Bark didn't interfere at all. He didn't have a good eye. He was too busy looking at himself. He relied on informants mostly. Bellboys, maids, but how often do they see anything at all?"

Sonntag stared at the books. "That answers a few questions," he said. "And raises a few more. Why didn't they just fire him? Who benefited?"

"Beats me," Mapp said. "He spent his life clipping movie magazines. Celebrities were his thing."

Sonntag's thoughts were restless and reaching into the wild blue. "You think he intimidated his managers some way? Did he ever talk about the hotel's managers?"

"All the time, Sonntag. Always about what cowards they were."

Sonntag thought he ought to wander through the Lakeshore's business offices, looking for a Spencer Tracy.

"Let me tell you something, lieutenant. The morals cases in municipal court. I've studied the dockets for years. Mostly it's couples nabbed in cars. They slip into cars at night and think that's safe enough. But any cop knows how to approach, park far away and walk up. They're booked for lewd and lascivious, fornication, all that stuff. All the rest, including the soliciting arrests at hotels and bars, don't amount to beans. The Lakeshore doesn't even top the list."

"You knew him better than anyone else in this town. Surely you got some sense of the man."

"I did. You want to know what drove Bark? Movie stars. Sonntag, no man alive knew more about every Hollywood actor than Bark. It drove me nuts. If Robert Mitchum got busted in

Los Angeles for smoking dope, Bark would know of it. If some actress was a dyke, Bark would scope it out."

"I keep feeling that if I could understand Bark, I could solve this murder."

Mapp seemed lost in memory. "He wanted to be one, once. At least an actor. He told me he went to the Pasadena Playhouse. Ever heard of it?"

"Nope."

"A nice old Spanish-style playhouse in Pasadena, a sort of training place for Hollywood. Go there, learn your stuff, get seen, get signed up by a studio. A regular theater course. Seems to me a whole bunch of people got started there."

Sonntag wrote the name in his notepad. "Did Bark say when?"

"Before the war."

"Did he quit? Did he finish? Did no talent scout pay him any attention?"

Mapp smiled. "You'd have to ask his ghost."

"Was he bitter about it?"

"No, not bitter, but something else. Deeply disappointed. Life had passed him by. There he was, knocking on Hollywood's door, and life passed him by. Once he told me he was better looking than Gable. There he was, sitting right where you're sitting, and Bark says he's got the stuff, and Gable was mostly bald and wearing toupees."

"Is that true? Toupees?"

Mapp sighed. "Hollywood is illusion. Negative illusion as well as positive. Gable might have a fine head of hair, but all it takes is a gossip columnist to turn him bald."

"I hadn't thought of that."

"He wanted to move Hollywood to Milwaukee, know what I mean?"

"I haven't the faintest idea."

"He talked the Lakeshore Towers into comping celebrities.

That was his idea. He told management that celebrities make the hotel, so get word out to travel agents, studios, that certain people can stay in the Towers for nothing; room, meals, bar all complementary."

Sonntag registered that. Here's Bark, talking management into drawing movie stars and stage stars and notables to the Lakeshore, and here's Bark, in his web, waiting to sting the first one that got out of line.

"Did it happen?"

"Oh, hell, yes. During the war, all those stars on the war bond drives, Carole Lombard, all the rest. They stayed at the Lakeshore Towers. Every time an actor on a publicity tour comes to town, it's the Lakeshore Towers. There's been a whole parade. Broadway people, English actors, and not just show business, either. Alfred Lunt and Lynn Fontanne have a place at Genesee Depot and there's a regular parade of guests. Some get put up there, at the Lakeshore. Big-time politicians, big-time newsmen. Walter Winchell, he was there once. Authors on tour. Fitzgerald, Hemingway, Sinclair Lewis, You name 'em, they came through and stayed at the Lakeshore. I have to give Bark credit. That little game made the place famous. Bobbysoxers, they still wander through the Lakeshore, looking for Frank Sinatra or Vic Damone on tour. Big bands, they get comped at the Lakeshore. We've had Claude Thornhill, Les Brown, Guy Lombardo."

"Some of those photos in his suite looked like they were signed for real, not just a studio reproduction."

"I've never been in there, Sonntag, so I can't help you on that one."

"Okay, here's the big question. Did Bark sting any of them?"

"It would've been in the papers, don't you think, lieutenant?"

Sonntag was going to say yes, and suddenly decided it was worth some investigation. "Did Spencer Tracy ever stay there?"

"Beats me, Sonntag."

"I should have looked long ago."

"Show your badge. You'll see whatever they have."

"I think I will," Sonntag said.

Sonntag braved a bitter lake wind, and hiked over to the Lakeshore Towers, glad when he plunged through the doors into abundant warmth. He trotted down the long flight of stairs to the lower level, and corralled the operations VP, one Marcus Greaves, a handsome devil who eyed Sonntag impatiently, and seemed eager to put the interview behind him.

"I'm still on the Bark case, sir, and have a few questions."

"We're cooperating every way we can, lieutenant. We wish the police would cooperate with us. We'd like Bark's quarters back."

"Soon, Mr. Greaves."

"It costs us in imputed rent about a hundred dollars a week."

"Does this hotel comp celebrities?"

Greaves pursed his lips. "What does that have to do with anything?"

"Comp celebrities? Draw them here? Add to the, atmosphere, you might say? Make this a notable place?"

"That's proprietary information, lieutenant."

"I'm conducting a homicide investigation. Now I'll ask again—"

"Oh, well, on rare occasions, yes. It's a matter of, shall we say, polishing our escutcheon."

"Was it Bark's idea?"

Greaves laughed softly. "Now what would a hotel security man be doing setting hotel policy?"

"Was it Bark's idea?"

"Surely you don't expect answers to silly questions."

"Was it Bark's idea?"

"Bark had no ideas. His brain wasn't capable of generating hotel sales strategy."

"Was it Bark's idea?"

Greaves heard the rasp in Sonntag's words, and smiled blandly. "Oh, in an offhand way, lieutenant. He thought we ought to put up those flashy sorts in our penthouses."

CHAPTER SIXTEEN

Greaves exuded patience, and something else that Sonntag had no trouble interpreting. The operations manager thought he was talking to an idiot.

"Now you understand, Sonntag, this is *entirely* private. It is not for *public* consumption. Yes, Bark did offer a *crude* idea, comp celebrities, but that of course needed *refining* into a marketing plan. Comping celebrities had some potential. It might draw interesting people and give the hotel some *ambience*. I should say, some atmosphere." He smiled slowly, soft creases in white dough. "But we can't let the public know that some rich people are getting rooms for free at the Lakeshore Towers."

"I'm interested in Bark. His proposal. Why you adopted it. What else did he say?"

Greaves smiled blandly, and sat composing his every sentence. "Why, Mr. Bark thought we ought to put celebrities in the two penthouses. They top the north and south towers, you know. A penthouse is customarily the most luxurious of our suites, and of course commands the highest *tariff*. That is, the highest price. I should say, charges. Rental. Yes, rental. That's the word."

"It's okay. I can lip-read," Sonntag said.

"We had to take a crude idea and turn it into something viable—that would work," Greaves continued. "It proved to be—ah, effective. It didn't so much improve our vacancy rate as it

114

did our peripherals. We lost income by comping our real estate, but regained it."

"Good for business," Sonntag said.

"The bar receipts, restaurant, you name it. And we brought the big bands to our ballroom, and that proved to be, ah, a moneymaker. It changed the ambiance, the hotel metamorphosed. So yes, with managerial design, Bark's raw concept turned into an asset. It raised our profits."

"So Bark was your fair-haired boy."

"Oh, no, he didn't matter in the larger scheme of things."

"Mind if I look at the penthouses?"

"Ah, I'd just as soon not."

"Mind if I see a list of who's stayed there the past two years or so?"

"That's proprietary, Sonntag."

"I guess I'll have to talk to the city attorney about a subpoena."

"Ah, lieutenant, that won't be necessary. I'll give you a two-minute look."

"Why the secrecy?"

"We don't want our celebrity program known."

"Wait a minute. You just told me the presence of all the celebrities you could lure here had changed everything."

The lips pursed. "Very well. Frankly, I'd rather not deal with the police."

"I'll have a look. Now, Mr. Grievance, was Bark invited to these penthouses?"

"Ah, sergeant, it's Greaves, not Grievance. Good heavens, no. Those people never heard of him, and what was he? Just a security man with dandruff on his shoulders. Why would they?"

"That's what I want to know," Sonntag said.

"I tell you what. Let me call housekeeping to see whether you may penetrate one of the penthouses, and meanwhile I shall have my secretary transcribe a list of occupants for the past two years."

"Tell you what. Just show me the ledger and I'll copy anything that interests me."

"I can't imagine why it should interest you, Sonntag."

Sonntag smiled. "Homicide."

"I don't get it. It's quite beyond me."

"Neither do I at the moment."

Greaves steepled and unsteepled his fingers, and finally arose. When he returned he had a list of penthouse occupants recorded by months for 1948 and 1947. There weren't very many. The penthouses had largely stayed empty.

Spencer Tracy was not among them.

It was some list. Public figures, like James Forrestal and Henry Wallace and Alban Barkley. Theater people, like John Gielgud and Irving Berlin and Ethel Merman. Film people, like Henry Fonda, Van Johnson, Greer Garson, Gene Kelly. Singers, like Helen Forrest and Kitty Kallen. Band leaders, including Tommy and Jimmy Dorsey. Notables, such as Cardinal Spellman, Norman Vincent Peale, Averill Harriman. Quite a hostelry, the Lakeshore Towers.

"Thanks. Have your secretary copy the names and occupancy dates and whether the guests were in north penthouse, or south, please. While she does that, I'll take a look at one."

"I can't imagine what this has to do with Bark," Greaves said.

"I'm not sure it does. That's what investigations do, you know. Look for threads."

The manager vanished again, and returned with a key. "North penthouse. Please don't touch. It's been readied for occupancy. I'll come with you—"

"Rather go alone, sir."

"Very well, and return that key to me personally."

The brass-button elevator man responded to Sonntag's bell, and pulled the mesh door open.

"Penthouse," Sonntag said.

The man nodded, pulled his brass handle around, and the elevator rose abruptly and continued past ringing bells to the eleventh floor, and then slowed. He opened the elevator onto a fancy foyer with a white enameled door.

Sonntag slid the key in, and the door opened smoothly, revealing a handsome suite with a great view of the glistening lake. Two bedrooms, two baths, kitchenette, dining alcove, living room with an east wall of glass, real fireplace, stocked bar, fake Renoirs and Utrillos. A good Philco phono-radio console.

Sonntag lifted the white phone, the new kind with the mouthpiece and receiver swelling on either end of a handle. He got an outside dial tone. This phone wasn't connected to the hotel switchboard, at least not unless one dialed the operator.

None of Bark's busts had involved a penthouse. Every one in the ledgers had included a room number. Maybe the occupants of penthouses were exempt.

Sonntag toured the premises with a detective's eye, looking for oddities in that white phone, peering behind picture frames, lifting vases to see what was on their underside, such as microphones. He found nothing. Handsome place that gave a sense of owning the world. He could see the south penthouse across the roof, and supposed it was a twin of this one. There was a door that opened onto the roof, but his key wouldn't unlock it, and it seemed to be there for service only.

Another theory in the wastebasket. Bark wasn't stalking celebrities. At least not the sort who stayed in these penthouses. So what was Bark's game, and how did he end up sliding out of a barber chair with two bullets in him? The hotel was not discontent with him. Bark never bothered people in these penthouses. Nothing made any sense.

He felt a wild frustration, as if the answers were close, just beyond his grasp, just beyond limning, waiting for him. He punched the elevator button, and heard the rattle and whine of the cage as it rose to meet him. The door swung open, and the same wizened monkey nodded.

"Lobby," he said.

"No luck, eh?"

The elevator monkey stared straight ahead, as if he didn't wish to acknowledge that he had just spoken.

"Should I have been lucky?"

"You talk to the wrong people."

"Who should I talk to?"

"Me."

The cage dropped steadily, clanging past stations, and slowed at the lobby as the elevator man eased it to a halt. But he didn't open the doors.

"Bark used to have parties up there in the penthouses," the man said.

"Parties?" Sonntag could scarcely imagine a man like Bark having parties. Bark didn't have friends.

"Yeah, when no one was booking the penthouses. Of course, they never ask an elevator man if he has any clues, so I didn't say nothing."

"Parties? Who came to them?"

"Nice-looking people. Lots of nice people."

"Ah, could you describe them?"

"Young mostly, but some old. Men, women."

A buzzer sounded, and again, an impatient ringing.

"Gotta go. These people, they all had little cases, bags, like overnight bags."

"You took them up and brought them down?"

"Yeah, once in a while."

The bell rang again.

"Who were they? Were they booked at the registration desk? How many, usually?"

The guy shrugged. "Fifteen, twenty, real nice-looking. Nicely dressed, too. Good shoes. Nice permanents on the ladies. I'd take 'em up, and maybe ten or eleven, I'd bring 'em down."

"What were the bags for?"

"Got me."

"What did they say on the elevators?"

"Nothing. Just 'good to see you again,' stuff like that."

"And when you let them out, where did they go?"

"Out the door. Took taxis, some of them. One or two drove."

The bell rang imperiously.

"Now you know everything I know," the brass-button guy said. "Was it a good tip or not? You bet it was. I can tell. I'm Willie. Just remember Willie." He swung the two doors open. A crowd had collected, grimly waiting for a ride.

"I'll want to talk to you again," Sonntag said.

In moments, the elevator was whisking people to their rooms. Parties. Good-looking people carrying overnight cases. Men and women. Penthouses, when they weren't rented. Bark in the middle of it.

Sonntag wandered into the well-lit lobby, trying to make sense out of something that made no sense. What was in those overnight bags? He'd come back when he had a few questions for the operator. So Bark had a social life. Or some kind of life.

Back at the station, Ackerman pounced. "Where've you been? You're supposed to keep contact."

"Hotel, talking to management."

"What's that got to do with homicide?"

"There was a possibility that someone in the hotel didn't like him."

"Waste of time. Sonntag, you've got dozens more to talk to. You've hardly made a dent in the list of people Bark busted."

"Actually, I've covered most of the locals. The rest were from out of town. What have you heard? Any word about Kinnets and Wool?"

"No, we've put out word to every university in the country. No one has shown up. That's the hot one, Sonntag. Catch Kinnets, and we'll nail this one."

Sonntag doubted it but he had learned to button his lip.

"Forget the hotel. Forget Bark. That's all dead-end. You won't catch a killer by psychoanalyzing a hotel dick. You've got a nice list of suspects right there in that ledger."

There were a few local names left, people Sonntag had judged unlikely. But you never knew.

"All right," he said, but Ackerman was walking out, and Sonntag's words simply bounced off the man's back.

CHAPTER SEVENTEEN

No killer had surfaced. Sonntag wasn't out of leads but the case was getting cold. Ackerman was staring over Sonntag's shoulder. Rasher Kinnets and his girlfriend Abby Wool were the hottest prospects, and they had vanished. Tom Wool wasn't a bad prospect, either. Ackerman had alerted universities across the country to contact the Milwaukee PD if Kinnets surfaced. Routine investigation, of course.

The list of locals that Bark had busted on morals charges wasn't large. Local college boys and some imported Chicago girlies, a young harpsichord teacher seducing an adolescent boy, two New Years Eve celebrators who decided on an impulsive fling, a drunken old lady who decided she wanted some romance for her birthday and spent hours in the bar looking over the prospects, a store manager and his buyer who were stranded downtown by a blizzard, two maids who were doing customers as well as rooms, and two suburban couples, for whom the Lakeshore was a different and exotic world, and a place for an escape.

Routinely, Sonntag looked into them all. They had alibis. Bark had been killed on a weekday morning, a time when nearly all of them were at work or in class or were in their homes and could prove it. The remainder of the people on Bark's incident ledgers came to the Lakeshore from everywhere in the country. Probably most of those who had been snared in Bark's web had come from the coasts, where laws dealing with morals were more liberal, or at least their enforcement was more relaxed. Then there were the usual salesmen; the ones who traveled in style. If they got nailed, so what? Their sales managers probably footed the fines and gave them a promotion. The one or two salesmen Sonntag talked to thought that it had been a good joke. Usually they had conned a local receptionist or secretary into a little nocturnal adventure, and running past hotel dicks was simply part of the old game.

He approached Captain Ackerman cynically, knowing what would happen.

"I need some travel money," he said. "Lots of people I should be talking to."

"Lots of travel money, do you? Suspects residing on Waikiki Beach? Oh, excuse me, Key West? Or maybe just Sun Valley, Idaho?"

"All of the above. Hotels cater to people from out of town."

"Out of town, is it? Locals are all pure as driven snow, are they?"

Sonntag grinned.

Ackerman guffawed.

"The best prospects are not here."

"Give me a list. Some of this we can do without travel. We have resources. Now, Sonntag, write up a report. I want to take all this to the chief. I especially want to know why you're ditching the locals."

"Alibis, captain."

"Alleged alibis, lieutenant."

Sonntag liked Ackerman half the time. Plainly, this was going to remain a local investigation, and out-of-town guests got a pass. It was all about money. If an investigation cost too much, they put you on a cheap hunt. Like that woman's body they found on the South Side, at the fertilizer plant. The whole investigation had a geography of five hundred yards, and probably would begin and end in the nearby bungalows.

He poured some java from his thermos, and settled back in his squeaking chair. He sensed something. Bark's victims had not killed him. Something else, something floating beyond, just out of touch. That's how most investigations ended. The crime unsolved, the leads petered out, the tips thinner and thinner. Even the press quits pushing, and then one day you get pulled off the case, it's cold, and you get put on another one.

Lizbeth's coffee was still warm. She favored Maxwell House, good to the last drop.

Then Rasher Kinnets and Abby Wool walked in.

Sonntag knew at once who they were.

"Lieutenant Sonntag? I'm Dr. Kinnets. I understand—"

"Yes, we're looking for you."

"This is my wife, Abby."

Wife. Sonntag collected a spare chair from Silva's desk and settled the two before him.

Kinnets shed his coat and porkpie, and waited.

"Yes, we've wanted you to fill us in a little. I'm glad to see you. And I'm pleased that you chose to come here. It'll help. Perhaps you can begin by telling me where you've been."

Sonntag pulled his stubby pencil out, and opened a steno notebook.

"It's simple enough. The university let me go." He smiled. "They booted my ass out of Madison. Abby and I, we made some decisions, and the first was for her to divorce so we could marry. After that we'd see about a future. We headed for Reno, stayed at a dude ranch near Carson City. She got the usual quickie. We married hours later, a Reno JP in a gaudy wedding chapel, complete with recorded organ music. After that . . . it was time to look at our future. I made a few inquiries, and that's when we learned you wanted us. I understand why. The best way was to drive east, which we did. We stayed in highway courts and a few little hotels, until we got here, and here we are."

"Ah, congratulations, doctor. I'm right that you're a PhD, right?"

"Correct."

"Who tipped you off?"

"They did, Johns Hopkins, where my group's quartered."

"Why?"

Kinnets seemed startled. "Why, courtesy I imagine."

Sonntag let it go. Every biology department in the country had been requested to alert the Milwaukee PD, not alert Kinnets that he was a hunted man. But here he was.

"Why are you here?" Sonntag asked. It was a blunt technique. Go straight to the heart of it.

"To clear ourselves."

"Of what?"

Again Kinnets was rattled. "We heard you wanted to talk to us."

"Of suspicion of murder."

Kinnets swiftly shrank in his chair. His new wife wilted, and took his hand. She was wearing a plain gold band.

Sonntag let up a bit. "Start with the time you registered at the Lakeshore, and tell me what followed, every detail. Tell me how their house detective conducted himself. Tell me how you felt about it. Tell me"—he addressed Abby—"what your husband thought when he found out."

Kinnets reddened, obviously embarrassed.

Abby rescued him. "We were at a marine biology conference. We're in the same field. We fell in love. It wasn't . . . intended. We just did. Maybe it was wrong. But maybe it was right."

Sonntag nodded.

"We each got a room," she continued. "But the hotel gestapo decided people in love shouldn't be together."

"We didn't have any idea that this—barbarian would bust into our room, our privacy!" Kinnets snapped.

"Then?"

"The door swung open," he said. "I didn't even know what was happening. Some big cop with a camera, he took a photo. Abby screamed. Two cops and the hotel dick. And there we were."

Abby stared levelly at Sonntag. "We were making love."

"I don't need those details."

"You must know the rest. We were arrested and charged . . . my God, I didn't know there are laws, laws for everything."

Sonntag nodded. "There are. Where was Bark in all this?"

"I can't remember. Just try getting dressed with two cops watching you," Kinnets said.

"He was there, a spider who had caught us in his web," she said. "He seemed, not just pleased, but satisfied. He had done his duty. It was as if he was lord of the universe and the two policemen, they were his, his . . . I was going to say lackeys. It was as if he . . . he . . ."

"Were you angry?"

"I was beyond anger. I wasn't even thinking of that. Anger came later. And a lot of other things. Bad feelings. Tom. My . . . I was married. What a mess, and my fault, too. I didn't think. What a thing to have happen. Not then, not when everything was going to be good."

"My fault, Abby, not yours. I was the one . . ." Kinnets said.

"Maybe Bark's fault," Sonntag suggested.

They both turned silent.

"Maybe if Bark wasn't so nosy it wouldn't have happened," Sonntag said.

It was odd how that silenced them. They both slid into morose quietness.

Ackerman peered out of his office door, spotted Kinnets, and started to approach. Sonntag didn't want him there. This was going well, better than he had hoped. But Ackerman was a wall of blue, gold trim, and if he came over to Sonntag's desk, it would all be over. Sonntag caught the captain's eye and slowly shook his head. Ackerman picked up on it. Sonntag nodded faintly. Ackerman slid away, but then sat down at a desk behind the Kinnets, hoping to eavesdrop. Sonntag didn't like it, but Sonntag was not the day shift captain.

Abby Kinnets stared at the floor. "What was going to happen was going to happen. All Bark did was push it forward, when we weren't ready. I mean, I was going to have to tell my husband. So, I don't care about Bark, one way or another. All he did was speed it up." She lifted her gaze. "Look, I know what you think. I was cheating. That's true. But there's more . . ."

"There usually is."

Kinnets seemed in a hurry suddenly. "We were in Nevada when this, this killing happened. We were a thousand miles away. We can prove it."

"How did you learn of it?"

"Clippings from friends in Madison."

"Could I have their names?"

"Jay and Elsie Caldwell."

Sonntag wrote the names on his pad.

"Here, look, I've got the guest ranch receipts. Hotel receipts. We stayed in downtown Reno after we got married. I've got everything. You can talk to anyone there!"

Kinnets dug into his breast pocket, a dangerous thing to do around a cop, but the professor pulled out a thick envelope, and in seconds he spread the entire contents before Sonntag. The man's hands trembled.

Sonntag read the contents carefully. Date of arrival, date of departure, daily room, dated bar bills, dated meal bills, dated transportation to Reno and Carson City, Reno divorce, judge, divorce lawyer, all dated, certificate of marriage, black and white photos of marriage, photographer, date stamped on back, Rasher and Abby, sleek in wedding duds, honeymoon hotel, downtown Reno, long distance calls, two to Baltimore, all dated. Purchases, new dress, a swimming suit, wedding bouquet, all dated.

Rasher and Abby Kinnets were in Nevada before, during, and after someone shot Bark, and had as much paper as anyone could hope to have to prove it.

Sonntag wrote the names on a legal pad. The hotels, the marriage chapel, the photographer, the stores.

"All right," he said. "Thank you."

"Are we cleared?"

Sonntag hated questions like that. "We'll let you know," he said.

It was less than Kinnets had hoped, and his face turned bleak. "Are we free to go?"

"Of course. I'll want a way to contact you."

"The Caldwells," Kinnets said. "We'll leave word with them."

They stood, noticed Ackerman ten feet away, pretending to spool paper through the old Woodstock. They froze briefly, and walked away.

Ackerman watched them go. "I don't trust all that paper," Ackerman said. "Too much paper, all nicely organized. Full of nice dates. It's like a Vienna choir boy singing in falsetto."

Chapter Eighteen

Greaves on the phone.

"Lieutenant, if you don't mind, we really want that suite released. You're costing us money. We have a tenant lined up. There's been such a housing shortage since the war."

"I'm about done with it. The only thing I want out of there is the movie magazines. What are you going to do with Bark's stuff?"

"We have some storage. Mr. Bark didn't own much anyway. We'll publish a notice. If no one claims it in ninety days, we'll liquidate it."

"Fair enough, Mr. Greaves. I'll be over for the magazines. They'll go into our evidence collection. Say, while I've got you on the line, did Bark ever engage your penthouses for anything?"

"All the time. Once a month. He had some friends come in."

"For a party?"

"Just a party. We provided a tray of hors d'oeuvres. We gave him a discount, twenty for the evening, plus ten for the snacks, and the bar bill."

"Who were these people?"

"I haven't the faintest idea. Friends of his."

"What did they do?"

"Played the records we provide there, I know that much. Maybe they danced. Maybe they listened to Walter Winchell. Maybe they thought the penthouse was the Stork Club. Now, are we done with all of this?"

"No. How did he book the penthouse? What did he say?"

"I wouldn't know, sir." Greaves was getting testy.

"I'll be over. I'd like to see his reservations. What did he do when the penthouses were reserved by others?"

"Nothing. He simply waited. He always wanted the first Monday of every month. Sometimes he couldn't get it."

"I'll be over," Sonntag said.

He didn't know why he bothered. The case was cold and Ackerman was about to put him onto other and hotter ones.

The chief had nixed any travel, according to Ackerman. The lieutenant should rely on police elsewhere if he needed anything. Anyway, it didn't make sense. Who would come from afar to shoot the lousy hotel dick?

Sonntag slumped in his chair, the ancient frustration running through him. Walls, mysteries, barricades. How many cases did he actually crack? Ten percent, twenty? How often did an investigator figure it all out and nail the perpetrator? Maybe he should move to Tahiti.

He stopped in Ackerman's office. "I'm going to give Bark's suite back to the hotel. We're done," he said.

"All right, do it. The hotel's been on my neck for two days. I told them it's your call."

"I'm taking some movie magazines. I want to look through them."

"And Spencer Tracy will leap right off the pages and confess."

Sonntag smiled. Ackerman smiled. It was a way of acknowledging that they were down to the last thin straw.

There were maybe ten of the magazines over there. Few enough so Sonntag thought he could lug them in a canvas bag he kept for evidence.

He wrestled with an east wind as he trod Kilbourn toward the lake. Milwaukee had the lousiest weather in the country. Mean damp winters, nasty lake winds, overcast for weeks at a time. Numbing cold half the year, steam heat and June bugs the other half. Still, he didn't mind. It was where Lizbeth came from, and where they would die, and that was all he cared about.

The hotel glowed cheerfully this blustery day, lording over the city at its back. He trotted down to the business complex, and sat outside of Greaves's office. The man was making him wait; retaliation, he figured. Twenty minutes later Greaves admitted him. He sure was a handsome devil. Almost like a movie star himself.

"Ah, the stranger from the police department. You're going to release the suite and surrender your key, right?"

"Soon as I collect a few things. And you're going to show me Bark's penthouse bookings?"

"Well, there weren't any, actually. We just drew a line through that day, north or south penthouse, and that's all we needed."

"What did he call this group? He must have explained it to you."

"Friends. One time he called it the Beverly Hills Club."

"Why?"

"If I knew, lieutenant, I'd pour out every last intuition that lurks in my soul."

Sonntag smiled. Greaves allowed himself a slight improvement of his mood.

"All right. I'm going to collect some magazines and give you a receipt for them. Then I'll turn over the passkey. If anyone claims Bark's stuff, I want to know about it immediately. Will you promise me that?"

"Of course, lieutenant. Now, I'll come with you."

"So I don't steal any towels."

Greaves smiled discreetly.

Sonntag and the operations manager hiked down the hallway and entered Bark's silent and somber suite. The relics of a man's life dangled from the walls. What else defined him? It took only a moment for Sonntag to scoop the magazines out of the drawer and dump them into his canvas bag. He toured the silent place once again, aching for something, anything, to whisper to him. But nothing did.

He abandoned Bark's suite, pulled the yellow PD sticker off the door, and handed Greaves the passkey.

"I guess that does it," he said. "Oh, one last thing. Those parties Bark threw, they just keep nagging me. Could I talk to a chambermaid who's worked the penthouses regularly? One who cleaned up after Bark's parties?"

"Certainly," said Greaves. "There probably is one cleaning the penthouses right now."

One phone call later and Sonntag was riding to the roof once again.

"You still looking?" the elevator monkey asked.

"We never quit."

"You check out those parties?"

"I'm doing that right now."

"Nice-looking people," the elevator man said, and swung the mesh gate open, then the gate to the foyer. The penthouse door was open.

A short chambermaid was vacuuming. She looked up, puzzled, and cut the motor.

"I'm Lieutenant Sonntag, Milwaukee police. You mind if I ask a few questions?"

She looked frightened.

"Not about you, ma'am. About people who come here."

"I haven't been working here for very long."

"Quite all right. The security man here, Mr. Bark, usually rented these penthouses once a month and had some sort of gathering. We were just wondering if you knew what sort of party it was."

"Smokers, that's for sure, sir. I never saw so many cigarette butts."

"What did these people do?"

"Played records. They never put them back in the right albums."

"Did they tip you?"

"Oh, no, sir, this was Mr. Bark's group."

"What else? Anything that might help me understand these affairs?"

"Drinkers, sir. The glasses, lipstick all over them. I have to collect them all and send them down to the kitchen, and put new ones into the bar."

"Beds used?"

"Oh, no, sir, never."

"Anything else, anything odd?"

"Pictures, sir. Flashbulbs in the wastebaskets. Lots of pictures. Somebody sure liked to use up film."

"Now, what about the bathrooms?"

"Oh, that's the cross I bear, sir. They always went through every towel; the women used them to clean makeup. Those ladies sure did paint up. I would have to replace every towel in the bathrooms, and sometimes housekeeping couldn't get the stains out. All that makeup didn't wash out. Once a lady left some, you know, those little powdering things they use, compacts, powder with a little sponge inside? I took it to Lost and Found."

"Every party? All the towels?"

"Every party."

"Mr. Bark called them the Beverly Hills Club. Does that suggest anything to you?"

"Playboys maybe. I bet half of them were like Porfirio Rubirosa."

"Why do you say that?"

She squinted at him. "Chambermaids aren't supposed to know anything. But the stuff I see, the stuff people leave, you wouldn't believe, sir." Then she took alarm. "I'm going to get myself in trouble."

"No, you're very helpful. I might have some more questions later. You mind if I come back later? You might think of other things you noticed."

She stared.

"I'm Joe Sonntag, and you are?"

"Lola Kranz."

"Mrs. Kranz, thank you. You're doing a fine job."

That was as much as he could glean from her. He descended to the lobby and headed toward the station, utterly bemused by Bark's swinging penthouse parties. Booze, phono music, women loaded with makeup. Here was the other Bark, the man who loved the big bands, the man who loved ballroom music.

Sonntag arrived at the station in time for lunch, dug his black lunch bucket out of his locker, and spread his nooning over his grimy desk. Lizbeth's coffee was still hot and savory. He unwrapped the wax paper that encased the sandwich. Wax paper was cheaper than the little sandwich bags, Lizbeth said. It saved almost two dollars a year.

He masticated a roast beef and mayo sandwich, a rare departure from the usual. The station was quiet. Crime had moved elsewhere this November. He pulled a couple of the movie magazines out, and began leafing through them. What could Bark have seen in them?

Will Frankie reunite with Nancy? Why is Gary Cooper spending so much time on the East Coast? Will Fox do a Jimmy Durante film? Is it true that Rosalind Russell is feuding with Sam Goldwyn? Will bad boy Robert Mitchum be forgiven?

Then the photos tucked into the magazine slid into view. Eight-by-ten glossies, big, black and white, stuffed into the middle of the magazine. A dozen of them. Sonntag spread them out on the desk, amazed at what he was seeing. There was J. Adam Bark shaking hands with Clark Gable. The photo was signed, blue ink. "For my good friend Adam Bark, with best wishes, Clark Gable." Sonntag studied another. "For Adam Bark, old pal, king of the Samba, Cesar Romero." And another, this time a gorgeous Greer Garson, side by side with Bark, who had an arm around her shoulder and was gazing with admiration into her lovely face. This time the inscription was done in a small, feminine hand. "You are a dear, Adam Bark, and I will always remember your kindnesses. Greer."

There were others. Bark shaking hands with Richard Widmark. Bark being kissed on the cheek by June Allyson. All warmly inscribed to J. Adam Bark.

Sonntag stopped masticating his beef sandwich and studied these astonishing photos as if they had descended from Mars. Then he hunted through the pages and found some other glossies. One caught his attention immediately. For there, before his unbelieving eyes, was a black and white glossy of Spencer Tracy, an arm thrown around Bark's shoulder, the two of them laughing at the camera. "For my old pal Adam. We're a pair of Milwaukee deuces. Spencer."

The other photos Sonntag scarcely noticed or registered. He propped the photo of Bark and Tracy up and studied it while he munched. He ate the apple, and drank the coffee, and eyed the photo this way and that. That damned Bark had a secret life, running around with movie stars. The man knew half of Hollywood.

Sonntag screwed the cup back on the thermos bottle, stuffed it into his lunch bucket, dumped the debris into his wastebasket, and wondered whether the chief would spring for a trip to England, where Tracy was starting a film.

CHAPTER NINETEEN

Sonntag discovered a chocolate chip cookie that Lizbeth had tucked into the lunch bucket, and munched it appreciatively. She knew how to bake.

"By God, we'll put Tracy in Waupun for life," said Ackerman, who loomed over Sonntag's shoulder. "Where did you get these?"

"Tucked into some magazines I took out of Bark's suite."

"Well, ain't that something. Our boy Bark had a secret life. This damn near convicts Tracy. Hey, we'll nail a movie star. Milwaukee boy makes good, does life."

Sonntag thought that Ackerman sounded a little too much like Bark. It must be contagious. The hunt for big game. Shoot an elephant.

"Who are these here others?" Ackerman lifted the prints one by one. "I hardly go to movies. Actors are all phonies."

Sonntag wished Lizbeth had put three cookies into the lunch box.

"Well, what're we going to do?" Ackerman said. "If I was you, I'd start talking to Scotland Yard. Heat up that teletype. We'll need to go high up for an extradition."

"What makes Tracy a suspect?"

"This! Bark and his buddy. Tracy's identified by the barber. What more do we need?"

"Could be," Sonntag said. "I want to look into a few things. Like, where were these taken and when and who took them?"

"What good is that?"

"Blank wall. All these shots against a blank wall. And I want Gorilla to have a look. These bother me. And another thing. Why were they hidden in the magazine? Why not on the walls like the studio photos? These are the keepsakes, Bark with his actor pals."

"Oh, he probably intended to hang them. And a magazine's a good place to keep photos from curling."

"Could be," Sonntag said.

He packed his thermos into the lunch box, threw out the wax paper, and collected the glossies.

"I'm going to talk to Gorilla."

"Good. I'll tell the press we're hot on the trail. By God, we've got this one licked."

Sonntag knew better than to protest.

He trotted to the darkroom, and found Gorilla studying some crime scene photos.

"Got a moment?"

Meyers nodded. Sonntag spread the Bark photos. "What do you make of these?"

"Well I'll tell you straight off they're not focused. Bad cameraman or a cheap camera."

He pulled a magnifier from a drawer and studied the photos. "Not seriously out of focus, maybe even deliberate. Just a softening. Every photo softened a little. That's a style. I always focus hard, but maybe this guy didn't want to."

"Anything you can tell me about where these were taken?"

Gorilla studied the prints. "Standard Kodak paper. Very good film and enlarging, not grainy. All taken in the same place, it seems. Against a wall. Maybe at the same time. Who knows? Yes, probably at the same time, composed right there in front of that wall." He turned to Sonntag. "It could be anywhere. But there's this. No studio backlighting, no sidelights, no diffused light. This is flashbulb work."

"Taken around here? Some big event here, or maybe Chicago? Taken in Hollywood?"

"I'm a photographer, not a clairvoyant, Joe. There's this. The same light switch on the wall."

There indeed was a light switch showing in two of the photos at the extreme left.

"I guess I'll have to dig a little, find some big event that draws movie stars. They're all spiffed up, suits and ties, cocktail dresses."

"Well, that's movie people. They'll get into an evening gown to go grocery shopping."

Meyers ran his glass over the Clark Gable photo and paused.

"What?"

"I don't know. I don't know what's bothering me. Well maybe . . . makeup on the collars. Those actors, half the time, they get makeup on their collars during filming, and the makeup girls have to clean them up before each shot. This here one of Gable, I think maybe that's makeup on his shirt."

There was indeed a shadow of something along the rim of his collar.

"But Bark, he's dressed the way he always does?"

Meyers just shook his head. The focus was too soft.

"Do Hollywood still photographers use soft-focus?"

"I've never looked into it."

"What are these?" Sonntag asked, referring to the prints Gorilla has spread out.

"An unidentified woman found on the north side, shot through the head."

"Another murder? Here? Who's on it?"

"Silva. I took these two hours ago. They can't ID her; no drivers, no social security, no purse."

The woman lay sprawled in a bloodstained suit with boxy

shoulders. She was young and had long hair. Her face was ruined by a bullet between the eyes but she looked vaguely like someone Sonntag knew.

"I think Ackerman will transfer me to this one," Sonntag said.

"Sorry I couldn't help," Gorilla said.

"You helped. The trouble is, I'm on a sidetrack."

Sonntag abandoned Gorilla Meyers and puzzled his way back to his desk. Nothing made sense. That Spencer Tracy would show up in Milwaukee and shoot a hotel detective was so improbable that Sonntag should be dismissing it, not nurturing it.

Sonntag propped the photos up at his desk and stared at them, but the photos revealed no secrets. Bark had apparently been running with actors. If he had traveled to the West Coast, there might be some train ticket information. Probably down to Chicago and then the Santa Fe Super Chief, unless Bark flew. Never underestimate the powers of a hotel dick.

But the longer Sonntag stared, the more skeptical he became. These photos would have been framed and on Bark's wall, and would have been the showpieces of his collection. Why were these photos stuck in a magazine?

He remembered a long shot, the ticket stub. That was as good as any to pursue. He tugged his trench coat over his baggy suit, and clamped his fedora over his head. He stopped at the dispatcher's warren. "I'm going to the burlesque show," he said.

That won him a grin.

Then he was out in the cold, hiking down to Wisconsin and Third. Some Christmas decorations were appearing in store windows. The gaudy Empress blazed with lights. Women hurried by, their gaze straight ahead.

The usual fat granny was in the ticket window.

"Hey, could you help me?" He flashed his badge.

She eyed him, nodded, and he watched her hand snake over to a small button, which would ring a small bell, telling the performers to clean up their act.

"This ticket. Can you tell when it was sold by the serial number?"

"Me, I can't add two and two."

"I thought so. Number is 10972."

She yawned and smiled. "I guess you're out of luck. The manager's gone."

"All right," he said, stuffing the mug shot in front of her. "This guy comes here now and then. Is he familiar?"

She glanced at Bark's mug photo, artfully done by Gorilla.

She shrugged. "Not that I know of. I never look."

"You never look?"

"Mister, they come here, they look anywhere but at me, and I look anywhere but at them. So maybe he came here once a day for ten years. I still wouldn't know it."

"I'd like to talk to the performers."

She yawned. "Who'm I to stop the cops?"

He headed through double doors into a small lobby. The noise of bump and grind rose from within. A poster announced the two internationally famous and legendary dancers direct from Paris as Dawn and Blaze, with a cast fresh from Minsky's, comedy by Mark Pill and Sammy Vail. Piano, alto saxophone, percussion. Slow, wailing, tired.

He pulled open the theater door and stood just within. Some fortyish brunette was still mostly dressed, red silks, red feathers, and was grinding away. This was grind music, the sax wailing, the percussion muted. Now a bump, that was a percussion moment. Bang the bass drum, bang, bang. She was smiling at the boys. Mostly these were boys playing hooky, and a few drunks sleeping in the rear. This was a truant officer's paradise, but none ever showed up here. Sonntag wondered whether truant officers knew where boys vanished to when they had fifty cents and carfare. They were supposed to be eighteen, but no one ever noticed.

After his eyes adjusted to the gloom, he spotted the side door, and eased over to it, past the musicians, just out of range of footlights, and then into the gloom of the back stage. The lady was grinding slowly, parading back and forth across the stage, winking at boys, and toying with her gaudy brassiere.

Sonntag watched.

"You want something?"

It was the comedy man. There were usually two vaudevillians in each show, telling smutty gags. This one wore baggy pants hung from suspenders, about right for erection jokes.

"I'm just looking for some information. That okay?"

"You're the cop."

"I guess it's not okay, huh?"

The comedian shrugged.

"Come here where there's light," Sonntag said. "You ever see this guy?"

"I see everyone in the whole world."

Blaze, or maybe it was Dawn, was losing more attire. Sonntag could tell by the snare drums. When the snares rattled, off went some rayon.

"I could use your help. This guy bought the ticket. Did he hang around here?"

"Acts come and go, pal. We've been here five days. Talk to the musicians. They're full-time."

There was a lot happening on stage. A teenage whistle or two. Snare drums. Throaty sax, building up to the last. She would quit with pasties and a G-string, or maybe leave much more than that with a cop backstage. They did a lot of stuff with feathery fans to improve the illusion.

"How do I find out when this ticket was sold?" Sonntag said.

"Beats me."

"When does the break come, so I can talk to the musicians?"

"This act just started. Dawn's first."

"Half hour?"

"Forty-five."

"Can I talk to the musicians when you're doing comedy?"

"Look, have you ever seen a routine that didn't have cymbals and drums, eh?"

Dawn's act reached some sort of apex, lots of piano, saxophone, and a few whistles from the schoolboys, and then she wandered by.

"Ma'am?"

She stopped, warily. She had stayed within the law, but there was plenty of corduroyed flesh in view.

"Just a few questions, if you don't mind."

She looked annoyed. "It's your deal," she said.

"Ever see this guy?"

She took the mug photo of Bark, and nodded. "Yeah, he's a regular here, always over on the left. Just sits and stares. You can't miss him. Suit and tie and hair combed back. Why?"

"We're trying to locate friends of his."

"He's no friend of mine, that's for sure, sweetie."

"He came here often?"

"How should I know?"

"Was he alone?"

"I never saw him with nobody."

The comedian had vanished, and now Sonntag heard light applause, and some fanfare.

"Was he a stage-door Johnny?"

"Yeah, once. He barged back here and asked to see me. Then he says, 'You look like Ethel Merman.' Thanks a lot, buster, that's what I'm thinking."

"Then?"

"He says, come to a party, the hotel penthouse, Beverly Hills Club, first Monday of the month, and I says scram, buster. Just another jerk. I never saw him again."

"No party?"

"I left the next day."

"Any other girls go to his party?"

"Beats me," she said.

He heard some cymbals, laughter, and a few bangs of the bass drum. He thanked her and then he was out of there, and into a clean November.

CHAPTER TWENTY

Joe Sonntag intuited who the stranger was. The man in the camel's hair topcoat, with the maroon silk scarf and soft brown leather gloves, looked like a banker, and if Sonntag were to put a fine edge on it, an East Coast banker.

The desk sergeant, Mo Mills, made the introduction. "Lieutenant, this is Grayson Bartholomew. He asked to talk to the man who's on the Bark case."

"Mr. Bartholomew," Sonntag said, waving the banker to the wobbling wooden seat next to Sonntag's desk. "You've come to town."

"Yes, a banking meeting," he said. "I have friends here, Ed and Polly Wade. They told me the hotel detective at the Lakeshore Towers had been shot. An interesting case."

An interesting visit, Sonntag thought. "It is. Do you have something to contribute?"

"Yes. But I'll have to plow through some embarrassing history first. I was here in Milwaukee last summer on private business, and stayed there—at the Lakeshore Towers. I'll be quite frank about it: My former wife and I rendezvoused there. We were thinking of remarrying. It didn't happen. The things that broke us apart still were looming there, but the meeting was valuable—or would have but for a most outrageous episode. Perhaps you know of it? If you are pursuing this case, I imagine you do."

"I probably do, but tell it to me, if you would."

"Yes, well, this man J. A. Bark, whose name I didn't know at that time, burst into my room, where my former wife and I were discussing our past and future—she had her own room up a floor—while we relaxed on twin beds, perfectly well dressed. But in comes this, this baboon with two officers, flashbulbs popping, and next we knew, we were being hauled off to this station house and booked. I never was so angry in my life."

"I've seen the photo," Sonntag said. He dug through a file folder, pulled the photo, and showed it to Bartholomew. There indeed were a well-dressed man and woman, he in shirtsleeves, his shoes off, she in her suit, her pumps off, each occupying a twin bed.

Bartholomew studied it. "You would think this would be exactly the evidence to nullify the whole thing, wouldn't you?"

"I can't say I see anything illegal going on," Sonntag replied. "But Bark seemed to have other ideas?"

"He and the officers who poked around decided that even if we were not doing anything illegal, we were about to, and therefore we ought to be charged."

The banker sat grimly, remembering all that. Sonntag didn't push.

"We pleaded no contest rather than innocent, to avoid the messy publicity that would result from a trial, and fled this bizarre city, bungalowville, I call it. The only favor in all of this is that it abruptly ended our talk of remarriage. Neither of us are, frankly, doing well in our present unions, but the whole miserable business here persuaded us that we would do worse together. Life offers its odd gifts, eh?"

The man was suave. Maybe that wasn't the word. Educated, well dressed, and able to express himself well. But Sonntag was growing a little mystified: why was he here?

"Now here's the thing," the banker continued. "That most unfortunate episode started me thinking. What sort of man was this damned hotel detective? Who was he? Why would he burst in on people to see whether they were, ah, engaged in liaisons? You ever think about that?"

"It has crossed my mind, yes."

"Well, I have friends in New York, cutting-edge thinkers, including psychologists, and of course I was soon describing the whole sorry episode to them. Lots of smiles, a little head-shaking. But one of them, my friend Ellis Adelman, began to mull it over. A fine mind, several doctoral degrees in the behavioral sciences, and also a clinical psychologist. What was this fellow like, this Bark? Why, dressed to the nines, looks like Adolphe Menjou, a little odd. So Adelman had me go all through the episode, and mulled it over, and here's where maybe I can help you. He thought this hotel detective lives his entire life vicariously. He also thinks this Bark fellow is helpless around women, maybe unmanned, if I may use that term. So he lives his life through others, sees the very things he wishes he could do, and hates all those poor victims of his, hated me, hated my former wife, and pushed hard to punish us. That make any sense?"

"Maybe."

"Well, it made sense to me. Ellis thinks this hotel detective is a hater of successful people. The upshot of all this is that you might hunt for Bark's killer among similar types, people who have no life of their own."

"You came to tell me that?"

"Yes, sir. It's an insight I got. I was so angered by that pinch—nothing like that has ever happened to me before—that I spent the next weeks thinking about lawsuits, messy, public, right out in the open. That's when I was poking around, asking questions."

"I see. What brings you here?"

"Got in yesterday. A consortium of banks is putting together a line of credit for Renault. Its plants were badly damaged during the war, and it's virtually moribund. I just got back from a conference in Paris. Three weeks of discussions, Hotel Ritz, the Renault people, Chase Manhattan, and others banks. I came here to work out details with local banks."

"You sailed to Paris?"

"No, flew, Pan Am Clippers, very nice way to go."

"I don't think I could manage it," Sonntag said. "And then you flew here?"

"Two days ago, yes. That's when my friends the Wades told me about this bizarre murder, the very man whose outrages almost drew me into a lawsuit. I thought I ought to share Adelman's insights. Maybe you can gauge what sort of social life he had from them."

"We're looking into just that, Mr. Bartholomew. But it does seem unusual for a man like you to stop by here."

"Well, I wanted to do it. I'm heading back later this afternoon. We've obtained a ten million line of credit here. Renault needs a hundred million U.S., to rebuild, and another ten million to sustain itself for a year or eighteen months. A new plant won't help if no one in Europe has the money to buy a car. It may be nineteen fifty before Europe gets past the war."

"You know, I'm still a bit confused. Why exactly did you come here?"

Bartholomew stared at Sonntag, no doubt considering whether to put his ideas into pidgin English. Then he smiled tightly.

"I came to share some psychological insights into the late Mr. Bark that I got from a top man in the field. You can investigate this killing in two ways: look at all the man's victims and find out if any were mad enough to kill him. Or you can look at Bark as a sort of whacko, a nut, and see who he associated with, and why. I thought if you were pursuing the most obvious course, you would be checking out the man's victims. Check out me, if you want, it doesn't matter. But here was my learned friend saying this Bark had no life, and was angry at those who did have some sort of life—home, family, esteem, friends. Ellis Adelman thought this man Bark might be obsessed with theater, and that's what I'm trying to convey. Actors. See if he was involved with a local theater group. This Bark might even have been an actor himself. Actors are all whacko. Show me an actor and I'll show you someone who has no center." Bartholomew smiled that tight smile again. "People with no center fly into rages."

It was odd, Sonntag thought, how closely the banker was skirting Sonntag's own thinking. But maybe the banker was trying to cover something. "You've done a lot of thinking about Bark, and even asking questions back there in New York. That's not very usual, sir."

"Of course it's not usual. The regular thing would be to try to forget about that hour of torment we went through, the smug accusations, being hauled off, accused of nonsense. So what? Get on with our lives, right? But I have an inquiring mind, and it's been fueled by sheer indignation, if you want to know why I've brought the whole episode up to a dozen friends in Manhattan for weeks on end. I also talked to lawyers about these ordinances. I didn't know they existed. Why do governments get involved? Maybe you can tell me, sir."

"Public decency, sir. Milwaukee is a clean city." Sonntag squirmed. He didn't want this to go further.

"It must embarrass you sometimes, lieutenant."

Sonntag sighed and smiled. The banker was no dummy.

"I'm a little baffled, sir, how Dr. Adelman arrived at so much about Bark just from what you told him about your own encounter."

"Well, it's speculative, of course. And it wasn't just one

encounter. It took me no time last summer to discover that this hotel dick fills the dockets of your municipal courts with cases like ours. He's a pouncer. So, yes, I told Dr. Adelman that our case was one of scores, maybe hundreds like it. That helped. A pattern, you see."

"But how does this lead to theater, that's what I want to know?"

"It's where people pretend to be living a life."

"Well, maybe. Most actors enact; they play roles. They return to their own lives offstage. Gary Cooper doesn't become the characters he plays."

The banker smiled tightly. "I thought to pass along what I had heard, speculatively, from an expert. Maybe you should argue with Dr. Adelman. I'll give you his number."

"Thanks."

"I've some odds and ends and then I'm off to Mitchell Field."

Bartholomew stood, drew his coat shut, and tightened his scarf. "It's getting cold," he said.

"I'm glad you came in."

Sonntag pulled his lunch bucket and poured some Maxwell House out of the thermos. The funny thing was, the suspect Bartholomew was offering prospects that might be more fruitful than anything Sonntag was pursuing. Theater groups. Why hadn't Sonntag thought of it? Actors. Not the movie actors hanging on his wall, but Milwaukee actors. Little theater. Did Bark ever attend a play? Did he hang close to those people?

Sonntag unwrapped a chicken salad sandwich from waxed paper, and eyed it. Lizbeth always spread it thick, the way he liked it.

Patronized, again. There was the banker ready to spout pidgin English; there was that operations manager, Greaves, routinely reducing the English language to Cub Scout level supposedly for Sonntag's benefit. Sonntag arose abruptly, headed for the men's room, and stared at his image in the mirror. Was there anything in his square mug that invited these people to address him as if he couldn't understand a word with more than two syllables?

He could find nothing, but meant to pursue it. Maybe he wore the wrong tie or something. Lizbeth didn't like his tie with the Evinrude outboards on it, but he wore it anyway.

He downed the sandwich and the apple and the cookie, which was actually two Oreos in wax paper.

He had to admit he invited it. Here he was, a lieutenant and actually the deputy chief of the investigations unit, a rank and position that had come to him inexorably through seniority and doing a good job. But he hated administration and loved the hunt, the clue, the fitting of things until suddenly he had a case. He was supposed to be in charge when Ackerman wasn't around, but somehow he never was, and the chief liked it that way. It left power in the hands of those who enjoyed using it. But it also left Sonntag with a little freedom, especially the chance to pursue his own inquiries. If Ackerman had been the one interviewing Bartholomew, Ackerman would have tossed out the banker's thoughts entirely, considered them an effort to throw the Milwaukee PD off the scent, and Ackerman would have ordered a full-scale probe of the banker, right down to the last unaccounted-for minute.

Maybe Ackerman would prove to be right, Sonntag thought, polishing off the last of the lunch and washing it down with the last of the java.

Chapter Twenty-One

Sonntag studied the teletype from the Pasadena PD:

JAY A BARK STUDENT AT PLAYHOUSE 1936–37. DROPPED OUT REASONS NOT KNOWN. ACTING MAJOR. PARENTS FRANK AND ELSPETH BARK, ALTADENA, NOT THERE NOW.

That was something. Bark had a theater background. How did it lead to what he became? The transformation from actor to hotel detective was all the more mysterious. Still, it was something to work with. And he could request a search for the parents. At last, J. Adam Bark was becoming a person.

There was one little theater group on the north side, in a converted movie house off Downer Avenue.

"What have you got?" Ackerman asked, from over Sonntag's shoulder.

"The house dick went to the Pasadena Playhouse and wanted to become an actor."

"What's that got to do with anything?"

"I'm not sure it does."

"What have you got on Bartholomew?"

"He was in Paris, all right."

"What do you have on Kinnets?"

"Definitely in Nevada. His wife too."

"What do you have on Gruen?"

"She looks a little like Spencer Tracy, but she sleeps too late to bump off Bark at ten in the morning."

"Keep hitting on those bedroom victims. One of them got mad."

"Give me travel money and I will."

Ackerman laughed and vanished into his office. He and the chief had offices. The rest shared a bullpen. Then Ackerman reemerged.

"Oh, Sonntag. I'm putting you on with Frank Silva. We still haven't ID'd that woman shot in the face."

"Quit the Bark case?"

"No, just back burner."

"I'm closing in on something. This is all coming together: movie star photos, actor, his penthouse parties."

"Sure, and Spencer Tracy sailed into Milwaukee and plugged Bark. Give Silva a hand."

Ackerman disappeared rather than listen to any more resistance.

That's how it always was.

He plucked up a *Journal*, looking for the movie and entertainment news. In particular, an ad saying what the little theater, the Milwaukee Players, was showing. He scanned the movie ads, the play ads, the clubs featuring singers. Vic Damone was in town. Lizbeth would like that, and he wouldn't mind listening to a set or two. Nothing. The playhouse was dark. Maybe they would be rehearsing tonight, and that would be good. They would be there, they would have a show going, and he could ask some questions, show the mug shot of Bark. Look for a Spencer Tracy in that bunch. Rehearsals usually started at seven in those places. It'd be another late night. He'd call Lizbeth.

He went to the evidence room and withdrew the stuff they'd found on Bark. It was all in a manila envelope. He poured it out on the counter there, looking for the social security card. Jesus

Adam Bark. That was it. Not Jay A. Bark. Maybe Jay was the man's real name. Maybe the man was embarrassed to be called Jesus Adam, and made the switch. He stuffed the possessions back in the envelope and handed it to the clerk.

"Jesus," he said. "Jesus Adam Bark."

"It takes all kinds," the evidence man said.

He wondered whether to report to Silva at once or track down one last item on his current list. He opted to nail down the Beverly Hills Club if he could, and hiked toward the lake front in numbing cold. Christmas carols were issuing from Gimbels and the Boston Store and Chapmans.

He plunged into the welcoming warmth of the Lakeshore Towers, descended to the business offices, and caught Greaves at a good moment.

"We're looking into these parties, Bark's penthouse gang. I hope you can help us," he said.

Greaves gave Sonntag a right profile view. "Mr. Sonntag, I've given you every scrap of information I possess, and I am very busy at the moment. We have four wedding receptions in the next two weeks."

Sonntag doffed his fedora and smiled. "You're most kind to spare me a moment or two. Just offhand, did anyone call Bark 'Jay.' Did he ever call himself that?"

"Adam."

"You never heard anyone call him 'Jay'?"

"Good god, detective, you are pursuing chimeras—fantasies."

"I have a thesaurus, Mr. Greaves. Now, what did he say when he reserved a penthouse? What did he call this bunch he was entertaining?"

"I'm supposed to remember, am I?"

"Yes, you are."

"The Beverly Hills Club. Yes, he would say he wanted the usual Monday slot for his Beverly Hills Club."

"And what did he say about the club?"

"I never asked. Beverly Hills is full of actors and Communist directors and screenwriters, so why should I ask?"

"Actors. He was entertaining actors up in the penthouse?"

"Lieutenant, he could have been entertaining orangutans for all I knew or cared."

"Did he ever talk about it?"

"Once we sent him a cleaning bill. The women in his little club had ruined every hand towel, and most of the bath towels. We had to send them out; the makeup wouldn't wash out. I asked him, do they all paint their faces? He just laughed and nodded."

"He nodded?"

"Sure, he was entirely agreeable and paid the dry-cleaning bill without a quibble."

"No explanation?"

"Oh, sure, he said the bunch was always in war paint."

"War paint?"

Greaves looked pained. "Women are always calling their makeup war paint, lieutenant. I trust you are familiar with ladies?"

"Never met one," Sonntag replied. "Tell me again what they did up there."

"Ate. Ate and drank. Ate the best hors d'oeuvres money could buy. Beluga caviar. That's top stuff, lieutenant. Glenlivet single malt, that's a fine scotch, you know; Jack Daniel's, Dickel, you name it, top-flight whiskeys."

"Moneyed people, they order that stuff, right?"

Greaves pulled himself up and addressed the lieutenant. "People with taste, sir. Moneyed people rarely have taste."

"Who paid?"

"Ah . . . I'm not sure. It could have been anyone."

"You prepared the snacks for how many?"

"I'd have to dig that out."

"Who served the snacks? I'd like to talk to the waiters."

"The snacks were taken there before Bark's guests arrived. He insisted on it."

"Why? What reason?"

"An orderly man, sir. Adam Bark insisted on order. As he put it, he wanted everything on stage before the curtain went up."

"Curtain went up on what?"

Greaves sighed, and then stared. "I've wasted quite enough time, and I'm sure you have too, sir."

"It was a figure of speech, is that what you're thinking?"

"Just so."

That was as much as Sonntag could get out of the man, but it was something. The mysterious guests got topflight nibbles and booze, spread makeup on towels, and sailed in and out of the penthouse without being seen by the hotel staff. And who paid for it?

Sonntag abandoned that for the time being, but with a sense of being tantalized, reaching toward something just beyond his cognizance.

He found Silva in Gorilla's photo lab. Gorilla had somehow created a mug shot of the dead woman, managing to fill in features that had been ruined by the bullet. The face was that of a young woman, with prominent cheekbones, deep-set eyes, full and lustrous hair, color unknown.

"That's it; that's as close as you'll get, Gorilla. I've been studying her for hours, and that's it."

"Frank, Ackerman's put me on your case," Sonntag said. "Fill me in. Tell me what you want next."

Silva turned to Gorilla. "Thanks, pal. I want half a dozen of these printed up."

"Got it," Meyers said.

"It's simple. Young woman gets shot once in the face on the

beach. We don't know who she is. No missing persons reports, so far. We can't trace her dental work. No one telling us someone's mail and newspapers aren't being collected. Pretty girl, twenties is all we can say. Dyed red hair, roots medium brown. Forty-five-caliber slug extracted from her cranial cavity, ballistics pending. Found on the beach near North Avenue, fully clothed, woolen coat, no sign of assault or other violence. No purse, no ID, no cash or drivers license. No jewelry, no ring. No lipstick on her lips or in her pockets. Boston Store carries the Varsity coat line, Chapmans carries the La Femme line of suits. Her fingerprints don't match anything so far; FBI's digging deeper. We've run into a total wall, but these mug shots Gorilla constructed out of a messed-up face might help. She's rather pretty, right?"

"Maybe Irish," Sonntag said. "Let's call her Maureen. I see a little of Maureen O'Hara here."

"Maureen she is, until we can do better, Joe."

"I'm your patsy. What next?"

"What next is that we should work on these two cases together. Both shot in the face with forty-five caliber. Some ballistics would help."

"Have you tried hairdressers?"

"Good thought. Best thought yet. Dyed red. Now we got some mug shots, let's go. Start on the North Side."

"One mug shot, anyway."

They headed for a drugstore and a phone booth, and then checked the Yellow Pages. There were seven beauty parlors on the near North Side.

"You got any ideas?" Silva asked.

"Start with those closest to the crime."

"Ever been in a beauty parlor?"

"Most married men have."

"Hey, that's not what I asked. What I want to know is, how

do you talk to those women? Are they gonna be mad, some cops busting in on them?"

"Let's find out," Sonntag said.

Silva was driving old 406, and they rattled along Farwell until they reached the Prima Donna.

"You first," Silva said.

Sonntag remembered the young man had never married.

They plunged into dryer noise and chemicals. Sonntag had forgotten the noise, but he remembered the acrid chemicals. He sure wondered what in hell hairdressers used on women's heads. There were three customers in what looked like scaled-down barber chairs, and two operators. Three women sat under buzzing gray helmets, looking like they were getting some kind of electroshock therapy. One beautician, the owner, quit combing and confronted the intruders.

"Milwaukee police," Sonntag said. "We're just trying to identify a gal. Do you mind?"

"I have to get the dye out or her hair will frizz."

"Just need one moment. You know her?"

The impatient beautician studied the mug shot.

"Oh yeah, she comes in now and then, gets her hair dyed red. She has easy hair. You should see what red does to some of them."

That was good news, first shot, first salon.

"You remember the name?"

"How can I forget? She calls herself Greer, like in Greer Garson."

Chapter Twenty-Two

But Greer wasn't her name.

"She called herself that because it was a big joke. Sometimes people said she looked like Greer Garson," the operator said.

"She have a name?" Silva asked.

"Oh, yeah, Maureen, Maureen, let's see, Maureen O'Grady. She came from Oshkosh or some place up there."

"O'Grady? She come here much?"

"Oh, not often. I got the feeling she was counting her dimes. Hey, I gotta take care of this lady now."

The woman in the chair smiled up at them coldly, while the operator began combing the gel, or whatever it was, through the lady's long blond locks.

"I guess it'd be all right if we just talk a little, okay?" Silva asked.

"Well, this is my customer."

"I don't mind," said the lady. "I'm getting an earful."

"This is a big help," Silva said. "We sure want to locate this lady, Maureen."

"Well, she lives around here somewhere."

The other operator, working at the next chair, chimed in. "Oh, Maureen has that carriage house behind the big red brick on Prospect."

"You know the address?"

"No, but you can't miss it. Two or three blocks that way."

"Have you seen her lately?"

"Nope. But she's about due."

"We're looking into a disappearance. You have any idea whether this Maureen disappeared?"

"Beats me," said the first operator.

"And your name is?"

"Monica Klinger. I own the place." She was combing assiduously, now, as if to let her client know she was not being neglected.

"Tell me what Maureen talks about, if you would. Does she visit with you?"

"They all do. Maureen, she comes from a farm up there, and she's really eager to get ahead."

"What did, ah, does, she do?"

"You know, I don't know. I don't think she's employed now."

"Does she have a boyfriend, or girlfriends?"

"There's a guy or two. She comes in around the first of the month to get gussied up. She loves to go out."

"Where did this Greer stuff come from?"

"Oh, that was the joke. She's pretty and someone thought she looked like the movie star, and that's all she could talk about. She has brown hair, but we made it auburn for her, so she could be mistaken for the actress. But it was a joke, you know? She could let it go pretty long; the brown roots didn't show."

"She was a real movie nut," the other beautician added.

"Like an actress? Did she play in little theater or anything around here?" Sonntag asked.

"Oh, no. A fan. She was a big fan. Once she found out she looked like that Greer Garson, that's all she talked about. Some guy stopped her once and wanted her autograph. So she did it. She signed 'Greer Garson' on a slip of paper."

Silva laughed.

Two more women entered. The beauticians were backed up.

"We'll talk some other time," he said.

"Sure, glad to help. Now Agnes, dip down into the sink so we can rinse."

Silva and Sonntag beat a retreat. Sonntag sucked in clean air, imagining that his lungs were grateful to him. They piled into old 406.

"I guess we better look for a brick pile on Prospect with a carriage house behind it," he said. The old cruiser whined away, and Silva punched the clutch just before the engine died, let it rev up, and engaged the engine. They cruised three blocks south on Prospect, and then back.

"There," Sonntag said.

One old residence fit the bill. Silva parked in an alley, and he and Sonntag approached a small dark carriage house with a front door facing the rear of the property. No lights.

Sonntag knocked. Only silence met them. Again. Then the wail of a cat faint but clear.

"Hate to do this, but you mind looking through a window?" Silva asked.

Sonntag rounded the other sides of the cottage. He couldn't see the cat. He could barely see anything.

Silva hammered again. "You mind getting permission?"

Sonntag headed for the main house, virtually a mansion. It, likewise, was too dark for an overcast November day. He rounded the alley to Prospect and ran the bell. He stood on the broad covered porch, hoping a maid or someone would respond. No one did. Prospect Avenue traffic hummed by.

He headed next door, another large home, cream-colored Milwaukee brick with a greenhouse off the south side. This time, a man responded at once to his ring. Cheerful, gray-haired, a portly Milwaukee belly on him.

"Say, could you tell me whether the folks next door are home? I'm Lieutenant Sonntag, Milwaukee police."

"Police is it? Why, sir, that's easy. The McKinnons are in Key West. That's what they do every winter."

"Who takes care of their place?"

"Young lady around to the rear, there. Maureen's her name. That's her job, you know, keeps the place up and running, forwards mail, all of that. Nice gal, off a farm upstate, I think."

"Well, that's what we're looking into. We think maybe she's in trouble."

"Why do you say that?"

"Not at liberty to say. You, sir, are?"

"Oh, Gus Pilsner, just like the beer."

"Mr. Pilsner, have you a key to her place, or would anyone object if we had a look?"

"McKinnons are old friends of ours. If something needs checking on, why that's fine with me. I don't have a key, but I'd be glad to come with you. I think she hides a key around there. Maybe under a flower pot or something."

"Please do that, sir."

Pilsner donned an ancient olive drab topcoat that looked like a World War One relic, and hiked back to the carriage house, where Silva was waiting.

"Mr. Pilsner, this is Detective Silva. You mind if we try the door?"

"Go right ahead. I'll explain it to the McKinnons, or Maureen."

The door was not locked. It creaked open.

"Does she leave the door unlocked, Mr. Pilsner?"

"Blamed if I know."

The carriage house was chilly and dark. Sonntag flipped a light switch and the front room bloomed. Maureen O'Grady was a good housekeeper.

A cat whined and slowly emerged from the gloomy kitchen. It was a gray tiger-stripe. It whined and whined, and Sonntag knew at once it needed food and maybe more.

"That's Betsy, her alley cat. She looks hungry," Pilsner said.

Sonntag couldn't stand it. He plowed into the kitchen, found an empty water dish and an empty food dish. He filled the water first. The cat sprang to it and lapped water desperately, while he hunted around for some food. There was a box of Purina under the sink. He filled the bowl, and the cat pounced on the food even before he settled it on the floor.

"Hungry," Silva said.

"Three or four days," Sonntag replied. It had been three days since the body was found.

"She always pampers that cat," said Pilsner. "Funny she let it go so long."

"That's what we're looking into, sir," Sonntag said. "Have you seen her the last few days?"

"I don't pay that much attention, lieutenant."

"I don't suppose you notice whether she has company?"

"Oh, if she does, I don't keep track. I try to be a good neighbor."

Silva was patrolling the rooms, touching nothing.

"Boyfriend, maybe?"

"Might be so! You know, a while ago she began getting herself up better. She bought some stuff, good labels I think. She went from brown to red, let her hair go longer, began getting all prettied up." He smiled. "That's a sure sign of something hiding in the woodpile."

"Maybe a skunk," Sonntag said, and wished he hadn't. He was always blabbing when he should shut up. "Mind if I look at her wardrobe?"

Pilsner seemed doubtful. "I don't know, I just wanted to make sure she's okay, not get into anything personal."

"She's not okay, Mr. Pilsner."

The neighbor blinked and turned quiet. Sonntag found the

bedroom immaculate and tidy. He covered the knob with a handkerchief and pulled a closet door open. There were a few dresses, a couple of suits, and two pairs of pumps, black and brown. Maureen O'Grady had not spent much on clothing.

There was no evidence of violence in this cottage. No evidence of struggle. No evidence of surprise. The refrigerator had eggs, a quart bottle of Golden Guernsey milk, some apples, a crock of butter, and some cheddar. The enameled breadbox had half a loaf of Langendorf bread. She had walked out, left the door unlocked. Silva eyed the place and shrugged.

Sonntag wanted to tear the place apart, but the presence of Pilsner stayed him. He really should get formal permission or a search warrant, but that would take some doing.

"Should we call for help?" he asked Silva.

Silva cocked a brow and smiled slightly, which Sonntag knew exactly how to interpret. They would keep on, walking the edge of the line, right under Pilsner's nose.

The brown leather-bound album on the end table next to the horsehair couch caught his eye. It was a fancy album, with gilt trim. He pulled his handkerchief again, sat down in the couch, and opened the album.

And sat, shocked, at its contents.

There were eight-by-ten photos, each of them similar to the ones Sonntag had found among Bark's possessions. Movie stars, the whole lot. Joseph Cotten with Greer Garson. Katharine Hepburn with Greer Garson. Van Johnson with Greer Garson. Spencer Tracy with Greer Garson. Clark Gable with Greer Garson. Alan Ladd with Greer Garson. Red Skelton with Greer Garson. June Allyson with Greer Garson. Mickey Rooney with Greer Garson. Angela Lansbury with Greer Garson. And half a dozen more, all with Greer Garson, that Sonntag wasn't sure about, not being a movie buff. All shot against a blank wall, sometimes with the same light switch showing.

"To Greer. You're the love of my life, Spencer Tracy," in a spiky male hand. "My dear Greer, how I admire you, June Allyson," signed in a flowing Spenserian script. "For Greer, lots of the best, Mickey Rooney," in bold letters. "Hey Greer, what a life! Van Johnson," in a rounded and disciplined script. "For a great actress, Greer Garson, with admiration, Angela Lansbury."

He rose, as if a leaf spring had pitched him up, and carried the album to the kitchen where Silva was discreetly poking into cupboards and examining cereal boxes.

He laid the album on the worn kitchen counter and began flipping pages as fast as Silva could absorb them. Silva slowed him down, his hand stopping the page-turning as the detective absorbed the contents. Then Silva paused, studied the photo, and the signature. "That's not Mickey Rooney," he said.

"I doubt that it's any of them," Sonntag replied. "And Greer Garson seems to be our missing girl, Maureen." He pulled the mug shot from his pocket and slipped it next to the images of Greer Garson. The match was not conclusive. A lot of those photos of Garson surely were Garson. Or were they Maureen with some clever makeup?

"We need some of Maureen's handwriting," Sonntag said.

He poked around until he found what he needed, a box of Christmas cards that Maureen had started to sign, with notes to her friends. Small rounded letters. Maureen's handwriting looked a lot like Greer Garson's handwriting on the photo of Greer and Bark.

"Mr. Pilsner, we're going to have to borrow these for a while. And we'll need to seal this place. If anyone asks, refer them to me," Sonntag said. "Will you care for the cat?"

"Yes, of course. Old tabby's my friend. Is she all right, lieutenant?"

"I'm afraid not, Mr. Pilsner. But for the moment, I'd just as soon you say nothing to anyone."

CHAPTER TWENTY-THREE

They slid into the old cruiser with the stuff in Sonntag's evidence bag.

"That was big," Frank Silva said. "We'll have to notify her parents."

"Listen, these are tied together, Frank," Sonntag said. "Hollywood stuff. Turning herself into Greer Garson. Do you mind if we stop at that playhouse off Downer? I need to ask some questions."

"If anyone's there, this time of day," Silva said.

But he steered old 406 toward the theater that housed the Milwaukee Players, leaving a trail of blue exhaust gas behind him. Maybe someday the city would spring for a few more cop cars. The front of the stone and brick building was dark, but that was to be expected. They found the stage door unlocked and entered a dim backstage area. Someone rushed up.

"Sorry, this is closed," the man said. Younger fella, maybe in his thirties, built strong.

"Milwaukee police. You mind if we ask a couple of questions?"

"Not much I can help with. I'm finishing up a set. It's a lot of painting."

"You build sets?"

"Design sets, yes. This is for *The Importance of Being Earnest*. Like it?"

"You act, also?"

"Oh, sure, bit parts, we're a company, we all do what needs doing."

"I'm Lieutenant Sonntag, and this is Detective Silva. We're trying to identify some people. We're going to show you a couple of photos and see of you can identify them, okay? Your name is?"

The young man seemed wary, "cop caution" is what Sonntag always called it. When cops show up, people are on guard.

"Steve."

That wasn't an entire name, but Sonntag let it go for the moment. "Well, Steve, we're going to show you a couple of photos, and if you know these people, or have ever seen them, we'd like to learn about it."

He tried the photo of Maureen O'Grady first. Steve studied it, his face a mask. "Never saw this chick. What about her?"

"You've never seen here around the theater? Or on the street? Her home is nearby."

"She looks like someone familiar, but I can't say why. Am I supposed to know her? Sorry."

"Hey," said Silva, "if you see here around here, you give us a call, okay?" He handed a card to Steve.

"Now we got another one here," Sonntag said, handing Steve the mug shot of Bark.

"He sort of looks like a character actor. What's his name? Adolphe Menjou?"

"Have you seen him anywhere?"

"How would I know? There must be hundreds like this old guy. Add a few warts and he'd be another character actor."

"Have you seen him?"

"No, never saw him in my life. What about him? Is he a bank robber or something?"

That seemed disingenuous to Sonntag. The mug shot of Bark showed him in his usual cravat and immaculate dark suit.

Silva said, "Tell it again, Steve. You don't know who these people are, right?"

"Right."

"Why am I thinking you're not leveling with us?"

"What is this, an inquisition?"

"Steve," said Sonntag, "you got a drivers license on you?"

Reluctantly, Steve pulled his wallet out and handed the license to Sonntag.

"Stephen Barovich, right? This your current address? Cudahy?"

Barovich nodded.

Sonntag copied it all down.

"I don't know what this is all about. What are you doing here? I'm trying to get a set finished."

"Do you play leading roles? You're a good-looking guy, big and muscular, strong features."

For an answer, Barovich reached for some playbills stacked on a table. "See for yourself," he said. "I've never had more than a bit part. They want stars that look like stars. Do I look like one? I look like a longshoreman."

Sonntag took a playbill. Barovich wasn't in the cast of the next show. "Mind if I keep this?"

"Go ahead, but I sure want to know what this is about."

"Just identifying some people," Silva said.

Barovich ran a big hand through sandy brown hair. "Well, I'm glad I could help," he said.

"The cast rehearsing tonight?"

"Yes, all evening. We're a hard-working troupe that gets it right. If we don't do it right, we don't fill the house."

Sonntag smiled suddenly. "We might try these photos on the rest, okay?"

Barovich nodded.

"Yeah, thanks, pal," Silva said.

They climbed into the cruiser, and Silva pulled the choke and fought the engine to reluctant life.

"You thinking what I'm thinking?" he asked Sonntag.

"I've got his address. We'll start asking some questions. Maybe we can get in and have a look."

"That was like pulling wisdom teeth," Silva said.

Ackerman pounced on them the moment they entered the bullpen.

"What?" he demanded.

"A tentative ID on the girl. Maureen O'Grady, from a farm west of Oshkosh," Silva said.

"How?"

"Beauty parlor operator."

Silva explained. Sonntag added that there might be a link between O'Grady and Bark. And a suspect they talked to at the Milwaukee Players.

"What do you have on Barovich?"

Sonntag shrugged. "Hunch."

"We'll start with the military records bureau," Ackerman said. "I'll put someone on it. Let's find out a little, then ask him where he was the morning Bark got shot. We don't know for sure when the gal, O'Grady? Yeah, Maureen, got shot. And meanwhile we'll do some ballistics. There's not much left of what hit Bark and then flattened in the barber chair. But a little."

Sonntag pulled out the photo of Greer Garson and J. Adam Bark, the one signed by the actress.

"Now what?" Ackerman asked.

The lieutenant dug into the box of Christmas cards, found several in which O'Grady had written a note, and laid them out next to the Garson photo.

"Good. Good. It's a match," Ackerman said, studying the script. "I don't need a document examiner for that. So who's this gal? And what about the Greer Garson imitation?"

"She apparently liked being mistaken for the actress. Dyed her hair red. That's why we headed for beauty parlors. Have you ever been in one of those places? I get cancer just thinking about them."

"We need to ID her. I guess that's up to you, Frank."

Silva sighed. This would be the bad part.

Sonntag pawed through the addressed cards. "Several of these are addressed to people in Omro, Wisconsin, wherever that is."

"West of Oshkosh."

"I'll start there," Silva said. He stared at the phone, obviously not wanting to do what had to be done, and then gathered his courage and reached the operator. "I'm looking for a customer named O'Grady, probably near Omro, Wisconsin, west of Oshkosh. If he has a phone."

Most farms didn't.

Silva flipped a button on a squawk box so Sonntag and Ackerman could hear. Sonntag dreaded what was coming. Sometimes he wanted to be anything but a cop.

"There's a Michael O'Grady at Omro, sir."

"I'll try that."

"It's a party line, sir."

The phone rang several times, two long, two short, two long, two short.

"Hello?" A woman's voice.

"This is Detective Frank Silva, Milwaukee police. Who am I talking to, please?"

"Mabel."

"This the Michael O'Grady residence, and have you a family member named Maureen?"

A pause. "Yes, sir."

"I may have bad news for you, madam."

"Oh, oh, dear. I don't . . . Let me get my husband. He's hay-

169

ing the cows."

A man's voice next. "Yes, what? Milwaukee police?"

Silva closed his eyes. Sonntag felt like closing his.

"We hope we have the right person, sir. Could you tell us where your daughter lived?"

"Prospect Avenue, near the lake. But my god, sir, what is this?"

"We believe your daughter is dead, sir."

"Dead? Maureen? Of what? How?"

There was sobbing now, plain and cruel and sad, rising out of the squawk box.

Silva looked helplessly at Sonntag and Ackerman. "Gunshot, sir."

"Gunshot?"

The weeping was all the more audible now. There were several O'Gradys on that end of the line.

"Ah, we don't know things for sure. What we need is someone who could identify . . ."

A long pause. "You can bring her to us. I won't go down there to that evil place."

"We need . . ."

"I don't care what you need. Send Maureen home."

Silva looked helpless, sat staring into space. Seconds ticked by. Sonntag lifted the phone from him.

"This is Lieutenant Sonntag, Mr. O'Grady. Did your daughter have family friends here, someone who could help us?"

"Yes. Her married sister's there. Ethel Linger. In South Milwaukee."

"Have you a phone number for her, sir?"

"Look it up. George Linger."

"I'm so sorry to bring you bad news, sir. We'll be back in touch. We're so sorry."

The phone clicked dead.

None of them spoke.

Captain Ackerman rounded the desk and put an arm around Silva's shoulders for a long moment. Then he retreated to his office, and Sonntag could hear him barking commands. There would be plenty of focus on Barovich.

"My mind just quit," Silva said. "It just quit."

"It's always like that for me, Frank."

"It just quit," Silva said. "I didn't know what to say."

Sonntag tugged open the directory and found Linger in South Milwaukee, took a deep breath, and dialed.

"Ethel Linger, please," he said to the female voice.

Then, "Are you the sister of Maureen O'Grady?"

"Yes."

"I have bad news for you," he began, and forced himself through the rest. Gunshot, Maureen found on the beach, need for the body to be identified, talked to the parents, so very sorry. Pain. Disbelief. Mrs. Linger agreed to come to the station and be taken to the morgue. She was, he thought, more subdued and resigned than her parents.

"Thanks Joe," Silva said.

"I've been doing it for a quarter of a century."

"But are you used to it?"

"A knife that severs the living from the dead? The messenger who tears apart families, spouses? No, never. It's just that I'm older and have a thick skin. That's how it is in this business. I couldn't last a day without a tough hide," Sonntag said. "No, that's not quite right, Frank. I wouldn't last a day if I was so tough I didn't care. The reason I'm here, the reason I don't quit, the reason I wrestle the darkness, is that all those hurts we see each day are my hurts too."

CHAPTER TWENTY-FOUR

It was late and dark; Sonntag was off shift, but there was one more thing to do. Lizbeth was used to it, so it was okay. He hiked over to the Lakeshore Towers, hoping to catch that little elevator man in the silk pillbox hat.

He stood in the lobby, watching the arrow turn slowly, pause on ten, and then again on four, and finally drop to the lobby level. Three people got off.

"Got a moment?"

The little guy nodded, swung the gate closed, and pulled the brass handle until the cage stopped between two and three.

"Thanks. You ever see her?" he asked, showing the guy the mug shot of O'Grady, so carefully reconstructed by Gorilla.

The elevator man whipped out wire-rimmed spectacles. "Yeah, she was one, I think. For the penthouse parties, right?"

"That helps me. Did these people look like movie stars?"

"I can't tell one from another. Me, I'm nearsighted so I don't go to theaters."

"Did they talk about Hollywood?"

"Nope, they were just ordinary people."

"Did they have little bags or large purses?"

"Yeah, they were always toting something or other. Men too."

"Thanks pal. You helped me."

"Me, I see a lot," the guy said, and eased the cage down to the lobby again. "You want to know what's going on, talk to the elevator man."

Sonntag hurried into the night, hoping to catch the Wells car at its terminal a block away. There was one waiting, the bright light from the windows patching the cobbled street.

Sonntag settled into the hard wicker and felt the familiar lurch as the car rolled west, its acrid ozone smell blooming in his nose.

So there was a witnessed connection. O'Grady went to Bark's parties. Both were dead. Movie parties. Who else went? Where could he get a list of people? Did they look like movie stars, too? Who took their pictures? Was one the killer, and if so, why? He could not think of a motive.

The pancake makeup. Were these people made up to look like stars? Was that why the hotel towels were routinely smeared with the stuff? Did they get all made up to look like actors and then wipe it all off at the end of the party? Why? Who were they?

He was so absorbed with the enigma he scarcely noticed that the car was passing over the viaduct and approaching the west end of it. He didn't even grab the wicker seat ahead of him and hang on this time. The cliff rushed up, and he was riding on solid ground again. He stared into the night, thanking God, not sure how his world had changed.

He dropped off at 56th.

Lizbeth pecked his cheek. "I knew you'd be home about now. I just know it sometimes. Live with a guy as long as I do and I know."

"I made a quick trip after shift. Asked a few questions."

She smiled crookedly at him by way of an answer.

Good meat loaf, good other stuff, and Borden's vanilla for dessert, read the *Journal*, L'il Abner's not very good tonight. Al Capp's losing it. Noise in the kitchen.

"Okay," she said, wiping her hands on a dishtowel. "I want

the whole nine yards, buster. Then we listen to *Truth or Consequences.*"

She dropped beside him on the sofa. Some families came together staring across the table over hot food. Sonntag and Lizbeth connected when they sat side by side on a couch, not facing each other. Her hands were reddened from the dishwater. She tucked stray locks behind the collar of the blouse under her sweater. He wished suddenly that she could have more of a life; that she didn't need his odd and sometimes bleak work to fill her mind. Maybe she should read more. He stared at her rumpled skirt, soft gray wool, seeing the shape of her thin thighs and bony knees, thighs that had borne so much weight, done so much work, supported her through laundering, feeding, cleaning, vacuuming, shopping. Not entirely dreary toil, for she had found solaces, especially the films they went to, up at the Tosa Theater on North Ave, or the Times Theater on Milwaukee Avenue. They had friends, too, neighbors, some of the cops and their wives. Canasta parties. Sheepshead, or schafskopf, as they called it there. Cribbage, gin rummy, solitaire. What would they do without games? And picnics. She utterly loved picnics, especially the ones in the parks along Lake Michigan, where she could see the whole world. Young mothers with strollers, kids playing baseball, beach boys and girls flirting.

"Maybe a serial killer. He killed twice, and maybe will again."

"He?"

"Spencer Tracy."

"Did you track him down?"

"Yeah, the real one was in a drying-out place in Chicago, fancy North Shore joint, Wabash Clinic. That guy's boozing is out of control, maybe. He was there for three days, getting vitamins and lectures, secret stuff, supposed to turn a boozer into a sober man, or so they say. Then he caught the Twentieth Century Limited to New York. As far as we know. We're not through with him."

"Well, I guess you won't be sending up a real movie star. So who's the local version of Spencer Tracy?"

"Whoever he is, he's killed Greer Garson."

She stared at him, jaw slack, wondering if this was a joke.

"A gal from upstate who looked like Garson. We found her dead on the beach a couple of days ago, bullet through her mouth. Same caliber as the ones that killed Bark, but we can't do much with that, no good ballistics."

"Who are the others in those photos of Bark's? They're targets, don't you think?"

"I should've brought those photos home. There's some I can't identify. You'd spot 'em in a flash, but I hardly know Gary Cooper from a walrus."

She smiled at him and ran a hand across his cheek. "Poor guy," she said.

"We've identified the gal, Maureen O'Grady, comes from a farm west of Oshkosh. We hit the right beauty parlor."

"Huh?"

"Dyed her hair. Brown roots. Good place to start, right? Don't you ever go into beauty parlors, don't you ever get a permanent, Lizbeth. That's what gives women breast cancer. You ever smell all those chemicals, you're a cooked goose."

Lizbeth was running fingers through her brown locks.

"So?"

"This young lady, she discovered it paid to look like a movie star. Now here's the deal. She's the Greer Garson in Bark's photo. And the handwriting matches. We picked up some good handwriting, and it's the same as Bark's photo. So now we got movie fans killing each other off."

"Are you sure they're fans, Joe?"

"What else would they be?"

"Actors, taking advantage of what they've got. Maybe you

should be Gene Kelly for a while and see how it feels."

"We're working on that. We talked to a guy in the Milwaukee Players, and Frank Silva and I think he knows something."

"Maybe they're not fans or actors, Joe. Tell me again about Bark's penthouse parties, okay?"

"There isn't much, babe. Here's what we know: he rented the penthouse when it wasn't in use. They partied, drinks and hors d'oeuvres. They played music, maybe danced but we don't know that. They were mostly young and good looking, according to the elevator man. They called themselves the Beverly Hills Club. They wiped out a lot of towels with makeup. Some pictures were taken up there against a blank wall, nice glossies, of a lot of these fake movie stars. These were signed. Bark had a bunch of them but not displayed on his walls. He hid them, as if he was sort of embarrassed by them. Beyond that, nothing. Not a single name. The elevator man recognized a few he took up and down. No list of these people in Bark's apartment or the girl's little place. Nothing in their phone books."

"Joe! I know what they are. These people pretend they're movie stars. It's all pretend. Star for a night. They aren't fans. It's the Beverly Hills Club, see? Anyone who looks a little like a movie star and can use some makeup to complete the illusion is welcome, see? So there's the bunch, partying once a month, just the way they think movie stars party. Walk around up there, and here's Fred MacMurray, there's Henry Fonda, here's Betty Grable, there's Lucille Ball, sitting there is Veronica Lake. So they take pictures. Get signed glossy prints they can show around. See who I met! See, here am I with Lionel Barrymore, or whoever, and he signed it!"

He grinned. "You're promoted to captain."

She was looking pretty smug, all right.

That was it: People who looked like a famous actor or actress pretending to be that person. Making up in the bathroom for the party. Wiping it all off before they took the elevator down to reality. Messed up towels, records out of their jackets, a lot of drinking, smoking, and dancing. It fit. And it fit J. Adam Bark, too. If he couldn't party in the real Beverly Hills, this imitation would do.

"Bring those pictures home. I think I can name everyone on them."

"Okay, tell me this. Do they know each other?"

"Of course not. That shatters the illusion. It's not Jim Jones or Jane Smith all made up to look famous, it's Humphrey Bogart and Ingrid Bergman. Real names wreck everything, see?"

"So how did Spencer Tracy bump off Greer Garson—if he did, which is still an open shot."

"Love, dummy. Greer meets Spencer in the penthouse. They exchange real names, phone numbers, even if they're not supposed to."

"Okay, that works. So why did Tracy bump off J. Adam Bark?"

"Did he really look like Adolphe Menjou?"

"Sort of, but there's no evidence he ever put on makeup and became the actor. I think he just hosted these events so he could be in a fantasy world. Like he was the one real person there. But god only knows."

"So, what next, Spade?"

She called him Spade sometimes, after Dashiell Hammett's detective. It was always a compliment.

"Spade's gonna hit the photographers in town and see who got hired to do those shots. Somebody with a good camera and a darkroom. Now that I think of it, those photos were ordered and paid for. Bark must have ordered his and paid someone. We find the photographer, maybe we get names, and find out who Spencer Tracy is."

"What if he's one of the club, not a professional?"

"Gotta start somewhere, babe."

"Okay, now I've been thinking. What kind of person gets a charge out of pretending to be a movie star? Do you want to be Humphrey Bogart, Spade?"

"Me, I want to be me."

"That's my point. Each of these fakers needs to pretend. Jim Jones wants to be Robert Taylor."

"No man in his right mind wants to be Robert Taylor."

She grinned and elbowed him.

"Maybe they're all whacko. Don't you think?" he asked.

"Nope, I don't think. I think they're all living more or less orderly lives except for one thing. They are absolutely starved to be someone, someone whose life is one big glitter, someone who goes to Academy Awards, gets tons of money, gets invited to parties, all that stuff."

"So how do they find out about this penthouse party? Who tells them when it's canceled because the penthouse is rented?"

"Beats me, Spade."

"They have to have a way of connecting. And I still don't have a clue why the local Spencer has started to bump off the rest."

"He hates them. They're fakes and the parties are cruel. He knows he's not Spencer Tracy. He knows these are just regular people. He knows that being Spencer Tracy now and then doesn't do him any good. If the hotel dick organized this thing, the hotel dick's at fault, the hotel dick made him miserable." She paused. "That's as far as I can get with this, Spade."

"That's pretty far, Lizbeth. You're promoted."

"Good, I want a maid and a holiday. How about the Wisconsin Dells?"

It made him blue. "I wish I could," he said softly.

CHAPTER TWENTY-FIVE

Gorilla Meyers was pretty busy, but he listened patiently.

"What we need, Gorilla, is the biggest blowup you can make of Tracy. His face, as big as your enlarger goes. Maybe even go bigger, a quarter of a face at a time," Sonntag said, after handing the photographer the signed photo of J. Adam Bark and Spencer Tracy. "Forget Bark. Blow up Tracy."

"For what? What do you want to see?"

"Makeup. Facial theatrical makeup. Frank Silva and I want to see who's hiding under all that pancake."

"I can do that," Gorilla said.

"When we get that, we'll have a lady I know show us what's real and what's paint. And then I'm going over to Ziggy at the *Journal* and have him airbrush the paint. He's the best airbrusher in the business. With a little luck, we've got a photo of the killer without all the makeup. You got a better way, maybe?"

"I'll think on it. Let me experiment. You want any other photos blown up?"

"Yeah, but not today. We're going to show the rest to a few studio photographers. We want to know who shot them."

"Let me know what you find out," said Gorilla.

Sonntag and Silva headed for old 406, and Silva nursed it to life, not an easy task in the cold weather. They had a list of studio photographers, most of them on the North Side and downtown areas, for starters. Close enough to the hotel to come take pictures.

"Who do you know that knows about theatrical makeup?" Frank asked, once the old cruiser was stuttering north.

"My wife."

"How does she know? Little theater?"

"X-ray eyes."

Silva grinned tentatively and let it go. He parked in a no-parking zone near the Howard Family Photo Salon: "Weddings, Anniversaries, Birthdays, and Graduation." Passports also. The cruiser coughed its last, and rocked gently.

"You want to try it?" Sonntag asked. He thought Silva had more finesse than he did, a big, soothing smile and a camaraderie that might peel photographers open.

A door-activated bell jangled, summoning a bespectacled owlish gent who wiped his hands on a not very clean apron. He stood at a counter. Behind were dozens of artfully displayed black and white, or sepia tone, photos: portraits, family groups, and bridal couples and groups. The guy specialized in drama. Dark background, or spotlights, or bright overhead lights that put a sheen to hair. Not bad, Sonntag thought, maybe a little too much comic-strip lighting. Definitely not a photographer of the hoity-toity though. These people were mostly lunch-bucket types, sort of like himself.

"Mr. Howard? Milwaukee police department. We're investigators."

"Me? What have I done?"

"We're just looking for the photographer who shot some pictures," Silva said. "It would be real helpful to us."

"Sure, sure, glad to help," Howard said. He smelled of developer, or was it fixer? Acetic acid? He wiped his hands nervously.

Frank Silva laid out five photos on the counter.

"Know who took these? Any photographer in town? Or out of town?"

Howard studied them. "Movie stars. Why do you even ask me?"

"They might have been taken here."

"Well, frankly, these are crummy. Look! Direct flash. No highlighting. There should be a good bounce off the ceiling to put a sheen on the hair. These are amateur stuff. I don't know why those big shots hired some expert with a Brownie, but that's the look of it. Someone with a flash camera got some big enlargements."

"They look pretty well focused to me," Sonntag said. "Something a lot better than a fixed-lens Brownie."

Howard pulled out a magnifying glass. "They're all soft-focused," he said. "So it's some Brownie photographer with a fancy camera."

"So who might take pictures like that? Candid camera shots. Celebrity meeting someone local?"

"I sure don't know," Howard said. "He probably cleaned up, too. I bet he soaked 'em good, celebrity shots, lots of prints so people can boast. This one of Greer Garson, that's her all right, someone meeting her, signed. That goes right up on the someone's wall, you bet. But the photography is crap, just crap."

"Did you take them?" Sonntag asked, suddenly realizing he hadn't asked the key question.

"Me? I wouldn't be caught dead peddling this stuff. Look at those shadows. Look at the glare in the eyes, flashbulb too close to the lens."

"Who might have taken them? Any idea?" Silva asked softly.

Howard turned the photos over. "Not even stamped or marked. Whoever took these didn't want to advertise it."

"Do most studio photographers mark their photos?"

"Anyone who's proud of his work. Lots of ways. Stamped on the back, or written in the corner, you name it."

"Anyone in town who might do quickie unmarked work like this?"

"Press photographer. Maybe somebody at the *Journal* making a buck, take a picture, develop it fast, use company film and paper and chemicals and maybe paid time, peddle it, don't say a word to management. In fact, I'd bet on it. This is fast work, like a photographer at a football game, shoot the bodies and print it up."

That seemed about right to Sonntag. He knew intuitively that these photos weren't taken by any studio photographer in town. But that didn't eliminate the need to check them all.

They tried a few more salon photographers with the same result. No one would own up to taking them, and all of them pointed to the glaring absence of technique.

"Want to try the newspapers?" Sonntag asked Silva, after three strikeouts.

"If someone's chiseling photographic stuff from the papers, he's not about to tell us about it," Silva said. "Which is all the more reason to see what we can see."

They found Harry Bechtel at the *Sentinel*, up on the fourth floor in a warren off the editorial department. He was their head photo man and an old friend of Sonntag's.

"What sort of mayhem are we looking at today, Joe?" he asked.

"Just some photos. Movie stars. These were taken locally. You have any idea who took them?"

Bechtel donned his horn-rims and studied the glossies laid out before him. "Jeez, I never knew so many actors visited here. If I'd known, I'd have taken a few myself. I've always had a thing for Veronica Lake. I want to mess up all that hair."

"They didn't. These are fakes."

"You spoil all the fun, Sonntag."

"What's your impression of these?"

He studied them carefully. "Just ordinary shots. Someone put these people in front of a wall and shot. Single flash, no filler, no highlight, sharp shadows on the wall, and some of these have flashbulb eyes, you know, when the flash pops back from the eyeballs."

"Professional photographer?"

"How'm I supposed to know that?"

"Wouldn't professional shutterbugs take more care?"

"Depends. These are candids, shot in social circumstances. Maybe shot fast. These are not sharply focused, and that says something. But if you want to know if some pro shot these, I can't say. I wouldn't know for sure."

"Mr. Bechtel, do cameras have signatures? Can you find something unique or at least traceable on the photos made by one camera, but not on some other camera?" Frank Silva asked.

"Good question. The answer is, maybe. Now a hair or a spot on the lens might show up in a whole bunch of pictures. A defect, a light leak, a shutter that's not right, all that might show up. You think these were all taken with the same camera?"

"That's for you to say," Sonntag replied.

"There's other things, too. Depth of focus, focal length, all sorts of things," Bechtel said. He studied the glossies, using a magnifying glass.

"Clean lens," he said. "No hair, no spots, no little blurs. If you're hunting for a camera, these prints won't help you much."

"But what would you guess?"

"Oh, big Graflex camera. Good lens, no distortion, Speed Graphic, high-speed film, fine-grain enlarging paper. The photographer's fairly tall, right? See, the lens is pointing down slightly at women, even with the faces of men. The flash shadow on the wall is slightly lower than the top of the heads. I'd say a tall guy took these."

"Guy?"

"You know any woman over six feet?"

Sonntag tried a gambit. "You know any press photographers who'd freelance this work?"

"I sure would if I got to meet a few movie stars. Tell me again, what is this deal?"

"Hollywood's moved to Milwaukee," Silva said, "and we're looking for Commies."

Sonntag wished Silva hadn't said crap like that. "We're looking for a killer. Two people dead. It's connected to these photos but we don't know how."

Silva tried to redeem himself. "Mr. Bechtel, you know of anyone at the *Sentinel* or the *Journal* who'd freelance these photos? You got anyone moonlighting?"

"There's two guys and me and a part-timer. We don't freelance. Everything we shoot belongs to the paper. If I shoot my daughter's wedding, it belongs to the paper. If I hand my camera to my wife, it's the paper's camera, see? And she shoots a photo with it, company equipment, company film, it belongs to the paper."

"That's all the more reason for someone to freelance on the side, isn't it?"

Bechtel grinned. "Not here," he said.

"Who'd take these photos? Let's say this is a party full of people made up like actors. Who'd they get?" Sonntag asked.

"Was it secret, this party?"

"Well, not public."

"I'd guess they got one of their own to shoot these shots. But what do I know?"

"Who has a darkroom? Do lots of people have their own darkrooms?"

"Expensive hobby. Enlargers cost plenty. The better films and papers do too. Then there's chemicals, print dryers, all the rest."

"Rich people?"

"Oh, no, not rich. Just someone who can divert some of a

paycheck each month. Say, if there's a party with people made up like movie stars, I'd like to shoot it. That's news, you know. Freaks dress up like Gable and take pictures. Any chance?"

"You'll be the first we invite," Silva said.

Bechtel laughed.

The *Journal* was only a few steps away, so they hoofed it.

Sonntag wanted to lecture Silva: You shouldn't joke around with people you're interviewing. That's because we're cops, and they take everything seriously. You should be straight with them. That's what was forming in his mind as he and the young man pounded pavement. But then he remembered how often he put his own foot in his mouth. There was hardly an interview he'd ever done in which he hadn't accidentally said something inane, or misleading, or that revealed more than he wanted to.

"Hey, kid, you have a way with people," he said.

"I knew you'd criticize me, Sonntag."

"Me, I just get stuffy when I'm poking around. You drew Bechtel out. Where'd you learn that?"

"Handing out socialist tracts when I was a boy. I had to take it and dish it out."

"You get beat up?"

"I learned how to dodge it."

They plunged into the stately and formidable *Journal* building, the home of one of the nation's finest metro dailies. Sonntag was always a little awed there, as if its reporters and editors were divinities, and its omniscient eye, like the eye of God, saw all things, even down inside the hearts of men. He always felt himself to be in the presence of greatness, and more. The *Milwaukee Journal* was the conscience of the city and state. He came seeking information, and suspected before it was over, the paper would give him the third degree.

CHAPTER TWENTY-SIX

Sonntag and Silva didn't get through the newsroom unscathed.

"Hey, lieutenant! Got a moment?"

It was Matt Dugan, their veteran police reporter, barreling like a dreadnought through the newsroom, past golden oak desks full of cigar melanomas.

"Not now, Matt."

"Just talk a little?"

"You get your daily briefings at the station."

Some ancient editors in green eyeshades were squinting at the cops in their midst, their gazes calculating.

"What you got for us? Maybe I can help you," Dugan volunteered.

"We just want to talk to some of your cameramen a bit."

"Well, I'll take you back and introduce you."

"Thanks, but they're friends of mine, Matt."

"Lieutenant, are those two murders connected? The girl on the North Side, and Bark?"

"We're looking into it."

"I hear some stuff about a lot of pictures. Did Bark have some unusual pictures in his place? Movie stars, stuff like that? Is there a Hollywood angle?"

"Later, Matt."

Sonntag edged away, prodding Silva in front of him, but Dugan leapt up and headed toward the photography labs.

"I'll help," Matt said. "I know my way around back there.

Are these two murders also connected with that woman found
next to the fertilizer plant?"

"No," said Silva.

"How do you know that? Bark and the North Side lady were
both killed with a forty-five-caliber bullet, right? How come
there's no word on that South Side woman?"

Sonntag elbowed Silva, who clammed up.

But Dugan saw his chance. "Is it true that Bark had wild parties in the penthouse? Like, orgies?"

"Not true," Silva said. Sonntag realized there was no stopping Frank Silva now.

"Were there dirty pictures involved? Was Bark running a
porno ring?"

Silva smiled. "Where'd you get that idea?"

"Is that what you've got there, some pictures Bark took?"

"He didn't take any pictures that we know of," Silva said.

"What about when he was breaking down hotel room doors.
I suppose he has plenty of photos of all that. I've been waiting
for this to blow open for years. Bark and his gangbuster raids.
He was the biggest turd in Milwaukee."

"We found no photographs of hotel guests in his possession,
Matt."

"I bet he had a bunch of juicy ones down in that den of his.
He never let me in there. Bare-ass naked pictures, and maybe
he got shot for trying to convert them into cash, right? Making
a little moolah on the side, blackmailing guests?"

"Wrong," said Sonntag.

The lieutenant herded Silva toward the photo labs, but
Dugan had leeched on and wouldn't let go.

"I just got a tip you were talking to the photo guys at the
Sentinel," Dugan said. "What was that all about. Don't you like
the *Journal*?"

"How'd you get a tip like that?" Sonntag asked.

"The Hearsts don't inspire loyalty," Dugan said. "I pay a buck a tip, and I knew you were in there before you got out their front door."

Sonntag laughed, suddenly. Actually, he liked Dugan and wished there were more ferrets like him, sticking their pointy noses into public business. "Matt," he said, "I can't talk officially, and this is not for public consumption, but sure, the girl on the North Side—I'll give you her name, we've got an ID on her now, Maureen O'Grady—and J. Adam Bark were probably killed by the same person."

"Spencer Tracy."

"Why do you say that?"

"I bribe witnesses, namely barbers. You even did a mug-shot test. Barbara, he says he picked out Tracy straight off."

"Spencer Tracy was drying out in a Chicago sanatorium, if that's the word for the joint, when Bark bought it."

"Maybe he slipped out. It's just ninety miles. Two shots and he's back in Chicago drying out."

"The idea did occur to us."

"How come you've been asking everyone in the hotel whether they've seen Spencer Tracy around there? Here's how I see it. Bark got some goods on Tracy, and Tracy blew him away. Gives me a headline, right?"

"Hey, Dugan, let's switch jobs since you know all the answers. You get to be a detective, and I'll be a reporter and hassle you."

Dugan smiled, Cheshire cat smug. "I didn't really think it was Tracy, unless he'd gone nuts and quit banging Hepburn."

They reached the photo department, and Dugan showed no signs of peeling off. Sonntag realized he had no way to unload the reporter.

"Matt, I guess we'll mosey on. We found out what we needed to know over at the Hearst empire."

"You don't want me to see what's in that envelope."

"Not now, no."

"Could it be Bark with a bunch of movie stars? Like, Bark with Spencer Tracy?"

"Where'd you hear that?"

"I pay photo studios for tips. Every time some babe wants a swimsuit portrait, I'm the first to hear about it."

Sonntag sighed. "No, these aren't photos of Bark with a bunch of movie stars," he said, which was bare truth, he supposed. "Frank, let's beat it. We open this envelope for anyone around here, it's public in ten seconds."

Silva edged close to Dugan. "You almost got it solved, man."

Dugan was grinning again.

They hightailed out of there. At least Dugan didn't climb into his war-surplus khaki wool topcoat with the sergeant's stripes pulled off the arms and follow them out.

The exited into a sharp cold, a north wind and scudding gray overcast moving like a freight train.

"Gonna snow," Frank muttered. "Nice warm place, friendly reporters, and you haul my ass out into the weather."

But Sonntag was laughing. Skunked by the best crime reporter in the Midwest.

Silva dived into old 406, and Sonntag followed.

"Hey, I got an idea," Silva said. He cranked the beast to life, pushed in the choke lever, and started north.

"Where are we going?"

"Milwaukee Stagecraft. A little dump of a place near Schlitz."

"Why?"

"You'll see."

The odor of hops and brewing lay strong in the air near the old brick Schlitz brewery. Sonntag didn't mind the smell, but it repelled people who hadn't grown up in beer city. It was a quirky odor, almost hospital-like, sometimes a little skunky.

It took Silva only a minute or so to find this place, whatever it was, and grind the ancient cruiser to a halt on a brick-paved alley.

"This here's the holy grail of the theater set," he said. "Costumes, props, makeup. It's the makeup we're interested in."

"Why didn't I think of that?" Sonntag said.

The proprietress turned out to be the gaudiest lady in recent memory. She was in her sixties, Sonntag guessed, but wore a bleached-blonde wig, huge gold earrings, and Dorothy Lamour lipstick.

"This here's Gertrude," said Silva. "We're old friends. I ask questions, she dodges answers."

"Cops and show biz don't mix," she said. "But I'll rat on anyone for a nice guy like you."

"I'm Lieutenant Sonntag. Some place you have here."

"Yeah, I can outfit any freak in town. I can even outfit a nudist colony."

Sonntag found himself studying rack after rack of costumes, some of them elegant, some sleazy. Did one need to be gowned as a Carmelite nun or a Tibetan monk or Queen Elizabeth or Blackbeard the Pirate? This was the place. One whole section was devoted to women's hats: big straws, little pillboxes, flowers galore. Organized chaos.

"Gertie, you sell pancake right?" Silva said.

"Max Factor."

"That's the brand, right? Okay, who's your biggest customer?"

She smiled coyly, her gaudy earrings bobbing. "The Brown Deer Country Club set, that's who."

Fanciest golf club in town, north shore.

"Yeah? Who buys?"

"Every grande dame on the north shore."

"Pancake?"

"No, my udder balm wrinkle cream."

"Gertie, who buys the pancake, the theater stuff? Do you have a few steady customers, people loading up on it?"

"Oh, sure, Frankie, and most of them are guys, too. You never know about guys, do you?"

"What's their names?"

"How the hell should I know?"

"What do they say?"

"They say stuff like, 'Tonight I'll be Clark Gable.' "

"Yeah? So they buy the greasepaint and become movie stars?"

"Movie stars? Jeez, Frankie. They're a bunch of farts who want to be someone else for a while. Hey, it's not greasepaint. It's pancake. Max Factor, that's the company. It doesn't shine, it pats on, and you get to color your mug any way it looks pretty. Wanna try some?"

All of the bells were clanging in Joe Sonntag's cranium. "What do they say? These guys, they come in here and buy some pancake, and what do they talk about?"

"The soirees. What a party bunch!"

"What parties?"

"The Beverly Hills Club. They belong to some club. I know one guy, he gets the stuff so he can turn himself into Robert Taylor."

"Anyone turning himself into Spencer Tracy?" Sonntag asked carefully.

"Oh, him! He's in here a lot. He doesn't like the red wig, says it's too obvious. He wants more subtle. I tell him, on stage nothing is subtle. Want red? Go red!"

"Any of them look like movie stars?" Silva asked.

"Oh, sure, some of them."

"Does this Spencer Tracy guy really look like the actor?" Sonntag asked.

"No, that's the thing. He needs to paint himself up pretty good."

191

"What does he say? Where does he come from?"

"Oh, he doesn't say much. I don't think he has much money. He's always careful about spending. Some of them, you should see them buy makeup. The women, they all think some pancake's gonna turn them into Ingrid Bergman."

"Or Greer Garson?" Silva asked.

"Yeah, her too. There's a gal, she wanted some shadow to put under her cheekbones and some highlight so her cheekbones would show up like Garson's."

"I think I know her. Pretty gal, younger than Garson, I imagine," Silva said.

"Sweet child. She's another with hardly a dime. I don't know her name."

"You don't know any names at all?"

Gertie sighed. "No, hon, these people don't want to be themselves."

CHAPTER TWENTY-SEVEN

Captain Ackerman didn't like detectives to work in pairs. He figured that when two detectives teamed up, they headed for the nearest coffee shop and squandered public payroll sipping java and talking about him behind his back.

"So where have you gents been hiding?" he asked, when Sonntag and Silva returned to their roosts in the bullpen.

Sonntag always had to take the brunt of these hostile probes. He was the lieutenant, after all. He raised himself sternly from his seat.

"Talked to studio photographers and then some newspaper people about those Bark photos. What we got was, this was no studio job, and probably no news photographer either. He's tall, maybe over six feet. The guy who took those photos has a good camera and a good darkroom. We might try some photo stores to see if there's some heavy users."

Ackerman yawned, his favorite insult. From long experience, Sonntag knew how to gauge those yawns. There were drop-dead yawns, quit-wasting-my-precious-time yawns, and then there was this other kind of yawn, which was Ackerman being oh, so polite and delicate. He was always polite when he wasn't one bit interested in what Sonntag had to say but was busting to tell Sonntag something. Sonntag decided to let him wait.

"We got a handle on Spencer. Big, big news."

"He's in London." Ackerman was staring through the grimy window.

"No, Milwaukee's version buys pancake makeup at that costume shop near Schlitz. That's what he wears when he goes out and kills friendly people."

"I didn't know there was a costume shop."

"That's because you're not a cross-dresser, captain. You can get Max Factor makeup there, the stuff that drove the hotel guy nuts because it fouled their towels. And Dorothy Lamour, who runs the joint, says that Spencer Tracy loads up on the stuff now and then."

"Now wait a minute, Sonntag. Dorothy Lamour?"

"Well, a reasonable facsimile."

"Has Milwaukee lost its marbles? Is this Hollywood?"

"She also sold some pancake to Greer Garson. Some shadow and some highlight to bring out the cheekbones."

"The girl? O'Grady?"

"The same."

"So how come you haven't pinched Spencer Tracy?"

"No names. Dorothy Lamour, her name's Gertie, hasn't got any names. Customers come and go. I told her to give us a ring immediately if she sells any more Max Factor to Spencer. And to get his name any way she can."

"Dammit, Sonntag, make some sense, will you? Who's Max Factor?"

Sonntag was enjoying this. "That's a brand, captain, like General Motors. Max Factor is the General Motors of pancake."

"And I suppose Spencer Tracy is the Buick. Why don't you get back where you belong, wringing confessions out of hotel guests that Bark busted in the middle of you know what."

Sonntag smiled. "You have something for me?"

Ackerman handed Sonntag a brief telex. Army records bureau. Stephen Barovich, born 1907, was drafted in 1942, proved to be intractable, contemptuous, wouldn't take orders, threw tantrums, and was finally sentenced to a stockade in

California, went through the war busting rock, and was dishonorably discharged in 1946.

"I've got more," Ackerman said. "Your set designer is not gainfully employed, and he lives with his father in Cudahy. His father's a tool-and-die maker, his mother's dead. He tried a few jobs after the war, all he could get was janitorial, but he got canned for insubordination. He would not take direction and usually ended up lecturing his employers about whatever pissed him off, and stalking away. He's hung around the Milwaukee Players for a year or two, does bit parts, and has a real talent for set design. He seems to have found a niche at last, at least until the next blowup. His father supports him, or at least gives him bed and board."

"Any interest in photography?"

"That didn't come up."

Too short, anyway, Sonntag thought. The photographer who took all those Beverly Hills Club photos was over six feet.

"We'll go talk to him again," Sonntag said. "Maybe we'll do a search. A gun, a wig, pancake. Our local Spencer Tracy wears a red wig; we got that from Dorothy Lamour."

"Jesus, will you start using real names, Sonntag?"

"Gertie. The costume lady. You got any more odds and ends for me?"

"Yes, if you're man enough to listen, Sonntag. You got wax in your ears. Why do I have to say everything twice? Ballistics. Now get this. Get it the first time so I don't have to repeat. The slug that penetrated Bark's sternum was mashed, so the lab doesn't have much. But it's out of the same box, they think. They did some chemistry. Same alloy. It's possible the same pistol killed Bark and O'Grady."

"Spencer Tracy."

"And maybe the pistol's not in the bottom of the river."

"Could be," said Sonntag. "Could be in Barovich's drawers."

"Ha, ha," said Ackerman. He was always withering when he was not being appreciated.

"We'll work on Barovich."

"No, there's something you're missing. The Beverly Hills Club," Ackerman said.

That was true. But Sonntag had mulled it and hadn't the faintest idea even how to approach the club.

"There's no names or addresses we know of. Nothing in Bark's possessions. You got any ideas?" Sonntag said.

"Public announcement. Classifieds. Organizations, next meeting."

"Near the end of every month, yes, that's good. Gertie at the costume shop mentioned the club by name. She'd heard of it."

"Start with the newspapers," Ackerman said.

Sonntag did. He headed for the *Journal* first. It was late in the day. He'd be late for dinner again, but Lizbeth was used to it. Or maybe she wasn't. They kept the previous month's papers on display in the marble lobby, bound by a big wooden spine that clamped them together. The wind whipped through his coat, and he wished he had worn his scarf. He wondered why he didn't dress sensibly in wintry weather. The wind chased him into the lobby, and he headed for the back issues. One could buy the previous month's back issues at a reception desk. But he might have to go to the classified department to dig any deeper.

These were October papers. This was November. The last possible announcement, if they met the first Monday of the month, would have been September. He gave up, headed for classified, hoping to dodge Matt Dugan, and entered the overheated bullpen, where there were a dozen ladies with telephone headsets, typing out the ads on big upright Underwoods while listening to customers. He headed for the sexy receptionist at the counter. It might be late fall, but she was wearing a blouse that didn't quit at her neck. Never underestimate a newspaper, he thought.

"Do you wish to place an ad?" she said, and beamed at him.

"I want to look at back issues of classified sections. Starting with September," he said.

"I'm sorry, sir—"

"Lieutenant Sonntag, police department," he said.

The beam vanished. "Just a minute," she said, and headed toward a bald male in a glassed office. Sonntag saw the boss staring at him. Then the seductive babe appeared again.

"This way, sir. Please put them back in order when you're through."

These classified sections had been collected on one of those wooden binders, like the whole papers downstairs. He found the September collection, and began hunting through the announcements for the last two weeks. Rotary, Kiwanis, Elks, Soroptimists, Optimists, St. Agnes Altar Guild, potluck supper at St. Michael's Greek Orthodox, Lions Club, Eagles, Sons of Norway, Franklin School PTA supper. No luck. Then, on 28 September, Beverly Hills Club, north penthouse, first Monday.

He tried August. Beverly Hills Club, south penthouse, but second Monday.

So that was the summons. No membership lists needed. Yet there must have been some way to recruit these alleged movie stars.

Sonntag hauled the bound classified sections to the receptionist. "I need to know who placed these Beverly Hills Club ads, ma'am."

"Oh, the hotel, sir. I took some of them myself."

"Anyone at the hotel?"

She smiled, a hundred kilowatts, great incisors. "I'll look it up just for you." She sort of wiggled. It was a purely female gesture. He had never seen a male sort of wiggle. "It'll be under

Lakeshore Towers," she said. "I'll pull the file."

She sashayed off to a file cabinet, wobbling on glossy pumps. Her swaying behind was mesmerizing. No wonder the *Journal* was rich. Reporters were paid worse even than cops, but reporters had some compensations, he thought. When do cops ever enjoy the scenery?

She returned with a ledger, handwritten entries marching down lined columns.

"You see? Here they are. Every month of the year. The hotel ordered those ads, sir. It was a Mr. Greaves. He signed the checks, too, the ones I sent to Accounting."

"Greaves? Not Bark?"

"I never heard of Bark. Woof! Woof!"

She leaned over the counter, displaying her voluptuous ledgers, disconcerting Joseph Sonntag, sending sensations through his loins. "Ah, Greaves, then. He would call and place the ad? Were your invoices directed to him?"

"Yes, sir, care of, let's see, Marcus Greaves, operations vice president."

"Did he come in? Did you see him, or was it all over the phone?"

"Oh, sometimes he comes in. Isn't he the perfect ringer for Cornel Wilde?"

"Ah . . . what does Cornel Wilde look like?"

"I guess you don't see many movies."

"I see lots, but my brain is scrambled from aspirin. Thanks anyway. This is a help."

It was quitting time. Sonntag hiked back to the Kilbourn Street station, collected his lunch bucket, and caught the streetcar. It was crowded this time, and he stood in the aisle, hanging on to the handgrip above. There were so many people aboard that he was certain the viaduct would collapse under the weight, and he closed his eyes all the way across, awaiting his fate. He got home only a half hour late.

"You made it," Lizbeth said. "Leave your coat on; you're taking me out to dinner."

"I am? But I have some photos to show you."

"The Greek restaurant," she said. "I want Greek."

"Do you know what Cornel Wilde looks like?"

"Sure. We saw him in *Forever Amber,* but you didn't notice him because you were seeing more of Linda Darnell than you ever thought you would, poor boy."

"Greek, you want Greek?"

She had that wild smile on her puss.

He took her to the Greek restaurant, where they had baklava for dessert. Then he pulled out the photos of Bark with the movie stars. "Who are these? I should have asked you long ago, since I don't know one actor from another."

He spread the glossies out on the table before her. She pulled her horn-rimmed glasses from their nest in her purse, and studied them. "I'm not sure about some," she said. "That's Cornel Wilde. Isn't it just like him? Now, let's see. Spencer Tracy, of course, and Tyrone Power. This is Veronica Lake, long hair. And that's your poor dear Greer Garson.

"This is Van Johnson, and that's Mickey Rooney and over here's Lucille Ball, and this guy is . . . oh, Farley Granger I think, and this other guy is probably Fredrick March, and this little twerp is Leo G. Carroll, and look at this! Bette Davis, and I think that's . . . whatever her name is, she looks like Bob Hope, and holy cow, Joan Crawford, and Lana Turner, but she doesn't fill sweaters as well, does she? And she's plucked her eyebrows, poor thing. Richard Widmark, and Robert Mitchum, and holy cow, Fred MacMurray. I didn't see this one before. There's a few others I'll think about. That's the A-list, honeybunch. The hotel's penthouse was really jumping."

"Yeah," he said, his voice husky. "Let's go home right now,

right this minute."

"I sure like to reel you in," she said.

CHAPTER TWENTY-EIGHT

The relentless phone ratcheted him out of sleep. Lizbeth clicked on a light, making him blink.

"It's for you," she said.

He nodded. It had to be for him. He poked bare feet into slippers and stumbled toward the stairs, even as the clamoring phone tolled the death of someone, somewhere. He finally found the phone, a black celery stalk, and pulled the receiver off.

"Joe, it's Frank. We need you. There's been another. It's Veronica Lake."

"Who?"

"Another Beverly Hills Club homicide. Veronica Lake. A cop found her on a picnic table near the lake. Lagoon Drive. Veterans Park. Shot in the face. But this time right through the mouth. Her face is intact. It's Veronica Lake. Same as in that photo of her and Bark."

It took a moment for Sonntag to register it. "Any ID?"

"Not a thing. And no bullet. She was shot somewhere else and taken there. They called me because of the O'Grady killing. Same deal."

"Who found her?"

"A cop, checking the park."

"What do you want of me?"

"We've got a killer loose, Joe, and he's going to bump off that whole club unless we get there first. Meet me in the park; no, make it the morgue. They're ready to move the body."

"I'll drive," Sonntag said. "Otherwise I'll have to wait for a night owl streetcar."

He stumbled upstairs.

"What?" she asked.

"Veronica Lake."

She bounded out of bed, threw on a robe, and hurried into the dark. When she returned she had the Bark photos, and showed the one with J. Adam Bark and Milwaukee's version of Veronica Lake. It was signed, "To Adam, Take me to your apartment some time, Veronica."

"Jesus," said Sonntag, buttoning a shirt. "Lock the door when I leave."

It was after four. He stumbled to the garage and started the old Ford coupe, a 1941 model because he couldn't afford a new car and the postwar cars were lousy anyway. The war had wrecked the car industry.

He usually didn't drive. Owning a car was expensive. He warmed the coupe and eased it out, backing onto the street. He headed for Wisconsin Avenue, which would take him straight in, and found himself riding an empty boulevard, his progress metered by streetlights that cast a weary white glow.

It came to him as he drove. He knew. He knew everything but the name of the killer. He knew exactly how this whole thing worked. This killing did it; he wished he had been smarter, but it took this killing to make it clear. The local Spencer Tracy was using the Beverly Hills Club to hunt women. He wanted to sleep with Greer Garson, and Veronica Lake. If he couldn't sleep with the real ones, these imitations would have to do. This rat, all powdered up as Spencer Tracy, romanced the poor damned women pretending to be stars—romanced them, and when they wouldn't go to bed, killed them because he hated them and himself. And Bark somehow found out he was stalking them and caught him, or told him to stop. So Bark had to go.

J. Adam Bark hated sex. He hated all types, married sex, unmarried sex, sex of all shapes and descriptions, and what had driven him year after year was not catching illicit sex in the Lakeshore Towers, but stamping out all sex. He hated sex done by younger people, sex by lovers, commercial sex, sex in movies. Strippers at the Empress. J. Adam Bark probably wished he could have been conceived in a test tube. Somehow, J. Adam Bark and Spencer Tracy had clashed. There were people like that, maybe people who never came to grips with their own bodies, their own desires. Right now he had one task, and that was to stop Spencer Tracy from killing any more women. And damned if Sonntag knew how to do it.

Maybe he was jumping to conclusions. That was the hell of being an investigator. Come up with a pet theory, and it would only get blasted to smithereens. He hoped Lizbeth had locked the goddamned door.

He parked in the empty lot, stepped into lakeshore cold, headed for the sheet-metal door, which was lit by a single security lamp under a green metal shade. The cold air would lay thick patterned frost on his divided windshield. He hoped he had a scraper. The defogger took forever, if it worked at all, blowing one little three-inch bare spot in a wall of white.

He rang the bell. Silva opened, and Sonntag stepped into a bleak warmth.

"She's here. It's her. I've got the photo, the one taken with O'Grady, the two of them smiling against that wall. Dead movie stars," he said.

Some doctor in scrubs was in there. So was the night chief, Lieutenant Pandro Brogan.

"Good," Brogan said. "You can ID her."

"Start from the beginning," Sonntag said.

"Look at her first," Brogan said.

He pulled a sheet back as far as her waist. Veronica Lake, long brown hair that fell to her naked breasts, a surprised look in her face, lips not ruined at all, but inside her mouth nothing was left.

Her clothing was spread on a steel table, lit by a single bare light. Pretty woman, wearing a brown gabardine suit. Fake pearl necklace, white blouse, girdle, nylons, low-heeled leather shoes. Sonntag felt a strange pity engulf him.

"Any other injury? Rape or sex?"

"Nothing. No semen. No visible rape. No bruises, no lacerations," the medic said.

"I'm Lieutenant Sonntag."

"Showalter, Doug Showalter. I'm filling in tonight."

"It's her, all right," Sonntag said. He pulled the glossy of her and Bark from his manila envelope, the photo with the flirtatious signature. It was her, a little made up. This girl had the wrong jaw line, but some pancake had sharpened it, shadow below, highlight above. "We've got some handwriting. Any ID at all? Dental?"

"At five in the morning?" Brogan asked. "We'll see about some dental matching. That's all we got."

"No missing reports. Like O'Grady. No one is missing her," Frank Silva said.

"No slug?"

"Exit wound back of head. No bullet. She was taken there and left on that picnic table."

"Who found her?"

"Carnavan. He was driving past, his headlights caught something on the picnic table. He investigated with his flashlight and phoned in. We got some lights and searched the whole area. No blood, no drag marks. She was carried, not dragged. Strong guy carried her. Nothing in the parking lot over there. No blood anywhere, but daylight might give us something."

"We're where we were with O'Grady," Silva said. "Which is nowhere."

"Dye her hair?" Sonntag asked.

They turned to the doc, a Marquette guy. "No dyed hair. That's her natural color right from the roots."

Silva sighed. "There goes that one."

Brogan looked baffled.

"O'Grady's hair was dyed red; we traced her through her beauty shop," Sonntag explained. "Not so lucky with this one."

"I don't get it," said Brogan. "Two women pretending to be movie stars, and the hotel dick, all shot by a guy pretending to be Spencer Tracy."

"I know part of it," Sonntag said. "It sort of came to me driving here. Our Spencer Tracy is on the make. He thinks he deserves movie stars. Man, he's been in bed with Ingrid, and Greer and Katharine! He goes to this club to meet the actresses. He wants to sleep with the queens of Hollywood, that makes him feel like someone, and this was as good as it was going to get. Bark figured it out and tried to stop him and got shot for the effort. Bark, he was a funny guy. I think he really didn't want a stalker in his club."

Brogan grinned skeptically. "You day-shift guys, you don't see the real world," he said. "The down and dirty world."

Sonntag held his peace. He had spent years on the night side.

He and Frank Silva trudged over to the station house bullpen. It was empty, forlorn. A telex chattered in the alcove. Not a soul occupied a desk. Overhead lamps every ten feet dropped pools of yellow light. Sonntag felt it again. Cops and pain, the two went together. Pain collected here in the station, permeated its walls, filled its restrooms.

Now the place was almost deserted. The drunks and vagrants had mostly been booked before midnight, along with the petty thieves, streetwalkers, night people, burglars, and boozy drivers. It was after five, a moment when crime took a break. The night guys were gossiping in the locker room.

"Maybe I shouldn't have called you," Silva said.

"If you hadn't, I wouldn't have come up with that. How the two gals and Bark got killed, and why."

"It's as good as any," Silva said. "Now what do we do? Looks like we're starting a couple hours early. Maybe Spencer's not in bed yet. Maybe he's cleaning up the place where he shot her."

"It's Barovich," Sonntag said.

Silva grinned. Hunches were okay in Silva's world.

"I'm going to check the darkroom. I hope Gorilla's done that blowup of Tracy."

They descended into the dark and empty lab, and got lucky. The blowup was lying there, beside the print dryer. "I'll tell Gorilla I got it," Sonntag said.

Up in the bullpen, they took a closer look. It was a great blowup, sixteen by twenty, a little blurred because the original was soft-focused.

"Joe, this makeup on him, it's plain as a wart," Silva said. And he was right.

There was highlight along the jaw, shadow under the cheekbones, highlight down the long nose and some putty or something to enlarge it, some highlight on the bridge of the nose, some penciling of lines here and there.

"Our Tracy's younger than the real Tracy. Look at these penciled-in frown lines on the forehead," Silva said.

"Do you see Stephen Barovich here?" Sonntag asked. The truth was, he didn't himself, but he didn't have a good eye for that stuff.

"Oh, sort of."

"I'll have Ziggy at the paper airbrush the makeup. Then we'll see."

"Look at the hairline, Joe. It's a wig, see?"

Wavy hair, the edge of the wig covering any real hair. An odd line along the forehead.

"It's got to be Barovich. He fits. He's a human shipwreck. He dreams of sleeping with movie stars. He makes himself up to be a movie star so he can pretend he's on top of the world, when all he is, all he'll ever be, is some guy sponging off his hard-working father and dreaming big dreams, big movie-star fantasies." He eyed Silva. "You think we're ready for a search warrant? His father's house in Cudahy, and the Milwaukee Players?"

"No, I don't," said Silva. "We've got nothing on him. The judge would say it's a fishing expedition."

Sonntag reluctantly agreed. "All right. That's for tomorrow. Today we're going after Greaves at the hotel. He lied to us. He's been to those shindigs. He's covering up. He's been paying for the newspaper classifieds announcing the meetings of the Beverly Hills Club. I went over to the *Journal,* and we looked at those accounts. It wasn't Bark, it was Greaves. I don't know why. We'll find out. He looks like Cornel Wilde. If I knew what Cornel Wilde looked like I'd have spotted him long ago, but Lizbeth saw it. We saw *Forever Amber* a few months ago, and she said I was too busy looking at Linda Darnell's chest to notice Cornel Wilde."

He eyed Silva pugnaciously, waiting for a retort that never came.

"Cornel Wilde and J. Adam Bark, nice eight-by-ten glossy. It's signed, too. We'll see if this signature lines up with Greaves's handwriting. If he gives us a runaround, I'll tell him he's lying to the police, obstructing justice, getting himself into trouble, and maybe that'll shake a few green apples out of the horse's ass."

CHAPTER TWENTY-NINE

They cornered Marcus Greaves the minute he arrived at his office. Greaves eyed them, sensed he was cornered, and nodded them in. He had a fine, spacious office but without windows, a lot of blond wood tinted gray, very modern.

He looked trapped, which he was.

"Gentlemen? I've been wondering how the investigation is coming," he said. "I'm glad to see such interest in the case."

Sonntag didn't acknowledge the greeting. Instead he dropped the glossy on Greaves's blond desk. It purported to be a photo of Cornel Wilde chatting with J. Adam Bark. It was signed, "For Adam Bark, from your friend, Cornel Wilde."

"Want to show us some of your handwriting, Mr. Greaves?" Sonntag asked. "Or would you rather we get a search warrant?"

Greaves clutched the desk, stared at Sonntag and Silva, and slowly sagged into his cream-colored swivel chair.

"I went to a couple of those penthouse parties," he said. "Just two. I was curious."

"Start from the beginning," Sonntag said, not unkindly. "Or start this way: you look a little like Cornel Wilde."

"I do. I hadn't paid any attention until a couple of years ago, when Adam told me I was a ringer. Well, I'm not. I had never even thought of it. He was obsessed with movie stars, you know. Two or three years ago there was a movie star look-alike contest here in the hotel. It was fun. People got prizes. I don't remember who sponsored it. But the idea of the parties started then. They thought it would be fun to show up at a party full of celebrities, or at least made up to look like celebrities. It's been going ever since. Bark set it up."

"That's how people joined?"

"Sure, Bark contacted a few contestants. Later, it was all word of mouth. But you know, real names were forbidden. If you were coming as Clark Gable, you never said you were Stan Williams. In fact we did have a Gable a couple of times, a pretty good imitation, but he never showed up again. Most don't. They come as someone, Loretta Young, James Cagney, who knows? I'll tell you something: a few of those people thought it was a hoot. The rest are, well, deprived. They live miserable lives, and being a movie star for a night now and then gives them something to live for. Only it doesn't. It's a cruel experience. They never stop knowing they're Stan Williams and Mary Smith."

"How about you?"

"Oh, I doctored my face with a makeup pencil, went twice, got photographed with a few of them, saw that it was harmless, and quit. But it was also a good income for the hotel, so I arranged for the parties to continue. Me, I'm just Marcus, and not a minor movie star."

"What did these people do?"

"They had the phonograph going all the time. Sometimes they danced. They stood, maybe postured is the word. They drank. They told jokes. They pretended. They complained about the caviar and champagne and being slaves of the studios. Stood around, wanting to be noticed. Or cozying up to someone whose photo they wanted."

"Who took the pictures?"

"We have a hotel photographer, Adam Kinkaid. You want to get married here? We'll supply the pictures."

"There's money in it. He must have gotten checks for his pictures."

"No, that was against the rules. No one revealed who they were, so everyone paid cash."

"This guy doesn't have any names?"

"Not unless someone dealt with him privately, and not at the parties."

"We'll get his address later. What about Bark?"

"Oh, he went to every one. He didn't look like anyone. People kept telling him he should make himself into Adolphe Menjou, you know him, character actor? Well, he didn't. He simply attended. Said he was hotel hospitality, simple as that. Actually, he was hotel security. There were a few people in that bunch worth keeping an eye on."

"Like the local Spencer Tracy?"

"Especially that one."

"Why?"

"Moody sometimes, on the prowl, always around the women. Let someone come as June Allyson and he'd be right there. And we knew he was violating the rules. He was trying to get to know these gals, get their real names."

"Why did you tell us you knew nothing about these parties?" In other words, why did you lie to cops?

Sonntag watched Greaves squirm, pluck words out of the air. "To protect the hotel," he said.

"When the barber said Spencer Tracy shot Bark, you didn't step forward. When Tracy ran through the hotel and vanished somewhere, probably the men's room down the hall, where he became someone else and then walked out, you said nothing."

Greaves nodded.

"You had valuable evidence. But you kept it from us. Maybe you're obstructing justice. Maybe you're an accessory after the fact, right? Maybe you covered up a murderer."

Greaves shrank into himself. "I will do everything in my power to help you."

"We'll see," Sonntag said. He used that phrase often. It left things hanging, and inspired a lot of truth-telling.

"Two women are dead," Frank Silva said. "Another last night. Veronica Lake. Maybe you could have spared the lives of those women."

"Veronica? Oh, god. She was always at the parties. Oh, god."

"Maybe you'll cooperate before another one dies." Silva was as tough as Sonntag now.

"Anything! Anything you ask!" Greaves said.

"Spencer Tracy," Sonntag said.

"God, if I knew his name, I'd tell you in a split second."

"Was he well made up?"

"That one wore a red wig that wasn't real. You know, visible along the forehead, too red. Too bright."

"What color hair underneath?"

"Dark hair, like neck hair around the collar."

"He fooled the barber."

"I think he was the best makeup man at those parties, except for the wig. He was an artist, a Rembrandt. He could do illusions with a little pancake. Some of them, it was obvious. But not that guy. He could walk down the street and people would mistake him for Tracy. So, yes, our barber was fooled. I'd be fooled."

"What did this guy talk about at the parties?" Silva asked.

"Movies. Stars. Titles, Hollywood, all that stuff."

"What about plays? Theater?"

Greaves thought about it. "I don't think so. Believe, me, I'd remember."

"Did he ever talk about local theater? Road shows? The Milwaukee Players?"

"No, never."

"Okay, at these parties, did he play the game? Was he actually being Tracy? Saying, like, 'When I was on the MGM backlot,' stuff like that?"

"No. He wouldn't try to be Tracy. Some of them, they tried to be the stars. They'd say things, like, 'I told Sam Goldwyn what a prick he is,' but this guy just talked Hollywood, like a fan would."

Sonntag wanted to know more about the photos. "This photographer, tall guy, right? He would take some pictures and bring the prints to the next party?"

"Yeah, and then people would sign them. That poor dead girl, Greer Garson, signed a lot of them, 'Love, Greer,' or 'To my old friend, from Greer,' things like that. Bark bought a whole bunch. They weren't cheap, five dollars, but people walked out of there with signed photos of movie stars."

"One more question, Mr. Greaves. Spencer Tracy's nearly fifty. Is this imitator older or younger?" Sonntag asked.

"Definitely younger."

"How do you know?"

"I can't say. People's real age is there, and no makeup hides it very well."

"Frank, do you have anything more to ask?" Sonntag asked.

Silva shook his head.

"Am I in still in trouble?" Greaves asked. He was plenty nervous.

"Big trouble," Sonntag said. He had no use for people who misled cops, obstructed an investigation, hid stuff that needed to be looked into.

The operations manager stiffened, stood up straight, and nodded. At least he was being a man, Sonntag thought. He collected the address of the photographer, and they quit the Lakeshore Towers.

"Should we talk to the photo man?" Silva said.

"I guess so. Maybe he knows some real names."

Silva drove old 406 west to a run-down area of Wells Street, and parked in front of a storefront. "The Candid Camera. Anyplace, Any Time. Overnight Photos," announced a sign painted on storefront glass. The shop looked like it could fold in an hour, any hour.

They jangled a bell above the door and were met with developer fumes. A big guy emerged from a curtained rear area.

"You're Adam Kinkaid? Milwaukee police here," Sonntag said.

It went fast. Yeah, he showed up at every party. Yeah, the hotel got a cut of every shot, yeah he was paid in cash, yeah, the photos were quick and dirty. Yeah, he had a name or two, people who came to the shop later and wanted duplicates. Let's see, there was a Maria Rice, and a Lawrence Scobey. Rice was doing an Angela Lansbury imitation, and Scobey was doing a Mickey Rooney.

"Those are the only real names?"

" 'Fraid so," the guy said.

"You got these filed by what, by actor?" Sonntag wanted to know.

"By actor, how else?"

"You got a bunch of Spencer Tracy negatives?"

"I do. I took a bunch. He was one of the best, I thought. My god, he not only looked like Tracy, he had the mannerisms. You should have seen the women flock around him. They flirted, he smiled, cocky guy, and you could see where that was going."

"How many negatives of Tracy?"

"Oh, maybe twenty."

"Could you do a contact sheet while we wait?"

Kinkaid stared. "If anyone killed the hotel dick, it was that guy."

"Why do you say that?"

"There was a fight at the last party. Not a fight, just something that happened between Bark and the Tracy guy, and old Spencer, he quit and went home."

"Hey," said Silva. "Did these people make up there or beforehand?"

"The men made up there. They didn't want to be seen in public wearing all that pancake. The women, they mostly arrived all made up."

"So you saw this Spencer Tracy guy without the makeup?"

"No, he was always made up. But he put his wig on when he arrived. He'd duck into a bedroom and come out a redhead. But sometimes . . . he wasn't wearing one. He's red-haired himself."

"Could you pick him out of a lineup?"

"No. I have no idea what that sucker looks like under that pancake. Come on into the darkroom, and we'll talk," said Kinkaid.

They did talk, and soon they were looking at a sheet of contacts. Mostly candid shots of Spencer Tracy and women. All sorts of female movie stars. All of them young and pretty. Sonntag and Silva studied the whole lot with a magnifying glass. Here were candid party photos, not the posed ones taken against the blank wall.

"We'd like one eight-by-ten print of each Tracy negative," he *(which?)* said. "Tell me how much and I'll get a voucher."

"Oh, two bucks each. Fourteen here."

It would come to twenty-eight dollars.

"You want 'em fast, I guess," Kinkaid said.

"We want them like, oh, yesterday," Silva said.

"How about a couple of hours? Quick and dirty?"

"Mr. Kinkaid, I like you," Silva replied. "We'll be back."

CHAPTER THIRTY

Kinkaid's candid photos were startling in just one respect. In every one of them, the local Spencer Tracy was conversing with attractive women. These were not the posed photos before the blank wall, but groups and clusters, taken as the photographer roamed the parties. And there was Tracy, conversing with a Greer Garson, now dead, a Veronica Lake, now dead, a June Allyson, and some women neither Sonntag nor Silva had seen in other photos, including a Rita Hayworth, a Betty Grable, an Irene Dunne, and a Lana Turner. Superb look-alikes, every one, young and incredibly seductive. Right there in the beer city, the world capital of porky hausfraus.

The image of Rita Hayworth jolted Sonntag; he'd been in love with her for years. There she was, bright and leggy, with that sexy innocence in her face, wearing a boxy suit. These women, whoever they were, were all in peril.

Silva studied the enlargements. "We're going to have more murders on our hands unless we move. Maybe it's time to have a big talk with Barovich, bring him in, give him a little attention."

Sonntag had been wondering the same thing. "I'm tempted. But right now we don't have one thing on him. He might or might not be Spencer Tracy. There's this. The papers haven't leaked the secret. The public hasn't heard that we're looking for a Spencer Tracy look-alike. That gives us a little room."

"Pull him in. Get a warrant and do a search."

"Yeah, and what are we going to tell a judge? We're still fishing."

"We could ask him where he was. Alibis can be checked. We've got three murders, we know the exact time of one, and approximate time of another. Just ask him."

"Maybe they've doped out the new one," Sonntag said.

They had. Veronica Lake turned out to be Eileen Maginnis, a dental technician who worked in the First Wisconsin Building for a orthodontist trained at Marquette's dental school. She was supposedly on a vacation visiting her parents in Black River Falls, so she wasn't missed. But the match showed up at once from her dental chart. All the lower teeth in her jaw were intact, even if the upper teeth had been shattered. A ringer for Veronica Lake if Eileen had let her hair grow as long as the star's. Twenty-eight, separated for three years from a husband living out of state; she had lost a child who had died of rheumatic fever.

Silva volunteered to make the painful phone call to her family, and soon was rung through by operators. Sonntag stood listening, depressed by grief for some pretty woman whose life had ended with a bullet through her mouth. She had played at being a movie star. It wasn't such a bad dream. We all think we'd enjoy being a movie star.

He had to give Silva credit. The young investigator had almost fallen apart the last time, but now took it upon himself to let the family know. It wasn't easy. Silva was listening, trying to explain, time of death, cause of death, reasons unknown, no suspects, what could we do to help the family? He was apparently talking to a relative. That often happened. The parents or children or siblings couldn't deal with it and summoned an uncle or even a grandparent.

Silva hung up and stared into space. "That was her stepfather. They'll catch the train. Be here tonight." Something in him sagged.

Sonntag admired the younger man. He had faced down the thing he dreaded most and had shared the news and the grief as best he could. Someone had to do it, and he did it. Silva was as good a cop as the world had in it. Bad news was the other thing cops carried around with them at all times. Bad news and pain.

Silva joined him for lunch. Sonntag and the younger man had somehow been welded together by events, and they found they worked better as a team. It was okay to say something foolish. It was fine to speculate. Sonntag found a bologna and Swiss cheese sandwich along with his Maxwell House and a Jonathan apple in his bucket. Silva brown bagged, with a thick sandwich of his own devising, the contents of which Sonntag didn't dare inquire about. But he suspected liverwurst and a layer of onions and sliced tomatoes, along with a couple of dill pickles, and a Twinkie for dessert. They were eating in Silva's carrel, oblivious of the busy hustle of the bullpen.

"Why do I keep thinking about that red wig?" Silva asked.

"Gertie said it's too red. Greaves said it was bright red. I guess I'd bleach it," Sonntag said. "It advertises that Spencer Tracy is fake."

"Can wigs be bleached?"

"We can find out. Where is this leading?" Sonntag asked.

"Our man makes up better than anyone else at those parties. Why does he wear a red wig, when he's a redhead anyway?"

It was an idle line of thought, leading nowhere. But Silva jotted it on a pad.

They were halfway through when Matt Dugan of the *Journal* materialized. Dugan's porkpie hat seemed to show up wherever there was a crime story, and now the police-beat reporter settled his butt on a corner of the desk.

"Cops eat, but newsmen are too busy," he said. "So who's the dead woman?"

Sonntag saw Dugan reading the report in front of Silva upside down. Good reporters knew how to do that. They could read the damned text from any angle. He'd seen reporters memorize and then publish verbatim several sentences of a report on the chief's desk, readable only upside down by the reporter as he talked to the chief. Dugan was pretending to stare into the bullpen, but he had her name, no question about it.

"We're in the process of notifying her family . . . aw, hell, Matt, we've done that," Sonntag said. "She's Eileen Maginnis, age twenty-eight, from Black River Falls. Cause of death a large-caliber bullet through the mouth. A dental technician working here in town."

"Assault? Violence?"

Sonntag shook his head.

"Motive? Is this killing linked to the others?"

"Maybe. Pretty woman shot in the face with large-caliber weapon and left near the lake. We have no motive."

"And no leads," Silva added.

"Spencer Tracy strikes again," Dugan said, and waited.

The reporter got the response he was looking for. Sonntag stiffened. "If you break that open, we're screwed."

Dugan grinned, all bad teeth. "I figured. I'll keep your little secret for a day or two."

"I wish to hell you'd just stuff it in your porkpie and keep it there. There's a good chance we can nail the guy if we keep that quiet. I'd damn near haul you in for obstructing justice if you say one word about Spencer Tracy. I'll tell you one thing, Matt. It's not the real movie star."

"It's one of the Beverly Hills Club, the weirdos up in the penthouse. Bark's pals."

"Yes," said Sonntag stiffly. He hoped Matt wouldn't betray him. If he did, by god, he'd never get another story out of Lieutenant Joe Sonntag.

"You've got a serial killer, right? And I'm thinking you've

been looking at Kinkaid's photos and know a few more gals who are vulnerable, right?"

"Dammit, Matt, don't you mess up our investigation," Silva said.

There was heat now. Dugan pushing for all he was worth, Sonntag getting hot, and Silva too.

"I just talked to the chief. He says you're pursuing several leads and closing in, and hope to apprehend the killer shortly."

Sonntag laughed. Dugan grinned. "If you tell me what you've got, I'll behave myself, cross my heart and hope to die."

"I'll say this, Matt, on those terms. We have a suspect, and not a shred of evidence, and we're sitting here trying to come up with a strategy."

Dugan stared. "You really have a suspect? Just between us?"

"A hunch, a damned hunch."

"So what movie star is the next victim?"

"Lana Turner," Sonntag said, and wished he'd kept his trap shut. Why was he always blabbing?

"I know a Lana Turner," Dugan said. "The sweater girl, and is she ever!"

A prickle rose up Sonntag's spine. He stared at Dugan, and watched the reporter turn very quiet. "You know her name?"

"Get in line, Sonntag. There's about five hundred guys want her name." He revealed evil nicotine-stained incisors. "But for you, and just for you, compliments of the *Journal,* on promise of good behavior from you and your Socialist chum here, I'll pass the word. She's Lucille Erdmann, and she's in the medical library at Marquette. And yes, she's been having a ball at those penthouse shindigs. And yes, she's a pal of Spencer."

It took ten minutes. Sonntag and Silva puffed up the stairs to the Marquette medical school library, blowing frost out of their lungs, and there, by god, was blond, smoky-eyed Lana, in a sky-blue cardigan, carrying a stack of radiology journals hugged to her bountiful chest.

"Ah, could we have a word?" he asked, instinctively doffing his fedora in abject respect and homage.

She eyed them, smiled suddenly. "Hello, cops," she said.

"Well, that saves an explanation," Silva muttered.

"Matt just rang me up," she said.

"I'm Lieutenant Sonntag and this is Detective Silva. You know why we're here, then."

"Oh, sure. You want to know if I know Spencer. I sure do. He's been chasing me for two years. But I just laugh. 'Spencer, dear, I'm married,' I say, and he gets real gloomy. This is supposed to be fun, you know?"

"Back up a little. You go to the Beverly Hills Club parties?"

"Sure do, guys. It's a kick. I do the Lana bit, the others do their bit, and it's a ball."

"You come alone?"

"Oh, no, my husband's Tyrone Power, but we don't let on that we know each other."

"Did Spencer tell you who he is?"

"He always said he'd tell if I tell, so I just poked a Camel in his mouth and lit it and told him I only have one hump."

"What does he say to that?"

"He gets persistent, so I tell him this isn't Schwab's Drugstore, and he's not casting me, especially on a couch."

"No name? Not even a first name?"

"Nope! That's against the club rules. But someone told me he's Steve someone."

"Steve? An actor? A painter?"

She shrugged. "Got me. Actually, he's sort of a pest, and I might quit going. My husband and I, we're tired of the partying. These parties are supposed to be fun, you know?"

"Lana, ah, Mrs. Erdmann, what does your husband do?"

"He's interning. After he's done, who knows?"

"One more. How do you know when to meet at the penthouse?"

"The paper, the classifieds. It's announced the last week of each month. The Beverly Hills Club, time and place."

"Do you know the real name of anyone else?" Sonntag asked.

"We're not supposed to say."

"There might be people in danger, Mrs. Erdmann."

She stared bleakly, and put the journals on a table.

"That's a dangerous place for a woman," Sonntag persisted. "Every scrap of information you can give us would help. There's someone very, very dangerous stalking the women at those parties, and we think it's the Spencer Tracy guy."

"No! Those women in the paper!" She stared, stricken.

Sonntag nodded.

"Have you seen this guy without his wig?" Silva asked.

"Yes, several times," she said in a voice so small that Sonntag could hardly hear her.

Silva pulled out the airbrushed mug shot. "This guy?"

"I'm not sure. It's dark up there, you know. It could be."

That's as far as it went. Joe Sonntag and Frank Silva couldn't get anything else from her, and finally headed into the cold. But not before they warned her to be careful, and to contact them instantly if she heard from Spencer Tracy.

Silva sighed. "I wonder if there's another Lana Turner around," he said. "Maybe I'll go camp in Schwab's Drugstore on Sunset Boulevard and try offering someone a part."

But Sonntag's mind was crawling with a thousand dreads.

CHAPTER THIRTY-ONE

It was a pensive ride home that night. Sonntag was both frustrated and blue. The truth of it was that he and Frank Silva didn't have a solid lead.

He and Frank had gone over everything they knew about Barovich. The military record. His surly responses to questioning. His artistic ability. His familiarity with makeup and costume and theater. No one, not even Lucille Erdmann, who had dealt with Tracy the Romeo, recognized Barovich.

Silva had narrowed the evidence down to the weapon, the bullets, the wig, and alibis. Hunting for some pancake makeup wouldn't help. In the dressing rooms of the Milwaukee Players would be every imaginable species of makeup, which Barovich could freely use without getting caught. The red wig, with a follicle or two of Barovich's hair caught in it, would serve. So would prints on the pistol. But unless Barovich was unusually dumb, the weapon and wig would be nowhere near the playhouse or his father's home.

Get a search warrant? What probable cause? The best they could come up with would be to bring Barovich in and have him explain just where he was at the times of the various killings, which would be difficult with the two women because the exact time of death was not known. Bark, then. A little after ten in the morning. Where was Barovich at that moment, and could he prove it? He and Silva thought they would round up the set designer in the morning, take him to the station, and get tough.

Gloomily Sonntag considered the early phase of the Bark case, the days when they all thought Bark had been killed by someone who was aggrieved by Bark's ugly bedroom raids. All those investigations were still open. The upshot was that the weeks of investigation had not yielded much, and Ackerman was taking heat from the chief, the chief was taking heat from the aldermen and the papers, and Sonntag felt the whole weight of their frustration and head-shaking on his shoulders.

He parked the old coupe, grabbed his lunch bucket, and walked into his home.

"We're doing Chinese tonight," Lizbeth said after a perfunctory peck.

He wanted simply to pour a bourbon and sulk, and started to grumble. But she stared stonily at him until he nodded. The house seemed cold. He dropped down the basement stairs and found the fire in the furnace down to coals; the stoker was silent. It was a burned-out fuse, so he screwed in a new one. Sometimes when a chunk of coal was too large it jammed the worm drive that screwed coal into the burner. He took the iron poker and pushed into the coal bin and pried on the worm. You either freed up the worm drive or you called the furnace man. He was lucky. Something gave. He got the stoker going, waited until he saw some bright life in the burner, and headed upstairs. The furnace always grimed his hands, so he washed them. The stink of burning coal filled the house.

She was waiting in her cloth coat, a scarf wrapped over her hair and tied under her chin, thin and hollow-eyed. He escorted her to the coupe, got it running, and backed into 57th Street. The Chinese place was on North Avenue. She didn't say a word. He parked, escorted her in, led her to their favorite booth, and they studied the menu silently. He always ordered the same thing anyway, but this time the menu was something to hide behind.

He had the usual chow mein. She had the usual chop suey. She liked the tea, and downed several little cups of it.

They ate in utter silence.

"I have nothing to do," she said when they had finished.

"But you have a whole house."

It was the wrong thing to say. She stared at him.

"Yes, and a whole day, too," she said. "I get to wash the breakfast dishes and put them away. Then I can make the bed and vacuum. Maybe wash windows. And clean the toilet. And wait for the mail. Maybe the *Saturday Evening Post* will come. Or *Reader's Digest*. That's good for two hours if I read the condensed book. Or I can go to the library and get a book. That's good for a few hours. Maybe write my sisters. But I have no news. Or listen to a soap opera while I iron your shirts. Or hang up the laundry in the basement when it's too cold to hang outside. That's good for a while. Then I can start making a casserole and wait to see if you'll show up or whether I'll eat alone."

"We need a good vacation," he said.

"I need to do something more than exist. I want to get a job."

"I can support you just fine," he said, irritated.

She sank into quietness.

He regretted his outburst. Maybe she could be a volunteer at Milwaukee Hospital. "You could help somewhere," he said. "It'd be good. Get you out of the house."

"I don't want that. I want to earn money. I want each hour I work to get me something. Seventy-five cents an hour, that's what I want. I could get that at Gimbels. Or the Boston Store. I'll sell perfume to rich women. I'll have something all my own, more than the household allowance."

It was dangerous to say anything. Sonntag nodded and hoped her mood would pass. He toyed with the last bit of rice on his plate. He couldn't handle chopsticks and ate with a spoon and fork.

"I'd like to be a detective," she said.

He stopped breathing. There was no way he could pump air in and out of himself.

"You always say I'm good at it. You say that I solve your cases for you. So I want to be a detective."

"Uh, but you're a woman."

It was not Joe Sonntag's best moment. She stared, her face blank and bleak.

"Let's go," she said.

"You could be a prison matron. They're big and tough. But you're too beautiful to be one," he said, smiling.

She glared at him.

"You could be a secretary. But you'd need shorthand and typing," he said. "There are two in the chief's office. We have three or four cleaning ladies. They have to clean the men's rooms."

She stared at him.

He didn't know what the hell to say. He rose abruptly, stalked to the cashier, paid up, and plunged into the night. She rattled along behind him. He put his coat on outside, remembering at last that it was plenty cold.

The coupe was no haven, with her sitting in close proximity to him. But they were side by side, and that was when they talked best.

"Find out," she said. "Or I will."

"Are you sure . . ."

"Then I will," she said.

He drove through the night, his headlamps making cones of light in the darkness. They passed pleasant Milwaukee bungalows with four-sided roofs and porches in front. Ordinary, sane people lived in them, drank Pabst or Blatz at the bowling alley, listened to Fred Allen, and went to the Wisconsin Synod Lutheran church every Sunday.

"I'll ask," he said.

At home, he hurried around and opened her door for her, helped her out, and held her elbow as she navigated to the kitchen door. She smiled.

The smile stabbed through him like electricity.

"He shot that second woman, the Veronica Lake woman, right in the playhouse," she said. "No one would hear. He's there alone all the time. She probably did something to set him off, laughing at him, or something like that. Or maybe worse, you know what I mean. You should go there tomorrow."

"Ah . . . we were thinking about it."

She smiled now. "I could work part-time," she said. "They could use a woman detective part-time."

"I'll talk to Ackerman."

"If you don't, I will."

"I think there's a policy, nepotism. No members of the same family."

"We'll see," she said.

She still was cryptic, and seemed a stranger, but later when she crawled into bed in her white flannel gown, she reached for him and clung tightly. He feared he had too little to give, and he held her tight, hoping for whatever it might be that he should hope for, because he wasn't being very smart, and he thought maybe he had been blind to bad things between himself and Lizbeth. He'd always thought of her as the woman he came home to. Maybe she yearned for a man to come home to. He wished he wasn't so dumb.

The next morning Frank Silva called in sick with a sore throat, and Joe Sonntag found himself alone on the case for the moment. He wondered what to do next. He found the playbill that Barovich had handed him. Just as he hoped, it listed the officers of the Milwaukee Players, including the very wealthy lady who was its president. He wondered if she'd even be out of bed.

Ackerman was looming over him. "How many suspects are we down to, Sonntag? A thousand?"

Sonntag looked up at the captain. "We don't have any."

"Great. I'll tell the aldermen. I'll tell Matt Dugan."

"Do that. Lizbeth has a theory I'm going to check out. We don't have a thing against the one guy who might be the one, Barovich. But Lizbeth thinks I ought to look around that playhouse."

"So it's Lizbeth now. You've run out of leads, and she's supplying female intuition."

"She'd like to be a detective, captain."

Ackerman laughed. "Can she lift a hundred pounds? Bullseye seven out of ten rounds at thirty feet?"

"She'd like to be. I said I'd talk to you."

There was this about Ackerman. He sometimes opened up. "About ten times a week I wish I had a female investigator," he said. "Once in a while I'd like to put a female fink in the women's pen. A friendly little ear."

"I'll tell her," Sonntag said.

Ackerman's laughter crackled. It was a good joke.

Sonntag waited for the captain to vanish, and then dialed Marlys Houseman, who lived in the Wauwatosa Highlands, an executive enclave west of town.

"Mrs. Houseman, I hope I'm not calling too early. This is Lieutenant Sonntag, Milwaukee police."

"It's never too early for Marlys," she said. "I'm up at five doing my abdominal exercises. I am fighting my Milwaukee bay window tooth and nail. Now, why would a Milwaukee officer be calling?"

"I'm wondering if you could escort me through your theater

at a time when no one's there."

"That sounds cozy, doesn't it, lieutenant."

Sonntag retreated from his hoof-in-mouth disease. "Just a routine investigation. I need to learn all about how theaters work. I'll ask you some questions. Any chance you could meet me there in half an hour? This early in the morning would be best."

"Actually, that's best for me, too. I don't go there afternoons, not with that spooky painter there."

"Good. Half an hour?"

She paused. "I hope you're fun," she said. "Empty theaters are strange places."

CHAPTER THIRTY-TWO

Mrs. Houseman was late, so Sonntag sat in old 406 with the engine running to stay warm. When she did arrive, he shut down the ancient car and met her.

"You even look like a detective," she said. "Sort of Humphrey Bogart."

"I sincerely hope not."

She stunned him. A perfect oval Olivia de Havilland face, glossy brown hair, tall and slim and rich. But after she let him in and they doffed their coats on the theater seats, he discovered a disfiguring pod at her middle, all the more heartbreaking because the rest of her was sublime.

She noticed him staring. "I'll get rid of the damned thing," she said.

Rows of theater seats stretched forward to a stage. This was an old firehouse that the players had somehow converted to a workable theater. They had even converted the lofty hose-drying tower into flies, where stored drop curtains could descend to the stage. Now this lay in deep shadow, lit only by a bare utility bulb backstage, the only defense against total darkness.

"Well?" she said.

"I guess I'd like to look around backstage, if I might."

"You sure are silent about all of this. Maybe I could help if I had a clue or two."

"I'm not sure I can say much, just now. But how about the dressing rooms, and prop storage areas?"

"As you wish," she said. She was plainly hoping to be privy to some good stuff.

"You can tell me about Stephen Barovich while I'm poking around."

"I knew it! I just knew it! This is about him."

He neither denied or confirmed.

"I sort of feel I'm talking to myself. Are you here?" she asked.

She led him through a side door, up some steps to the bare stage, which had ample wings to either side. Sonntag stared into the shadows, and suddenly wished he had armed himself. There was something about the gloom he didn't trust.

"He's been with the company quite a while. Some of us get along fine with him, but he just worries me, and I don't know why. He doesn't seem to make a living. But he's a gifted set designer and painter, and he's good with costumes, I'll say that. It's just that, well, I don't know. It's the look in his eyes. I don't want to be alone with him."

"What does that look remind you of?"

"Bitterness. There's a lot going on inside of him. Could you tell me this much? What you're looking for, and what kind of crime we're dealing with?"

"I'll say a little, depending on what we find."

She eyed him, a worried look in her face. "You know, you didn't show me your badge. I would like to know you're you."

It was a valid request. He pulled his black leather folder and showed her his badge.

"Now I feel better," she said. "The dressing rooms are down these stairs, below the wings. And the prop room is on the other side."

She flipped a switch that lit the area, then took him down some concrete stairs and into a subterranean labyrinth. She flipped more switches and led him into one of the two dressing rooms. There were men's clothes hanging on pipe racks, benches, and walls covered with theater posters. Outside the enclosure was a brightly lit counter backed by a mirror; the counter held an array of makeup in tins and jars, as well as pencils, liners, eye shadow, bottles of spirit gum, and a hat rack full of wigs. He studied the rack, touched nothing, and saw no red wig among the specimens.

"Are there other wigs here?"

"I guess. Let's look." She took him to a closet with shelves, where a few more wigs gathered dust. He spotted a red one and slowly slid it out of its nest. But it was a woman's wig, with red braids. He put it back.

"If you see a men's red wig with short hair, I'd sure like to know," he said.

"Yes, Mr. Mysterious."

The makeup could easily have been used by Barovich and no one would know of it. He saw nothing there that pointed to him.

"Let's see the other," he said.

She took him into the women's dressing room, where costumes also hung from a pipe rack. It was just as plain and utilitarian as the men's dressing room, a sort of bullpen used by all the women.

"Let's try the prop room, okay?"

She smiled, a little miffed, and led him across a barren area directly below the stage, to the other wing, and here the whole area was crammed with couches, chairs, tables, lamps, framed pictures, various vintage telephones, and large props. But she threaded through these to an alcove, turned on a light there, and nodded. Lining the walls were plank shelves, and on these shelves were innumerable small props: vases, candlesticks, pitchers, most of them dust-laden. He saw at once what he was looking for, perhaps because there was not a speck of dust on it. An army-issue forty-five-caliber automatic, looking innocent of death, a theater piece. There was also a dusty short-barreled black revolver next to it, a harmless starter's gun for track meets, its shortened cylinder loaded with fresh blanks. And a pasteboard box of blanks, forty-five caliber.

He studied the automatic. The dust below it was disturbed. It had been pulled off the shelf and put back recently.

"I guess I'll need to go out to my car and get a bag of mine," he said.

"You found something?"

"Yes, there's something I will need to borrow from you."

"This is sounding serious!"

"Mrs. Houseman, this is plenty serious. I'll be back. Please don't touch a thing."

He got his evidence bag and returned. With rubberized tongs he lifted the automatic off the shelf, dropped it into his bag, and noted the locale and time in his breast-pocket notebook. Then he did the same with the box of blanks. He thought about the track-meet revolver and decided to let it sit there. He had what he wanted most, except maybe the red wig.

He studied the rest of the prop area and poked around every cranny, letting nothing escape him, while she kept on with an amused banter, the sort of talk that masks fear. No red wig hidden out of place. No box of real bullets, not even in the drawers of furniture. Barovich was smart.

Still, there was Lizbeth's intuition plaguing him now. She thought the set designer had killed a victim right here and carried her away. It was certainly the perfect spot. He examined the concrete floor and found neither blood nor an area recently scrubbed. He hunted down the housekeeping gear and found a dried mop and a push broom. He might come back for the mop, if needed. He turned to the walls and wood, looking for pockmarks, a buried bullet, bits of lead from a disintegrated slug. He reexamined the dressing rooms. Nothing.

"You certainly are on to something, detective."

"Yes, in fact, I am," he said.

She sighed. "I guess I'll know eventually."

"You are very helpful," he said.

He spotted a closed door off the dressing rooms.

"What's in there?"

"Bathroom."

He opened, turned on the light. It was a utilitarian room, a john and sink and counter, small broken mirror, naked light bulb, tiled floor, an electric hot water heater in one corner. An array of glass bottles lined the counter next to the sink. He studied them. Professional hair coloring. Pre-dye rinse, dyes, post-dye setting wash. For salon use only. Chestnut, black, strawberry, gray, platinum and bleach.

"Would players dye their hair here?" he asked.

"I never noticed."

"If they were to be, say, a blonde in a play, wouldn't they go to a salon for that?"

"Or wear a wig," she said.

With his tongs he lowered each bottle into his canvas evidence bag and noted time and place and what he was taking in his notebook.

"You sure have me baffled," she said.

"I'll write you a receipt if you want."

She paused to examine herself in the mirror. Women do that. The crack radiated from a tiny chip on one side. There was a chest-high pock in the cream-painted concrete wall near the counter, nothing else amiss. He studied the pock, a round gouge in the concrete, as if it had been whacked with a ball peen hammer. It had been painted over, cream like the rest. The tan tile floor shone, spotless and bright. There was a drain in the tile floor. He had a bad feeling here. Maybe he'd be back, maybe with a lab guy. He'd see what they made of the stuff in his canvas bag first.

"We couldn't afford anything fancy. It took a big drive just to get this building converted. We bought the theater seats from a wrecking-ball place," she said. "The restrooms for the patrons are nicer."

"I suppose I should look at them," he said.

She doused lights behind him and followed him to the lobby, which was flanked by restrooms. They both were immaculate.

"You have a cleaning service?"

"The players can't afford that. We have a rotating crew. You get a month doing chores. That's the theater for you, scrubbing johns. We also rotate ticket-taker duties." She eyed him. "I'm not exempt. I've done my bit."

They drifted upstairs to the theater seats, turning off lights along the way.

"Well?" she said. "Get what you wanted?"

It was an invitation to explain.

"Maybe. I tell you what. I need a day or so, and then I'll call you. I'll probably be able to say a lot more than now."

"I just know it's Stephen Barovich," she said.

He smiled. For once he was zipping his lips.

"You can do me one great favor," he said. "Say nothing. Not to your people here, not socially, not anywhere."

"Hush-hush stuff," she said, a bright smile building on that beautiful face. "Can I tell anyone that you behaved yourself in the empty theater?"

Sonntag felt himself wilting under her candid gaze. "Mañana," he said.

She sighed. "It was a long trip cross-town," she said as they left.

He handed her his card. "If anything, anything at all, that seems unusual happens, please call me at once. And meanwhile, please be safe."

"Joe Sonntag. You're a good Bogart," she said, pocketing the card.

He drove back to the station, headed for the lab with his canvas bag, and dropped it on the counter. "Hey, Willie, here's some stuff. First, dust these for prints, and see about a match with Stephen Barovich, army records. Second, I want ballistics just as fast as the lab can do a report. Compare it to the slug taken from O'Grady, and the damaged one from Bark. I think this forty-five is our weapon. It won't be easy to pick up prints from this box of blanks. I got this stuff at the Milwaukee Players prop room. But look it over and tell me about anything you find that's interesting. And fast, fast. If the suspect finds the pistol is missing, he may flee."

"I can do the prints in a hurry, but the ballistics can take a while, Joe."

He returned to the bullpen, thinking about an early lunch.

He sat in his carrel edgily. Then Willis Bando showed up at his desk. "Joe, that pistol is totally clean, not a print, not a partial, on it. And that includes the clip. Same with the bottles of hair dye. Same with the bullet box. The blanks are ordinary, with cardboard wads, pretty old. There's nineteen left."

"Too clean, that's what I suspected. A theater prop would be loaded with prints," Sonntag said. "But how do you prove anything from a clean weapon?"

"I'll have ballistics by tonight if you want," Bando said.

"I do."

He dialed Silva, and he answered.

"How's the throat?"

"Bad. Every damned Thanksgiving, give or take a week, it's this." Silva sounded waterlogged.

"I think we're closing in," Sonntag said, and told him where they stood.

Silva listened. "What are you going to do when Barovich

discovers the automatic is missing? A guy that careful, he checks daily. You can bet on it."

"I don't know, Frank."

"I guess you'd better know," Silva said. "Want my bad-cold, stuffed-nose advice? Get the bottles and gun back there fast. Don't tip him off."

"Good advice, Frank," Sonntag said.

Chapter Thirty-Three

Lizbeth's leftover Thanksgiving turkey sandwich on Wonder Bread tasted exactly the same as a hundred others Joe Sonntag had downed at his desk over the years. So did the Maxwell House. So did the apple. So did the Oreo cookies.

But he didn't notice. His attention was focused on the paradox of Stephen Barovich, guilty as hell but without a single bit of evidence proving it. The best evidence he had was like the dog that didn't bark: a stage prop pistol that was wiped clean even though no one needed to wipe it clean. Something Sherlock Holmes would play with, but not something real cops in a real world would put any stock in, because it didn't connect Barovich to anything.

Sonntag had thought about trying to sneak the bottles and pistol back into the playhouse, hoping the set painter wouldn't notice. But he ended up rejecting that nonsense. And besides, the automatic pistol was not available, not if he wanted some ballistics. They would shoot a few rounds into a barrel of water, retrieve them, get a ballistic "fingerprint," and then begin the comparisons.

So Barovich would be aware that something wasn't right. His hair dyes were gone. His weapon was gone. What would he think? Sonntag had no idea. He could not fathom Barovich. He didn't even grasp motives. What was the man doing, killing the hotel detective, killing women? Sonntag was tempted to arrest him, haul him in. The force had a few men who could bully a confession out of Little Orphan Annie. Arrest Barovich for what?

He sipped cool coffee and puzzled the matter, feeling more helpless than ever.

Well, shoot, maybe lure Barovich. Let him play Spencer Tracy once again. This was the twenty-sixth day of November. He wiped crumbs off his desk, crumpled the waxed paper and pitched it, closed his lunch bucket, and collected his trench coat and fedora. It wasn't so bad outside; he'd hike.

"I'm going to the hotel," he told Ackerman. "Talk to Greaves."

"I'm glad you're coming to your senses," the captain said. "It was a hotel guest. See where all this Hollywood stuff got you?"

Sonntag smiled. He was very good at smiling when he needed to, even though he had to use unaccustomed muscles. He headed down Kilbourn toward the Lakeshore Towers. This was a fine day, for a change, bright and mild, with a rare sun flooding the streets. People were smiling.

Greaves kept him cooling his heels for fifteen minutes, but finally admitted Sonntag to his blond oak inner sanctum.

"Mr. Greaves, how would you like to throw another party?"

Marcus Greaves stared.

"The ad would have to get into the *Journal* classified by tomorrow. There's barely time."

"You think it'd work?"

"We're down to that option. I think I know who the killer is, but he's been careful. But maybe Spencer Tracy shows up at this shindig. If he does, we can scrub his war paint and see what's underneath. If he's not the right guy, he can sue you and us."

"You think Spencer Tracy would actually show up?"

"There hasn't been a word in the press identifying Spencer Tracy as the man we want."

"Who is this fellow, may I ask?"

Sonntag shook his head. "We could be wrong. So no names."

Greaves weighed it, or pretended to. He found a reservations ledger and opened it to December. "North penthouse is free the first Monday of December. That's the sixth. Well, all right. The Beverly Hills Club will meet again. I'll call the paper right away. We do the regular? Hors d'oeuvres?"

"Go whole hog, Greaves. Club Brentwood. Club Bel Air, Club Holmby Hills, Club Santa Monica, Cabaret Malibu."

"It will be Beverly Hills beside the lake," he said. "With champagne."

"You'll do yourself a favor," Sonntag said.

"I sincerely hope so." The operations manager was obviously discomfited by the reference to possible charges of obstruction.

"Let me know if anything goes haywire. If the party's on, we'll need to do some planning."

"Certainly! We'll catch him! And oh, yes, I meant to tell you. We've moved Bark's stuff out of that suite. We're still looking for a new security man. If you know of anyone—"

"I don't."

"Is there a chance we can have his incident ledgers back? Those are hotel records."

"They're evidence, Mr. Greaves. Eventually, but not now."

The hotel man nodded.

Sonntag left, trotted up the steps to the lobby, instinctively headed for Bark's office back behind the reception desk, and found the light on and the Philco radio playing. It was Duke Ellington's "Mood Indigo." There were blue-ink mimeographed memos on the desk. One, from the CEO, said that it was management policy to make the Lakeshore Towers a safe place. All personnel should report odd or suspicious behavior to hotel security. Another said that hotel staff should head for basement shelters in the event of nuclear attack and direct guests there.

"Mood Indigo" was followed by Harry James's "Chiribiribin." Good stuff, Sonntag thought.

He drifted toward the barbershop, and through a corridor window he spotted Damon Barbara cutting someone's hair, but not in the chair where J. Adam Bark had been shot. He quietly studied the man. Everything rested on Barbara's description of what happened. Did someone who was made up to be Spencer Tracy really burst in at exactly the moment when Bark had a hot towel over his face, and plug him?

Was this whole business of finding a killer in the habit of turning himself into Spencer Tracy utter nonsense? Was Barovich guilty of nothing but a lousy history and being uncooperative? Sonntag dug his hands into his trench coat, feeling his usual powerlessness and frustration, and slid away before Barbara discovered him staring through the glass.

He abandoned the lobby and headed into the streets. A lake wind was picking up, and it would drive him west to his lair. But instead, he caught a streetcar to Tenth and Wells, where he popped into Kinkaid's photo emporium. The tall picture-taker popped through a curtain.

"Lieutenant?"

"Kinkaid. Something you can do for us. Another Beverly Hills Club party in the north penthouse on Monday. I'd like you to go. They're used to you. If we send our own man it'd cool the action. You up to it?"

"Sure."

"I have a specific request. If our local Spencer Tracy shows up, and I'm hoping he will, I want photos. Unobtrusive, discreet photos. Candid stuff. Tracy talking to people. Never obvious. Just the way you usually take your candids, but somehow slide him into the picture. And if you can manage, get the faces of those he's talking to. Okay?"

Kinkaid smiled. "Sounds like a few bucks in it."

"That's my boy," Sonntag said.

"Count me in," the photographer said.

Sonntag retreated to Wells Street and hiked back to the station, feeling itchy and blue. Trying to net a killer in a trap was a last resort, and he knew it. At the station he settled into his carrel, wanting to be alone. He felt the stares of the other investigators, but it was just his imagination. They were out, they were busy. He really was staring at himself, the senior man who'd muffed another big one.

Bando materialized beside him.

"Joe, we went ahead, didn't wait for the state lab. We put two bullets into a water barrel and had a look. There's a match with the round taken from the O'Grady woman. There's not enough left of the slug that we scraped out of Bark's barber chair to make a match. That one's a probable, at best, but don't count on it."

"That helps. Thanks, Bando."

"We'll get this stuff to a lab, and they'll do better," Bando said.

"You've given me what I need."

Sonntag itched to climb into the old cruiser, drive to that playhouse, and throttle Barovich until he began coughing up a confession. Grab Barovich and pound him. But Sonntag knew that would never happen. It amazed him that he could feel such a surge of cold rage, a rage that would brook no fences, no boundaries.

He hoped O'Grady's alley cat was doing okay. He should check with Pilsner.

He pulled the phone book, found Pilsner's number, and dialed. The phone rang only once.

"Gustav Pilsner here."

"This is Lieutenant Sonntag, Mr. Pilsner. Actually, I'm calling about the cat. I just wanted to make sure—"

"Oh, lieutenant, Maureen's family took the cat back to Omro, I believe the place is."

241

"I guess I missed it. The funeral's up there?"

"It was there several days ago, sir. My wife and I thought of going, but it's a long drive. They tell me there's about a thousand flowers covering the grave."

Sonntag felt bleakness crowd him. "I wish I had gone. It got away from me. Thanks for taking care of the cat, sir."

"Glad to. The McKinnons came back to deal with this. They're looking for a new house-sitter."

"Well, fine, thank you, sir."

Sonntag hung up abruptly, not quite knowing why.

He commandeered old 406 and drove to the picnic table where the body of Veronica Lake had been found. It had all been gone over. He went over it again. It wasn't far from the Milwaukee Players theater, but too far to haul a body there without a car. Barovich had a drivers license but no car. Did his father, the tool-and-die maker, have one? Sonntag skirted back to the playhouse off Downer and parked his nondescript and unmarked old cop car. The playhouse sat somnolently in the November half-light. It had no marquee, but a poster announced that *The Importance of Being Earnest* would open in January.

He braved the cold and studied the cars parked beside the playhouse, noting licenses and makes. But the car that interested him most, a blue Nash sedan, was parked in the alley behind the building. There were a lot of Nashes in Milwaukee. He took down the license, then tried the door, which was locked, so he could not have a look at registration papers. He studied the rubberized floor for bloodstains, and then the gray fabric upholstery. There were dark stains. He wanted to examine the trunk. It was tempting to probe that car, but he refrained. If Barovich was as careful about the car as he had been about everything else, there would be nothing incriminating in it.

The playhouse, the lakefront, the beauty parlor, the place

where Maureen O'Grady lived, the picnic bench where Eileen Maginnis was found, were all within a ten-block square. He thought that sheer laziness is the Achilles heel of killers. Barovich had a revealed a pattern after all.

Back at the station, he ran the Nash through, and found it was registered to Barovich's father. Get a warrant and bust into it, check for blood, or wait for the Beverly Hills Club? He opted to wait. It would be better to pounce on Barovich, scrub his disguise, and arrest him.

Lizbeth was waiting when he got home.

"Well?" she asked, drying her hands in her apron.

"We're going to throw one last party for the Beverly Hills Club," he said.

"I don't mean that. I mean me."

It took him a moment. "Uh, I talked to Ackerman. He said if you can lift a hundred pounds and put seven of ten rounds into a bulls eye at thirty feet, you might make it."

She stared stonily.

"He also said there were ten times a week when he could use a female investigator."

She turned away, and he could not read her reaction as she vanished into the kitchen.

She returned with his bourbon and water, and a Manhattan for herself. This time she was smiling. "They'll take me on. It's just a matter of letting it sink in."

He truly hoped they wouldn't take her on. He wanted her at home, someone to come home to each evening, someone there with a meal and a smile. But that made him uneasy, too. She was not happy. She had little to do. She had for years been absorbed in his work, and she knew how to do it as well as he did. And she wanted to do that with her life. And he was standing in her way. He sipped. The bourbon was welcome.

"You should apply," he said. "I'll introduce you around.

They're going to have to waive some things, strength requirements and size requirement, all that."

"I am strong enough," she said. "Here's to the Beverly Hills Club."

CHAPTER THIRTY-FOUR

Joe Sonntag didn't think he looked much like a bartender. He wore a white shirt and bow tie, and hoped no one would notice if he wasn't very adept with the drinks. Frank Silva was a natural. And he knew booze better than Sonntag. He would do the complex mixology; Sonntag would pour the bourbon and ditches or the scotch and sodas or pry open a bottle of Coke. And they hoped that no one would pay much attention.

"I'll damn well get union wages," Silva said, "or I quit."

Sonntag's first plan was to get plastered up as an actor.

"But you don't look like anybody," Lizbeth had said.

"I could be Humphrey Bogart."

"You could be Boris Karloff," she replied.

That did it.

The north penthouse was a classy place for a party. The east windows opened on the lake, a sea of darkness now, but from the west windows, Milwaukee lights twinkled far below. Sonntag had put some platters on the phonograph; a Glenn Miller collection, turned low. Kinkaid arrived early with a thirty-five-millimeter camera and a bag full of stuff. He would be a familiar figure even if the bartenders weren't.

The guests began drifting in around eight. Some of them headed for the bathroom or bedroom to put themselves into their makeup. Sonntag kept eyeing the penthouse door every time it opened, and people flooded through. Sometimes he glimpsed the elevator man swinging the doors shut.

It was an odd business. He poured a bourbon for Robert Taylor. He poured a scotch and soda for Jane Wyman. At least he thought it was Jane Wyman. But then Lana Turner arrived, smoky eyes and well-filled cocktail dress. She glanced briefly at Sonntag, smiled slightly, and drifted through the crowd. Tyrone Power arrived a little later, probably the length of time it took him to park the car. They both got Manhattans from Silva.

Then in came Ronald Reagan. At least Sonntag thought it was. The makeup job wasn't very good. Reagan was not as well done as Monty Clift, who wanted a glass of Bordeaux. Clift looked dour and unhappy. Sonntag thought it was easy to sort these people out. Lana, now she was having a fine old time and this was all a laugh. But some, like Clift, stood around looking sad-eyed, trying to live a fantasy.

Kinkaid was busy from the start. He pulled Reagan and Wyman over to the blank wall and shot a photo. This Reagan and this Wyman had apparently never met, which made the photo session all the more amusing.

But no Spencer Tracy. Sonntag eyed the door anxiously, waiting for the man to walk in, head for the bath or bedrooms to get himself into costume, and then circulate. There was an awful lot of Irene Dunne's chest on display, and Sonntag thought it would attract the stalker. He wondered how J. Adam Bark would have circulated in this place.

Sonntag poured a white wine for Lucille Ball, and another scotch and soda for Robert Taylor. The man really looked like Taylor. Sonntag could not discover even the mark of an eyebrow pencil. Well, if Milwaukee had a Robert Taylor, it probably had a Greta Garbo or a Katharine Hepburn.

Jimmy Durante wanted a whiskey ditch.

"Hey, that's a great schnozz," Sonntag said, pouring away.

"Rinkidinkidooo," Durante replied and headed for Rosalind Russell.

Sonntag drifted away from the bar, changed the records to an Artie Shaw album, and listened to "Stardust."

Still no Spencer Tracy. It began to grate on him.

He poured a Jack Daniel's for Douglas Fairbanks.

Robert Taylor wanted a refill.

"How's things at MGM?" Sonntag asked.

"Indentured servitude. They signed me for another five years, but at a lousy eighty grand a picture."

"I'd complain too," Sonntag said.

There was a lull. Frank arranged bottles and rinsed glasses.

"It's getting too crowded," he said.

Sonntag nodded. They were expecting the usual fifteen or twenty, but there were over thirty this time. Their plan was simple: once Spencer Tracy walked in, and they were both positive they had their bird, Silva and Sonntag planned to abandon the bar, grab Tracy, pull him into a bedroom, disarm him if necessary, pin him, and begin peeling off the disguise. There was plainclothes backup in the hotel bar if needed. But this shindig was getting so lively that people were filling the bedrooms. It was a worry.

"Maybe head for the bathroom with Spencer?" Silva asked.

"Play it as we see it," Sonntag said. "Don't forget that Barovich is ex-army, and knows how to fight."

Silva nodded.

Silva served a highball to Elsa Lancaster, who downed it in one gulp and smiled sweetly. "How about another, you doll," she said.

"Coming right up."

The music quit. Sonntag drifted out, pulled the pile of shellac seventy-eights off the spindle, hunted for more stuff, and found a Xavier Cugat album. Good. A little Latin would be just right. He loaded the records and watched the first one drop. It was a good catchy rumba.

He headed back to his station at the bar and poured refills for June Allyson and Rosalind Russell. They were getting pretty giggly. Sonntag glanced toward the door when it opened, but it wasn't Spencer Tracy.

Then he spotted Ethel and Lionel Barrymore, dancing the rumba off in a corner. He watched, enchanted. They were doing a distinctly bawdy rendition.

He surveyed the room, just in case he had missed something. Van Johnson was sipping a Coke and studying June Allyson's chest. Sonntag saw how this was going. The Beverly Hills Club was a place to pair up. Monty Clift was drinking hard and staring moodily out upon the blackness of Lake Michigan. And Fredrick March had settled onto a couch, looking ready to cry.

"This damned charade is hard on some of 'em," Sonntag said to Silva. "Look at the loners."

There were loners all right, people trying to live a fantasy and feeling miserable about it.

Still no Tracy. Ten o'clock and no Tracy. Ten-thirty and no Tracy.

"He figured it out," Sonntag muttered.

Silva manufactured a martini for Al Jolson and nodded.

Lionel Barrymore approached, leonine and old. "Just fill a glass with Dewars," he said.

Sonntag thought he'd have to arrest himself for serving a drunk, and poured only an inch.

"Goddamn cheapskate hotel," Barrymore said. He carried the booze to the corner, where Ethel was slumped in a chair and looked suspiciously comatose.

"Better check Ethel," he told Silva.

"Merman or Barrymore?"

Startled, Sonntag discovered Ethel Merman, all lipstick and brass, sitting in a chair with her skirts hiked thigh-high, smoking a cigarillo and drinking something sea-green. Leo G. Carroll was patting her bare knees. She was toying with his cravat and making googoo eyes at him. Sonntag thought that the pair would vamoose before the party was over.

Dana Andrews asked for an old-fashioned. Silva nodded and began mixing.

"And another for Teresa," Andrews added.

Sonntag shot a look. He was talking about Teresa Wright, standing just behind, and next to Sammy Kaye and Virginia Mayo.

Over at the blank wall, Kinkaid was shooting a few of Fred MacMurray, who had an arm about the shoulders of Joan Fontaine and Henry Fonda, while Reginald Denny watched.

"How's the studio treating you, Dana?" Sonntag asked.

"Don't ask. I just ended up on the cutting-room floor. It's all right though. They sent a limo and a driver for me for the Academy Awards."

Still no Spencer Tracy.

Sonntag put more platters on, mood music now, Jackie Gleason stuff, "I'm In the Mood for Love." Maybe that wasn't appropriate. Sonntag thought the bedrooms would be getting some use unless this shindig broke up.

But it did, suddenly. This was a weeknight. He watched men vanish into the bathroom, where there was a tub of Pond's cold cream and towels, and emerge a couple of minutes later with the pancake gone and another fouled towel left behind. It was the men, not the women, who didn't want to parade through the lobby wearing that stuff.

"Where's my limo?" asked Myrna Loy. "They were supposed to send a limo."

Within minutes the penthouse emptied. It was eerie. As if all these humble working people had to hit the sack and go back to their shop floors and desks early the next morning.

Silva looked annoyed, and picked up glasses everywhere.

The last to leave was Ethel Barrymore.

"Lionel's getting horny," she said.

"But that's your brother," Sonntag said.

She winked.

J. Adam Bark would have fainted.

Then, suddenly, it was quiet, and only the chaos left by fifty people testified to a soiree.

Sonntag got on the house phone, rang the bar, and got the backup. "You guys go home. We didn't score," he said.

"It sure was fun," said the backup, Ransom Jones.

Hotel housekeeping would take care of the mess. It was ten to eleven.

"Frank, I'll catch the eleven o'clock night owl car," he said.

"I'm damned sorry, Joe. I thought we'd nail him."

"So am I," Sonntag said. "We'll hear all about it tomorrow from Ackerman."

He collected his suit coat and slid it on, feeling the weight of the small service revolver in its pocket. It would have been useless in that crowded penthouse, but he wanted it with him. He pulled his trench coat over him. He had buttoned the liner into it and it was good enough for the weather if he added a good wool scarf.

He caught the elevator down. A new night-shift boy drove it. He stepped into a cruel lake wind, and hiked over to the Wells Street Terminal. He boarded the bright-lit car, paid his fare, and sat down near the rear. At eleven sharp the motorman cranked the door shut, pulled the handle, and eased the car westward.

The car toiled west, ingesting a passenger or two, regurgitating others, and then rolled noisily across the viaduct while Joe Sonntag closed his eyes and hung on to the wicker seat ahead of him. Then it was over and he was on solid ground, riding familiar rails down a familiar street, past familiar lights at the corners.

The driver dropped him at 56th Street, and he strode through the night to 57th, heading toward home, past the hulks of parked cars with frosted windshields.

The lights were on. She had waited up for him, shades drawn. Well, he'd have a tale to tell, and they'd laugh ruefully about the trap that sprung on nothing.

He unlocked, stepped in, and realized he was too dumb and too late.

CHAPTER THIRTY-FIVE

Lizbeth was bound tight to a dining room chair. Spencer Tracy had a black revolver stuck in her face. There was a wild despair in her eyes.

Tracy smiled. He was wearing his trademark black leather jacket and fedora. "Come right in, Sonntag. I've been waiting. This is the last act. Maybe you'll end up on the cutting-room floor."

The disguise was brilliant. There was Tracy, a dead smile in his face, holding that mean little revolver on Sonntag's wife.

Sonntag stood very still. The small service automatic in his suit coat pocket seemed a mile away from his hands. Don't rush, don't excite the man, don't do a thing, and try to keep him talking. The old lessons crawled to mind.

"You're so dumb, lieutenant. Trying to suck me in. How dumb can a cop get? Did you really believe I'd fall for it? What do you take me for?"

"You're very smart, Mr. Tracy."

"Mister Tracy, Mister Tracy." The killer smiled. "You don't even dare call me by name. It's good, isn't it? No one could do better. Except for the wig. I hate the wig. I prefer to dye. But you stole my dyes, didn't you? So you'll die, but only after watching the show."

"I'm dumb. I don't get it," Sonntag said.

"You still don't get it? Well neither do I! You wandered in here as if nothing would happen. The blue Nash is a block away

but you didn't bother to look. Some cop you are. It never occurred to you that you made me mad."

Spencer Tracy waved the revolver slightly. He circled it
around her face, pointing at her eyes, and then back toward her
mouth, the gun's mean little snout inches from her teeth. He
laughed, wiggled the weapon, letting him know she was facing
exactly the same death that had stopped the life of Maureen
O'Grady and Eileen Maginnis. He caught Sonntag's eye, read
Sonntag's thoughts, and smiled easily. The urbane movie star,
top of the world.

Lizbeth sat rigid, not moving a muscle. Her wrists were
bound tight behind the ladder-back chair. Her ankles were
wrapped in sash cord. Her eyes locked with Sonntag's and were
swimming with desperation.

"I guess I'm not very bright, Spencer. Now, tell me about
Adam Bark, okay?"

"The hotel dick! He was in my way."

Sonntag shook his head. "I don't follow you."

"You're dumb, dumb, Sonntag. The man was in my way."

Sonntag shook his head. "I don't understand Greer Garson,
either."

Tracy laughed. "I felt like it."

"But why?"

"Sonntag, you want reasons, as if reasons mattered. I felt like
it. Little bitch."

"Why was she a little bitch?"

Tracy sighed. "If you don't have it figured out, you're not
much of a man, Sonntag."

"No, I guess I'm not. I still don't get it."

"Then that's how you'll croak, dumb as the day you were
born."

Sonntag was running out of talk, and stood warily. He could
move, take a hit, two hits, try to pull his automatic and kill the

bastard before he killed her.

"Sonntag, you're running out of things to talk about. That's how you stall, right? Keep talking, talking, talking, stall, stall, stall, hope for a break, right?"

"Anything I can do to change things?" Sonntag asked. Keep on asking questions, any questions.

"No, Sonntag, Fate has decreed that this is your hour. But first, just so you got a front-row seat, I'll do this."

He turned toward Lizbeth, aimed at her mouth, and pulled the trigger. The shot racketed through the parlor. Lizbeth screamed. Her chair toppled to one side. She hit the floor, still bound. She coughed, blood leaked slowly from her mouth. She gasped, coughed, and slid into her own world.

Sonntag wished he had never been born to see this moment.

Spencer Tracy slithered toward the front door, his revolver on Sonntag, never wavering. At the front hall he paused, shot, and shot again. The first stung Sonntag's cheek, the second struck his chest. Tracy laughed. The third hit Sonntag's arm, the fourth shot caught Sonntag's hip, and the last shot ripped Sonntag's hat from his head.

Sonntag knew his life was gone. He reached under his trench coat, found the suit coat pocket, pulled the automatic, slid the safety off, and aimed even as Spencer Tracy turned to leave. Sonntag aimed at the man's back, shot, the automatic jarring his hand, and watched Spencer Tracy sag, red bloom at his back, and topple into the front hall.

Sonntag shot again, and Spencer Tracy twitched. His hands relaxed. The little black revolver clattered on the maple floor.

He wheeled toward Lizbeth, who lay gasping and coughing. She spasmed, spit out the cardboard wad, which had shattered, along with more blood. She gasped for breath, got the powder fumes out of her lungs, and quieted. Sonntag raced into the kitchen, found a knife, and cut the sash cord, until Lizbeth lay on her side, her mouth leaking blood, free from the ladder-back chair.

He felt his own cheek. It stung but he wiped no blood away. He found cardboard wads littering the floor where he had been standing. There was a tear in the arm of his trench coat. There were black spots where the wad had hit his coat.

He stumbled to the phone, dialed zero, and waited.

"Number please," the lady said.

"Get an ambulance to six-eleven 57th. My wife's been shot. Send the police."

"Sir? Sir, please confirm. Six-eleven 57th Street?"

"Do it!"

"Yes, sir."

Sonntag plunged toward the kitchen, soaked a dishtowel in cold water, and brought it to Lizbeth, who was mewling and coughing. He wiped away her blood, which still leaked slowly from her mouth. He wiped her face. "Okay, okay, okay," he said. "Okay, okay, okay."

He thought he heard Tracy stir, and leaped up to kick the bastard to death, but Tracy lay inert, his mouth a twisted circle.

He found a pillow and slid it under Lizbeth's head, not wanting her to drown in her blood. He wiped her face and told her it was okay, okay.

He heard the sirens long before he saw the flashing lights, and then they all arrived at once, the ambulance guys tumbling in, pausing at the body at the door, and then gently sliding Lizbeth on a stretcher.

Then the cops came, his brothers in blue. Let a man in blue fall, let a man in blue get into trouble, and the whole force is on it. They burst in, his guys in blue, weapons drawn.

"I killed him," Sonntag said.

"Milwaukee Hospital. You coming, sir?"

Sonntag nodded. He followed them out to the meat wagon,

held Lizbeth's hand, watched as they slid her in, and then crawled in beside her. She stared up at him, holding a wad of bloody cotton to her lips. Then the ambulance wheeled away. And a cruiser followed, its lights rotating.

His house crawled with the guys. They'd figure it out.

They carried Lizbeth into emergency, slid her onto a gurney, and one of the night interns loomed over her, listened to her heart, pushed her mouth open, studied her bruised lips, while a nurse got a blood pressure cuff on her. "What did it?" the intern said.

"A blank at less than a foot."

The medics set to work. They swabbed her mouth, looked her over. They had her sit up and wash out her mouth with a solution. They used a tongue depressor, looked around, and finally paused, addressing Sonntag.

"The wad lacerated her soft palate. That's the blood. Her mouth's been burned. Her lips and mouth area have taken a load of hot debris."

"You could talk to me," Lizbeth said crossly. "I'm not deaf."

"We could hold her for observation," the intern continued.

"Hold her for observation," Lizbeth said. Her voice was hoarse. "Maybe you should ask me."

Sonntag turned to her, a question in his eyes.

"Get me out of here!" she snapped.

"There's some things to do, Mrs. Sonntag. Regular mouth washes, and some salves I'll give you for your lips and face." He turned to Sonntag. "If she fevers, call us at once. There's some new stuff, hard to get, but we'll get some, penicillin."

"She? You mean if I get a fever," Lizbeth said doggedly.

The intern ignored her.

But Sonntag watched tears well in her eyes.

"I want to keep her for an hour," the intern said. "Shock, things like that."

Sonntag nodded.

They were waiting, the swarm of blue out in the hall. There was Ackerman in his pajama tops and cop pants, his face tear-streaked. There was the chief and Gorilla and his camera, and all the rest.

"How is she?" Ackerman asked.

"Feisty and foul-mouthed, captain."

Gorilla sat his camera down, buried his head in his hands, and wept.

Sonntag sat down and gave them the statement, blow by blow, and they said it fit with what they found in the house. The wads from blanks scattered the room.

Barovich was dead. They had knelt beside him, thrown light on him, and began peeling stuff away, something rubberized, maybe made out of powdered latex, they'd have the lab figure it out. They peeled it away, a magnificent big Spencer Tracy nose, perfectly done. The wig came off, the pancake washed off, and there was Barovich. His father's Nash was down the block. Sonntag's first shot had caught him in the side, pierced his chest. Barovich was using an athletic starter's gun, which lay on the hallway floor. Did Sonntag have any idea why?

"It was on the shelf with the props at his playhouse," Sonntag said. "I left it in place."

"But he knew better, army man like that. What was the matter with him?"

Sonntag sighed. "People who try to live fantasies sometimes confuse them with reality," he said.

And that seemed to be the only explanation.

"Did Barovich say why? Why you, why the rest?" Ackerman asked.

"We were all in his way. That's all he said. When I pressed him, before he shot Lizbeth, he said he had no reasons, didn't need reasons, and only dumb cops wanted reasons."

"I guess I do want reasons," Ackerman said.

But no one could think of any.

They waited for Lizbeth to be released.

"Sonntag, you won't want to go back to your house," Ackerman said. "The boys are busy there. So I just woke up Greaves. You have the south penthouse tonight, courtesy of the hotel."

"The penthouse?"

"Not the party joint, the other one. And I'm giving you an extra half hour off. You don't need to show up until eight tomorrow."

"Thanks, captain."

"We'll drive you and Lizbeth over."

"We'll need some stuff."

And it was done. Lizbeth appeared, looking fragile. Black smudges were developing under her eyes. They guys whistled and clapped. They all drove to 57th Street, where Sonntag and Lizbeth dodged men in blue and packed an overnight kit.

They were chauffeured east to the lakefront hotel and whisked to their penthouse suite. And then they were alone. It was very strange and quiet and sweet.

Lizbeth got into her white Mother Hubbard and crawled wearily into the big bed, where Sonntag soon joined her. They lay there, in that antiseptic place, staring at the ceiling, holding hands. He felt the ring on her ring finger, the ring he had slid there so long ago. Her hand was warm. She was subdued.

But then she leaned close and whispered.

"Do you think the ghost of J. Adam Bark's going to bust in?" she asked.

"Let him try it," Sonntag replied. "I'll tell him we're holding hands under the covers, and that is something that J. Adam Bark never did all his lonely life."

ABOUT THE AUTHOR

Axel Brand is a pseudonym. But his doppelganger has written about sixty novels.